CRITICAL ACCLAIM

"Among sports-based books, by far the best is Tarkenton's collaboration with Edgar Winner Herb Resnicow, *Murder at the Super Bowl*."

— *Time Magazine*

"A good, solid whodunit. *Murder at the Super Bowl*'s appeal stretches beyond hardcore sports fans to all those who feared the intricate, fair whodunit was extinct."

— *The Drood Review of Mystery*

"This is an entertaining story with surprises."

— *The Chattanooga Times*

"The dialogue sparkles; the technical background rings true; the characters . . . quite engaging; and, most of all, the puzzle hangs together well."

— *Mystery Readers of America Journal*

"Football fans know Tarkenton as one of the great scrambling quarterbacks; now mystery fans can watch his wizardry as a storyteller!"

— *Crime Times*

"Although the famous quarterback, Fran Tarkenton, has top billing in the author credits, the story reads like a Resnicow novel, and a very good one it is, indeed."

— *The Armchair Detective*

MURDER AT THE SUPER BOWL

Fran Tarkenton
with Herb Resnicow

CONCEPT BY BILL ADLER

PaperJacks LTD.

TORONTO   NEW YORK

PaperJacks

MURDER AT THE SUPER BOWL

PaperJacks LTD.

330 STEELCASE RD. E., MARKHAM, ONT. L3R 2M1
210 FIFTH AVE., NEW YORK, N.Y. 10010

William Morrow and Company edition published 1986
PaperJacks edition published January 1989

This is a work of fiction in its entirety. Any resemblance to actual people, places or events is purely coincidental.

10 9 8 7 6 5 4 3 2 1

ISBN 0-7701-1050-9
Printed in the USA

To my son, David Alan, who started the whole thing
—HERB RESNICOW

Grateful acknowledgment is made for the technical advice and assistance of Stephen Engelbert of *The New York Times*, Stan Isaacs of *Newsday*, and Mike Gigante of the N.F.L.

1

AND THE LAST SHALL BE FIRST

It was the moment of truth and it would take eight seconds. Eight seconds to decide who would live and who would die, with no time-outs left. Would the Brooklyn Wizards, the Cinderella team, the team of raw unseasoned boys and tired, broken old men, the team of rookies and castoffs, would they be able to breach the solid wall of giants that stood between them and the white line that meant life?

Or would they die on that strip of grass, inches short of, grasping at, reaching for the goal that no one, four months ago, no one, not even themselves, had believed remotely attainable.

The Wizards, so aptly named by their head coach, Zachary "Magic" Madjeski, the expansion team, the fifteenth team that would equalize the uneven divisions of the American Football Conference and give New York City its own team, had been destined for the cellar by the sages of sport who doubted that the Wizards would win even one game that season.

The Wizards had the lightest line in the NFL. The Wizards had a skinny quarterback barely six feet tall, the waived Alvin "Crazy Al" Tilley. The Wizards had played together only two seasons. The Wizards had been awarded twenty-point handicaps in their first three games.

These Wizards were now, in absolute ignorance of their incompetence, angered by the insults of the Brooklyn fans, audaciously executing the wild plays Magic Madjeski was forced to employ, by virtue of the wild card system, which made it possible for a team that had lost 8 games out of 16 to play a team with a 15–1 record for the right to be in the Super Bowl, these Wizards were within eight seconds of becoming the AFC champions. If they could. . . . And they did!

The Brooklyn Wizards playing for the world championship in the Super Bowl? It was unbelievable! It was insane; it was witchcraft. It was crazy; it was magic. It was Crazy Al and Magic Madjeski, the pride of the Wizards.

Julius Witter laid the word processor printout down precisely six inches from the edge of his desk, thoughtfully ran his right thumb over both halves of his pepper-and-salt military mustache, then pulled his gray cardigan straight over his long, skinny torso. The standard ritual over, he pushed his half glasses back over his bald head, focused his cold blue eyes carefully a foot over the top of Marc's head, and sighed. "It's beautiful, Marc. A work of art."

"You don't like it," Marcus Aurelius Burr said. He pushed his limp brown hair back over his high forehead, his small, slim, compact body rigid, suppressing the tension a confrontation with Witter always produced.

"Poetic. Lyrical." Witter put his big feet up on the chair he kept next to his desk for just that purpose and leaned back, his eyes now on the ceiling.

"You hate it." Marc's soft brown eyes failed to catch Witter's focus. "You despise it."

"That headline is really apropos, Marcus."

"Just a suggestion, sir."

"You figured our headline writers might not think of it?"

"The thought had crossed my mind, Mr. Witter."

"You're right, Burr. They never in a million years would have thought of it. They would have put in something really blah, like WIZARDS BEAT LONGHORNS, 15–14. Your headline provides just the right touch of reverence for the holy game."

"Why don't you like my story, Mr. Witter?"

"I told you, I love your story, Burr. It's just not news."

"Everybody in Western civilization watched that game, Mr. Witter, every second of it. They know exactly who did what to whom; they don't need it rehashed. What they really need is a story to highlight the emotion, the essence of the conflict."

"What they *want*, Burr, is a description of what they saw as you saw it, with some of the finer points of strategy analyzed. Stuff the TV announcers didn't have time to see or understand. So our readers can do their Monday-morning quarterbacking on Monday morning and figure how they could have done it better. Plus all the data the TV crew didn't give. In a thousand words."

Marc paused for a moment and drew a deep breath. Calmer, he said, "I did put in some statistics, sir."

"True, Burr. You even got the name of the matador right—Crazy Al. But you missed a great opportunity to describe how he nonchalantly baffled *el toro*—they are the Texas Longhorns, after all—with his fancy veronica just before the thrust home the sword at the moment of truth and the gallant beast fell dead at his feet, the tip of the left horn just grazing his suit of lights."

"A little too obvious, Mr. Witter."

"Hemingway wouldn't have done it, eh, Burr?"

"No, sir." Burr leaned forward and looked his editor straight in the eye. "Is it because you don't like me personally, Mr. Witter, that you're turning down the story?"

"I dislike all my reporters, Burr. It goes with the job, but I still print their stuff, after it's translated into English. Why did you bring in the story instead of having your computer phone our computer? Don't you know what the deadline is?"

"I had plenty of time, sir, and the rewrite men often change the story. I figured if I brought it in personally, I might be able to discuss it with you."

"The long words, Burr? The literary allusions?"

"No, sir. Just convince you that our readers might like—"

"Persuade, Burr, not convince. You will *never* convince me that you know what our readers want better than I do. Why don't you apply to *Sports Illustrated*? They have really good writers there; you could learn from them. You'll have a whole week to get a story in, not like our poor little rag where you have to get your copy in every day. On time."

"*The Daily Sentry* is a good paper, Mr. Witter. I just want to add a little variety to the sports section. Some interest. A little class."

"Our readers don't want variety, Burr. Or class. They want the news, in the same place every day. They want to know who won and how, and by how much." He smiled wickedly at Marc. "So *Sports Illustrated* turned you down, eh, Burr? Guess why."

"They're fully staffed right now, sir. But I don't want to go to *SI*; I'd really like to stay with *The Sentry*. I just wish you'd—"

"Cut the crap, Burr. What do you really want? Why are you so polite all of a sudden? What's with the 'sir' and the 'Mr. Witter'? Why no wisecracks, no put-downs, no snotty answers? Are you trying to get a raise?" Witter snorted at the idea. "From *me*?"

"No, sir, Mr. Witter, just ordinary politeness to my revered editor. You know what I really want, sir; I want to be an investigative reporter."

"Who's stopping you, Burr? You get me a good story, fully documented, facts not bullshit, and I'll print it. Bookies paying off to keep the score within the spread? Players betting against their own teams? Drug pushers in the locker room? What have you got, Burr?"

"Nothing like that, sir. What I really want is political investigation, like Watergate. Or say, a multinational corporate scandal."

Witter leaned back in his chair and slowly filled his pipe. After he got the smoke going, he leaned forward and said, "You know how you got hired, Burr?" He blew the smoke into Marc's face.

Marc moved his chair back. "Yes, sir. You phoned me and offered me the job while I was still in Munich."

"Now, why would I offer a job, a reporter's job, to a twenty-two-year-old kid who had never worked on anything but a school paper before and who I had never even seen when there were a hundred good newspapermen, real pros, walking the streets, begging for work? Men with families, kids, responsibilities? Men who would do their jobs and be happy doing it; never make trouble. Why, Burr?"

"Because I was at the top of my class in journalism school?"

"Really, Burr? I never knew that. Congratulations."

"Then why?"

"Because Mr. Heisenberg, who happens to be our publisher, was interested in gymnastics at the time. He was sore that in '72 the Japanese swept men's gymnastics and the Russians took women's gymnastics. The only American who even showed in the top twenty individual scores was named Marcus Aurelius Burr. Mr. Heisenberg checked and found you had just graduated with an M.A. in journalism and suggested, *suggested*, mind you, that I might be able to use you in the sports section. As a reporter. He also suggested—would you believe it?—that I should teach you the business. Which explains why I've been so patient with your childish antics and your lousy sneering attitude. I'm getting very tired of waiting for you to grow up, Burr. Either change or get out."

"Transfer me, Julius. I'll take a cut in salary. I'll do anything you want."

"What I want, Burr, and this is an order, is for you to live with the Brooklyn Wizards from now till the end of the Super Bowl. A color story and a news story every day. Five hundred words and a thousand words, every day. Including Sunday. On time. And I'm disapproving your taxi fare from the Gruber Dome. You should have phoned in the story by computer."

"So you're not going to use my story on the game?"

"Did I say that, Burr? Did I? Didn't I just say I loved it? Sure I'm going to use it. But not in Monday's paper. It's going in the Sunday edition. With your byline, Burr—your full name, Marcus Aurelius Burr. So when a hundred readers write in to say what fancy crap it is, they'll know who to blame and where you're coming from. Now get your ass over to your terminal and write a proper story of the big play-off game. You've got less than an hour, so shake it. I'm holding a thousand words open."

Marc Burr took two sheets of fanfold readout paper from his inside jacket pocket and slapped them on Witter's desk. "Here's the story you want, Julius—a thousand words. It's trite, it's low-level, it's pure compressed barf, just like the rest of your crummy sports section. So I know you'll love it, Julius." He stalked to the door of Witter's glassed-in office.

"If you think so highly of your fancy literary efforts, Burr"—he waved the two pages—"why did you bother writing this story?"

"I knew you wouldn't appreciate the good stuff, Julius, even if I explained the big words to you." He opened the door. "What you've just told me, Julius, is that you *can't* fire me. And I'm not going to quit, no matter what you do. So if you want war, Julius, you've got it. And if you're not careful, I'll make it a war of wits. Which you're guaranteed to lose." He slammed the door. The glass rattled.

2

_____

"You wanted to see me, Boss?" Alvin "Crazy Al" Tilley flopped into the chair in front of Head Coach Zachary "Magic" Madjeski's desk. Tilley peered out like a mischievous child from the tangle of long dirty-blond hair that hung in front of his beard-stubbled face, his grainy, red-veined eyes like those of a Bowery bum. He had tried to eat the night before, that was clear, but the splotches of food on his jacket and shirt showed he had not succeeded. He had also tried to drink, and in that had done very well, as the smell that filled the office proved.

"I wanted to see you at ten o'clock," Magic Madjeski said softly, menacingly, his angry black eyes aimed at Tilley's slumped misery. "In uniform, working out with the rest of the team." Madjeski's nostrils flared. "You've also been smoking. I can smell it." Madjeski's small plump body was stiff with rage, his short gray hair bristling.

Tilley raised his eyes, a medley of red, white, and bleary blue, and grinned. "And wenching. And staying up late. Celebrating. I won, didn't I? Nobody expected me to win even one game the whole season, and now I'm in the Super Bowl, my first Super Bowl. So I celebrated."

"_We_ won," Harold "Boom-Boom" Drogovitch, the defensive coordinator, growled, pushing his inch-thick finger into Tilley's face. Boom-Boom's fierce dark eyes glared out from his brown-bearded face. His tightly curled hair, and the fuzzy brown sweater over the big broad torso, made Boom-Boom look like a grizzly bear, an angry 6-foot 4-inch, 240-pound grizzly bear. The slim quarterback squirmed away from the accusing finger. "*We!* *We.* The *team*, you crazy jerk, the *whole* team. Anytime you feel like doing it all by yourself against my defense, I'll go in myself as middle linebacker and tear your helmet off, with your swelled head in it." He whipped his horn-rimmed glasses off, ready to rip the quarterback in half right then and there.

"You talk like that out loud one more time, Tilley," Edward "Carny" Quigley, the offensive coordinator, shouted, lifting his lanky body out of his chair, "and I'll tell my offense. Once, just once, they hold back to let the Orcas' front four in and they'll be picking you up with a blotter." Carny's usually mild light eyes looked much darker to Tilley now and, though not as broad as Boom-Boom, Carny was almost as tall and looked even more dangerous. His seamed tan face under pale blond hair, his slit eyes and sharp features, reminded Tilley of the tales of the merciless western gunfighters he had read as a boy.

Madjeski put his hands out sideways, holding the tensed forearms of the men at his side with surprising strength. "I'll handle this," he said. He stared at his offensive coordinator until Quigley sat back in his chair, then gently put his hand on Drogovitch's shoulder and held it there until he felt the hard muscles relax. Madjeski turned his big gray head back to the slouching quarterback. "I didn't pick you, Tilley. You were shoved on me, you and two rookies, because we were an expansion team and nobody would give up an experienced quarterback unless he was an over-the-hill troublemaker. Your old coach called me to sympathize. He said getting rid of you added ten years to his life. I had to start

14

you because you were the only one we had with experience. The trouble is, Tilley, your experience is fourteen years of doing everything wrong. And what's worse, you're not even trying to do it my way."

"What am I supposed to do when no receivers are free and five hundred pounds of gorillas are coming at me? Half the time I completed the pass."

"And half the time," Carny Quigley pointed out, "we lost fifteen yards."

"We won, didn't we? We made the wild card play-off, didn't we?"

"Because the top four teams in the conference were so good, they clobbered all the other teams in their divisions. Because of lucky bounces. Because the artificial turf in the Gruber Dome is so new and fast, our lightness gives us a speed advantage, that's why."

"We still won," Tilley muttered, keeping his eyes down, not wanting to look at the straight, hard old man across the desk. "*We're* in the Super Bowl." He shot a quick look of apology at Boom-Boom Drogovitch.

"We won," Madjeski lectured, "because Boom-Boom and Carny trained their teams in fundamentals, over and over, until they automatically did everything the proper way. We won because they initiated defenses and offenses that made up for our physical deficiencies."

"Our starting defensive line," Boom-Boom said, "averages twelve pounds lighter than the next lowest team, and we're thirty pounds lighter than the Orcas' *offense*. You want to bang up against a guy thirty pounds bigger all game long?"

"I've got the slowest guards in the conference," Carny said, "by a full two-tenths of a second. And aside from the bullshit I give the press, neither one is an ounce over two forty."

"Don't tell me"—Tilley showed a flash of anger—"about

15

how lousy the line is. I weigh one eighty and I've been hit by a six-nine, two-ninety-pounder an average of three times a game. The fact remains that we're in the Super Bowl because I made that last play."

"And that's another thing, Tilley," Madjeski said. "We have a game plan; we have established plays. Carny worked hard on that I-formation surprise; you changed it."

"It worked, didn't it?"

"It'll never work again," Carny said. "Anytime there's a power I-formation, there'll be one big end pounding your hard head into the ground."

"But we won."

"Yeah, backpedaling," Carny snorted. "One leg stuck out of that crowd and you would have been on your ass. One bump by a linebacker and we would have lost everything. We play fundamentals, Tilley; we play the odds. You can't depend on luck."

"It wasn't luck. I saw the right-side linebacker keying on my left tackle. I knew if he got there fast, there'd be a pile-up. So I angled my feet and looked left, to show them that the play was going left. I knew the right side would be clean."

"You told them?" Carny roared, his face red, the tendons on his neck standing out. "You *told* them? That's why the hole closed up? You purposely keyed them to make my surprise play fold so you could be the hero? To make me the bum?"

"Mr. Tilley," Madjeski said calmly, "you are not a team player. You are not the kind of man we want on the Wizards in the future. You're barely six feet tall, you're thirty-five years old, and you've slowed up noticeably. You cause confusion on the field and dissension in the locker room. You break all the team rules, and this leads the other players to believe they can do the same. You are highly overpaid, which causes even more trouble with the front office. You think I must take all this insult because you're indispensable. Well, Mr. Tilley, it gives me great pleasure to inform you that you are dead wrong." Madjeski smiled with tight lips.

"What are you getting at, Magic?"

"From now on, Mr. Tilley, you're going to act like a member of a team. You're going to show up on time for every workout, every practice, every film session. You'll do whatever the coaching staff requires. You will be properly dressed and physically and mentally prepared to do your job at all times. And most important, you will follow the game plan precisely and execute the plays I send in properly."

"*Jawohl, mein Führer.*"

"You won't think it's very funny when I put you on waivers, Tilley. At your age and with your reputation, nobody will pick you up."

"You would waive me? Fire me? Now?"

"Not now, Tilley. Right after the Super Bowl. If you don't obey orders."

"You're telling me this now? Before the Super Bowl? Are you crazy?"

"No, Tilley, you are, if you think I'm going to coach a team any longer with a problem like you on its roster. I want a football machine where every part does what it's supposed to do. For that, I need a quarterback who does what he is told and does it the right way. Mr. Gruber promised me a major quarterback next year, price no object, if you fail. *When* you fail. I want that quarterback, and I mean to get him."

"But you're leaving this year. Retiring. Everybody knows that. What the hell do you care about next year?"

"I just may not retire; I haven't decided yet. But if I go, I want to go like the old Magic Madjeski. With respect, not as a lucky coach who happened to have a crazy quarterback. I want to leave a team in *my* style, a team I can be proud of. I don't want to phone my condolences to the new coach."

"Gruber won't let you fire me." Tilley sounded desperate. "I don't care what he promised you, Gus knows how many tickets I sell. The fans love me. I'm the most popular—"

"Our dear owner," Carny said smoothly, "also knows what you've been saying about him behind his back. In public. To the papers. He especially doesn't like what you said about his new light beer just before you made the commercial, so don't expect any residuals from that one."

"Everybody knows it tastes like weak piss. Only worse."

"That may be," Madjeski said, "but they don't say it out loud when the camera is running, especially when they're going to be paid a lot of good money to say how great it is."

Tilley sat up straight. "I always thought you were smart, Madjeski. You had a reputation as a tyrant and a dictator. No heart, no soul, but smart. I knew you didn't like me, but so what? I don't like you either. In fact, I hate you, and so does everyone who comes into contact with you. And that includes the ape on your right and the hyena on your left. No coach ever liked me, but every one I've played under knew how to use me. Except you. But even so, I managed to drag this team from the cellar to the Super Bowl in two seasons. But now, I don't think you're so smart anymore. Any head coach, anybody with even half a brain, wouldn't tell his only hope for winning the Super Bowl, two weeks before the game, that he's planning to fire him."

"Neither would I, normally, Tilley. But I have learned that you are very short of money, in debt, in fact, and there are rumors—I'm not done investigating yet—that you have bet on games in which you played."

"You lousy son of a bitch, you spied on me? Well, you're dead wrong. You'll never be able to prove I bet on any games, especially my own. And if you think I would throw a game, you're really crazy. There's damn few other quarterbacks who scramble, who risk their bones to get a first down."

"Even betting on your own team is not legal, Tilley, and you know it. And your lack of money—the bad investments, the kind of life you lead—it all costs, doesn't it?"

"I'll go to the papers with this, Madjeski. I'll tell them you're throwing the Super Bowl just for spite; that you're trying to break my spirit so we'll lose."

"Go ahead, Mr. Tilley, if you think you're so smart. But you may find that, if we lose, you'll be accused of using that excuse to throw the game yourself. Because, obviously, you bet against your own team. Your own teammates will kill you. I expect to have no trouble finding the man who will swear he placed a bet for you on the Orcas."

"You bastard. You'd frame me?"

"Me? Certainly not. I just want to make sure you'll play your best and that you'll follow the game plan we set up and execute the plays as practiced. And win. If I retire, or even if I don't, I want to win the Super Bowl. And you would too, wouldn't you, Mr. Tilley? Because if you have any hope of being picked up by another team next season, or of becoming a coach, you have to win. There'll be very few endorsements or cushy retirement jobs for Crazy Al Tilley if you lose."

"Why are you doing this, Madjeski? You're throwing away the only chance we have. Why?"

"Because you're a lousy grandstander," Boom-Boom Drogovitch said. "When you get away with one of your crazy tricks, the papers give you the credit, but when you mess up a good play, we get the blame."

"You're a headline hunter," Carny added. "Always shooting your mouth off to the papers: how stupid we are, how you always save the game in spite of us. This time, this last time, you're going to stick to the game plan and you're going to execute the plays exactly as practiced. Magic will send in each play, and you better not fool around unless the defense shifts while you're calling the signals."

"We'll lose," Tilley gasped. "Too rigid."

"If it gotta be," Boom-Boom said, "we'll live with it. You talked so big to the press that losing will be blamed on you this time. We've got a couple of columnists set to rip you apart at the first opportunity. You're not the most popular guy in the NFL, you know."

"So you better win," Carny said. "And if you do, everybody will know it's because of our game plan and our plays."

"And my defense," Boom-Boom added.

Tilley stared sullenly at the head coach. "I don't believe this. I just don't believe it." He raised his voice. "You tell me now you're planning to put me on waivers, *now*, right before the Super Bowl, *now*, just to get me to play it your way? Which you know for sure is going to cost us the game?"

"On the contrary, Tilley, the only chance we have of winning this game is to follow my game plan precisely, without deviation. And I've finally decided that this is the only way to get you to do it. . . . And there's a thousand-dollar fine for missing practice this morning," Magic said.

"After I won the play-off game? You can't do this—"

"Pick him up, gentlemen," Madjeski said to Boom-Boom Drogovitch and Carny Quigley, "and clean him up. Throw him into the shower as he is, with his clothes on. I don't want anyone else to see him in that condition; bad for morale. After that, it's into the whirlpool, good and hot, for fifteen minutes. Then have Rybek give him a good massage—Vincent himself, not his assistant. I want Tilley suited up and ready to go for this afternoon's scrimmage. Tell your assistants I want a full scrimmage, no loafing. In full uniform."

"Some of the guys are pretty beat up from yesterday," Carny said. "Those Longhorns are tough. How about a light workout instead, Coach?"

"A full scrimmage, Mr. Quigley," Madjeski said. "There will be no letdown on my team."

The two big men picked up the quarterback by the arms

and carried him to the locker room door. "I'll give him the massage myself, Magic," Boom-Boom said. "It'll be a pleasure."

"Do you think it sank in, Carny?" Madjeski asked. "Will he do what we want?"

"He's got no choice," Quigley said. "No choice at all."

3

The Oregon air was cold but the western sun was shining on the backs of the sweat-suited Orcas working out to the barks of the assistant galley masters. James "Jimbo" Tallifer, the Orcas' head coach, nodded once in satisfaction and, done with this unwonted display of emotion, walked back a few yards, flanked by his offensive and defensive coordinators, Dino "Scar" Scorzetto and Walter "Tank" Chrysczyk.

Jimbo Tallifer was still as straight and handsome as in his playing days: His brush-cut brown hair showed only slight touches of gray, his body only slightly thicker than when he was an all-pro quarterback three years running.

Jimbo kept his gray eyes, protected behind his trademark aviator sunglasses, pointed at the field of sweating athletes as he spoke, watching, weighing, judging. "Scar, some of your linemen are moving stiffly. Yours too, Tank. Have everybody who has the slightest pain report to the trainer. Massage, whirlpool, diathermy, cortisone, taping: whatever is needed. No heroes and no Novocain today."

"You trying to make sissies out of my boys?" Tank asked. The giant Tank, the greatest tackle of his day, dwarfed even the six-foot four-inch Tallifer by four inches. Tank still weighed over three hundred pounds and nothing jiggled on him as he walked. He had a shock of thick black hair that fell in all directions and needed to be brushed away from the thick lenses he wore in front of his tiny eyes. "They're just a little sore because they took a lot of abuse from the Piranhas yesterday, that's all. No big deal. Pain is part of the game."

"Pain takes attention, Tank," Jimbo said. "It takes a couple of hundredths of a second off your quickness and makes you move differently. Two weeks to the Bowl; that's enough time to get everybody in perfect shape."

"What about scrimmage?" Scar asked. Scar, at six feet, looked short next to Tank, and even Jimbo, and he was twenty pounds heavier than Jimbo. Scar had lost only a few tenths of a second's speed from when he was one of the best running backs in football. With his sleeked-back black hair, thin mustache, and pointed sideburns, he looked like the typical Latin gigolo of the old musicals, but when he was tackled, it was usually the tackler who was knocked backward as Scorzetto picked up an extra two yards. "You want to go easy on the scrimmages too? That could make them lazy."

"Tomorrow and Wednesday, light run-throughs," Jimbo said. "There's no way you can maintain game tension for two weeks. Then a slow buildup to the Saturday before the game. No practice injuries, you hear? Save it for the Wizards."

"Tuesday?" Scar asked. "I already gave them Tuesday off, Jimbo, as usual. They need a day to relax."

"Not this Tuesday. I want the buildup slow but continuous. They can have next Tuesday off. No way to keep them tied down then, right after the official NFL photo session in New York. But I don't want the boys going crazy their first day in the big city. Bed check that night and no getting drunk, no fighting and no trouble. They've got to be in shape for the Wizards."

"There's nothing to worry about with the Wizards," Tank said. "A bunch of kids and has-beens. Lightweights. They don't have a guy over two seventy. I could take on their whole line myself."

"Maybe twenty years ago you could have, Tank, but don't let their size fool you. What they don't have in size, they have in speed and stunts and games; Boom-Boom and Carny are damn good. What's more, I don't want to hear anybody attached to the team, *anybody*, knocking the Wizards. Any reporter asks you, the answer is that the Wizards are a great team and we're *hoping* we can beat them."

"Come on, Jimbo," Scar said, "the spread is going to be at least sixteen points, maybe even twenty. It'll set a record for the Super Bowl. The only question is, by how much are we going to cream them? The Piranhas could have taken them by twenty, and we beat *them* by thirteen."

"You want the spread to go to twenty, Scar? I thought you needed retirement money."

"Just talking theoretical, Boss. None of us bets on games, right? But okay, like you say, build up the Wizards every time. Maybe we can push the spread down to fourteen points. Only trouble is, who's going to believe us?"

"The place to put down a bet's gotta be in Brooklyn," Tank said seriously. "Those Brooklyn fans are so crazy, they'll push the line down to twelve or less, which as far as I'm concerned is an absolute lock. Only trouble is, I don't have any contacts in Brooklyn."

"I have an uncle," Scar said thoughtfully, "that I work with, sometimes. Occasionally, you know? But for small stuff, usually."

"Is he reliable?" Jimbo asked.

"Is he connected?" Tank asked.

"Absolutely straight, Tank, but he's never handled anything really big before, and the way I figure, this is one to put your shirt on. But he can't do it all by himself; no bookie will take him on for big dough."

"Talk to him, Scar," Jimbo said. "Maybe his uncle has an uncle. But no names. This could be retirement money for all of us. When are you going to see him?"

"If I can take off after the photo session too, Jimbo? I've

been watching films till midnight for the past two weeks, and I'll be doing that every night until the big game."

"You're a big boy, Scar. I don't tell you what hours to work. You know what you gotta do."

"Okay. My first day back in New York, my mother's going to make a big spread, *big*, and invite everybody, especially my uncle. I'll talk real business with him then. Of course, I'll be in touch with him by phone tonight, to start making the arrangements."

"Good. See how much he can handle. Now tell me again, boys, you're sure we're going to win *big*?"

"There's no way we'll win by less than twenty-one. I'll put my kid's college dough on that."

"Tank?"

"My line outweighs their offense by so much, it's like playing with midgets. Hell, my linebackers are bigger than their guards."

"Every team in their conference outweighs the Wizards, Tank, but they're still in the Super Bowl. They've got to have something."

"Luck, Jimbo, pure luck. I went over some of their game films last night. It's fifty percent luck."

"And the other fifty percent?"

"A combination of things, Jimbo. A little speed, a lot of tricks, and Crazy Al. You can't ever figure what he's going to do next."

"He's also smart," Scar said. "This is his fifteenth year as a pro, and there's nothing he don't know. He can read a pattern and find a hole for a receiver while he's scrambling."

"I can stop him," Tank said. "I'm working on the defense for the game right now. We're going to drop zone defense— that's too vulnerable to the short passes Tilley throws—and go man-to-man."

"That leaves us open for the bomb," Jimbo said. "Their wide receiver is very fast, even though he has no moves worth a damn."

"Tilley threw long only twice in the past season, Jimbo, and each time with the wind at his back. One hit and one went for an interception. I don't think he'll take that risk too often in a Super Bowl game. His arm won't take it, even if Magic lets him do it."

"Still, we've been very successful with zone defense, Tank. You think it pays to change?"

"Not completely, Coach. We'll mix in a little zone every once in a while, just to keep Tilley off balance. But I never liked 'prevent defense.' Sure it protects you from the bomb, but it lets those short passes eat you up, and all of a sudden you're on your own twenty, fighting to stop a goal and force a field-goal attempt. Three points ain't six or seven, but enough threes can kill you too."

"Okay, Tank. Work it up in detail, and we'll discuss it again. What do you have on offense, Scar?"

"Power, Jimbo, pure power. There's no way to work against speed and stunts effectively; you're never sure what they're going to do. We use what we've got: fundamentals and weight. When your offense is that much bigger than their defense, you force your way through. All the stunts in the world won't stop a big offensive line from opening a hole for a big fullback like Lester Willis. We'll average five yards a carry, guaranteed, maybe a little more, and just march down the field. No fumbles, no interceptions, just raw power."

"No passing?"

"Oh, sure, Jimbo, Pete Sandor will pass. Just enough to keep them honest. Any time their linebackers come too close to the middle, we'll pick up eight, nine yards in a short sideline pass. And if the safeties come up too close, Pete can throw the bomb with the best of them. Even if it doesn't hit, it'll spread out the downfield defense."

Tallifer was silent for a while, thinking. When he spoke his face was dark. "I want to have a big score, boys. A *very* big score. I want this to be Madjeski's last game and I want him to go out covered with mud."

"You hate him that much?" Scar asked.

"Everybody who ever played for him hates him. I learned a lot from him, but he took my blood and my life. He shortened my career by at least three years. If it wasn't for him, I could have had all the records: pass completions, goals, points, everything. I could have had three more years, four, of big money, endorsements, the works. This time I'm going to break *him*."

"Don't worry, Coach," Scar said, "we'll bury him by twenty-four. More."

"I want more than that, Scar. I want the biggest differential there ever was in a pro game. I want to rub his nose in it and make him eat it. I want his blood."

"Hey, take it easy, Coach," Tank warned. "We'll kill them, don't worry. But you can't do it while you're sore. You've got to think, plan, execute."

"I've been thinking, Tank, and I know exactly what to do. And you're going to do it."

"I already said I would, Coach. Relax."

"I'm relaxed, Tank, and I heard what you said. But it's not enough. Let me tell you what I've been thinking. First of all, I want the biggest, toughest men in your front line for the first quarter, linebackers too, but not the regular starters. I want them to pound the offense, lay them out, hit them with everything. The same for offense, Scar. Weight and power. When our guys hit, I want them to hit extra hard. When they tackle, I want them to slam the man down, not just stop him. Tell them it's their chance to show they deserve to be starters and that it's only for one quarter, not to save themselves for the rest of the game."

"I can do that, Coach," Tank said, "but it may cost us points. Our starting lineup is pretty damn big; I can tell them the same thing."

"No, Tank. I want our first-quarter men to weaken, to tire, to lay out the Wizard offense, and their defense too. Then, in the second quarter, when our regular starters come in, they'll be fresh. They'll be hungry and they'll worry about the first-quarter guys taking their jobs. They'll be good and sore. The Wizards' offense will be tired, weakened, hurt. Our guys will rip them apart, go through them like butter. The Wizards will lose the spirit; they'll fold. We'll get three quarterback sacks in the second quarter and at least one fumble. Guaranteed."

"We'll get that anyway with our starting team in there, Coach."

"This way it's worse. It not only ensures that we wipe them out, it changes the whole course of the game. In the first quarter they'll become overconfident; they'll think they're playing well and that it's worth the beating they're taking. In the second quarter, when we slaughter them, the sudden shock will kill them."

"I don't like to give up points we don't have to," Tank protested.

"You won't necessarily have to give up anything, Tank, but I won't cry if you do. It's not the first quarter that pays off, it's the score at the end of the game. There's more, though. Listen. I've been studying the Wizards' game films too, and I've discovered something. It isn't just luck that brought them to the Super Bowl. Sure they've had more than their share of luck, but they've also got a good coaching staff. Madjeski may be a bastard, but he's a smart bastard who comes up with plays that no one else in the world would think of. And Boom-Boom Drogovitch and Carny Quigley are just as good as you two. They've got some very smart veterans on the team. What they've lost in speed, they've gained in smarts. And they've got Crazy Al Tilley, the scrambler."

"He can't throw over either of my ends," Tank pointed out. "With their hands up, they look ten feet tall."

28

"So he'll scramble and run the end's ass off until he drops his arms and a receiver is free. That's part of what I found out watching the game films. Tilley is smart; he even thinks while he scrambles. The Wizard luck? Hell, it only happens when Tilley is quarterbacking."

"Yeah," Tank said. "I figured that too. You do enough unorthodox stuff, somebody's bound to make a mistake. So if your team is used to it and the other team isn't, Tilley turns that one mistake into a touchdown."

"Exactly, Scar. So the second part of my plan is this: When the offensive line is beaten, physically and mentally, I want blitzing, lots of blitzing. And when the linebackers get to Tilley, I want him hit hard. I want him scared. I want him to hear footsteps behind him, in his head, every time he drops back to pass. I want him watching his blind side instead of his receivers. And if you can do it, I want him caught between two tacklers at once."

"You want him out of the game?" Tank asked. "Crippled?"

"Not permanently, Tank—just out of the game. Look, he's a little guy, not even six feet, maybe one seventy-five or one eighty. It won't take too much to rack him up. Even if he stays in the game—and he might, he ain't short of guts— if he's bruised, shaken, punchy, worried, frightened, there'll be no more luck. And then, no Magic."

"Our boys will do that anyway, Coach," Tank said. "But we're all pros, all in the business together. We're not going to deliberately put a guy out of the game. We've all got to eat."

"I just said that, Tank. I don't want his knees broken. But I do want him hammered. Hard. And I hope your boys remember that in a Super Bowl game, the zebras won't call fouls on a slight, a very slight, stretching of the rules. No unnecessary roughness, Tank—just a little more *necessary* roughness."

"I already told them that, Jimbo. But I also told them

that a fifteen-yard penalty for unnecessary roughness costs a first down."

"Okay, we understand each other," Jimbo said. "I want the team to watch movies tonight, some of the Wizards' games." He turned to Scorzetto. "Scar, you'll find out how much your uncle and his friends can handle?"

Scorzetto nodded. "If he can't, I think I could find another guy too."

"Great. Now start thinking about the overall picture. The goal is to humiliate Madjeski by running up the biggest score in any pro football game. The strategy is to use our size and strength to wear down and overwhelm the Wizards. And the tactics are to make Crazy Al Tilley ineffective. Completely. One way or another."

4

"Go hang for a while," Dahliah Norman said, as Burr got off the elevator and entered the loft. "You look like you're too tired for supper." She turned down the gas range and walked to the front end of the building. The loose green smock puffed out over her tailored gray-tweed skirt and white cotton blouse. As she moved, her long auburn hair picked up glints from the bare bulbs hanging from the sixteen-foot-high ceiling.

The loft was thirty-six feet wide and one hundred feet long from the street front to the back fire escape. At the rear of the giant room was a small bathroom, the only enclosed room in the place, backed up by the open kitchen. The dining room was described by a table and four chairs, the bedroom by a wall of freestanding closets, which gave a little privacy to the oversized platform bed. The living room/study/office consisted of two desks, wall-to-wall bookcases, and soft modular seating units that could be pushed together in an infinity of combinations. A few low tables and an expensive stereo/TV center completed the home half of the loft.

The street half was a gymnasium, a gymnast's paradise: horizontal bar, parallel bars, side horse, still rings, and a wall-to-wall tumbling mat thirty feet long. All the walls were covered with huge blowups of champion gymnasts, caught at the peak of their performance, taken by Marcus Burr after he had stopped competing.

Dahliah walked ahead of Burr, her stride no longer than his, but her energy carrying her faster. At the horizontal bar she plugged in a radiant quartz heater and aimed it carefully where Burr would hang. As Burr approached her, she waved him away, her green eyes mock-stern. "I don't feel like kissing a man who's twanging tense. Relaxing first, kissing later. I took out your sweat suit already. The past week you've been coming home ready to detonate."

Burr went to the chest at the wall and pulled out an athletic supporter. "You're going to exercise too?" she asked. "It was that bad a day at the fun and games department?"

"Not physically," he said as he undressed. "But all the crap I had to listen to, the hustling and the hype, the outright lies. And on top of everything, Witter has been driving me crazy. He's out to get me; trying to make me quit."

"Why does he hate you, Marc? Have you ever analyzed that?"

"He doesn't hate me any more than he hates a pebble in his shoe; just wants to get rid of an irritation."

"Maybe he wants a truce? Face-to-face?"

"Julius? He never gives up. The other guy has to cry uncle."

"Then cry uncle, Marc. Fake it, if you have to. It isn't worth all this tension."

"And turn into Julius Junior? Would you stay with me if I hated myself, Dahliah?"

She sidestepped the question.

"What's on the agenda for tomorrow."

"The official photography session."

"Are you taking your good camera?"

"There won't be any action—just posed pictures of everybody shaking hands. Just my little autofocus, in case something interesting happens before Super Sunday."

32

Dressed for action, Marcus jumped up, caught the horizontal bar with both hands, put his head back, and went limp. As she watched, Dahliah could see Marc's body lengthening, his toes reaching down, down, as his muscles slowly stretched and relaxed. Dahliah had never seen anyone so relaxed. A cat, maybe, not a human.

"Can I talk to you?" Dahliah asked, adjusting the radiant heater so that it shone directly on Marc's body. She opened a folding chair and set it next to the heater.

Marc grunted.

"I gave two classes today"—she settled back in her chair—"psychology of violent crime and defusing hostage situations, both graduate studies. I had a real bit of luck. One of my students, a lieutenant who's had some experience in crisis management—talking down would-be suicides and the like—told me that the course was really good, practical, that it jibed with his experience. All this, right after my chairperson came in to observe me."

"Does that mean you get a raise?" Marc asked, kipping up to a rest position on the bar. "So we can afford to heat the whole place?"

"Raises come annually, Marc, not daily. But this came at just the right time. After you get tenure, there's always a worry period when they get second thoughts about whether or not they did the right thing. Especially with a woman. Not that the Oliver Wendell Holmes College of Criminology discriminates, but police work is still very much a man's world."

Marc began doing drop kips, twenty in a row, then he swung into a tight backflip dismount. "Little do they know what a prize they have in Dr. D. Norman," he said, "most beautiful professor in the whole city university. One of these days you should show up in real sexy clothes instead of a suit; you'd make full professor in a hurry. You have my permission to kiss me now."

"After a shower, animal." She pushed him away. "And show a little respect, pig. I didn't get tenure on my looks."

"Give me five minutes. A little work on the parallel bars, a little on the horse, and a minute or two on the mat. Make that twenty minutes. I want to soak in a hot shower. Then put the food on the table. What are we eating tonight?"

"Caesar salad, thick three-bean soup, and spicy noodles. For dessert, clementines. Perfect balance."

"I need complete protein, Dolly. I do a lot of running around."

"There's plenty, Marc. I even put a coddled egg in the salad dressing."

"Ecstasy." He winced. "One of these days, I'm going to sneak some chopped liver into your muesli, give you a taste of the real world." He moved to the parallel bars.

"So what's the big deal?" Dahliah asked. "From the way you describe it, it's what you've been doing all your life, your adult life."

"That's the whole point, Dahliah. There are only so many ways you can say Team A won over Team B, or Player C hates Coach D. After a while it becomes one big gray mess. Blah. Boring. Deadly."

"But you love sports, Marc. I know you do. Otherwise why would we live in a gymnasium?"

"Sure, sports. I love to do sports, even to write about them. I've always wanted to be a journalist. But almost all of what we call sports today is games, professional games. And they're all highly commercialized."

"Nobody forces people to attend sporting events; they do it because they want to watch the best athletes in the world performing. And to share, even vicariously, in the beauty and the thrills of the game. Some of the moves"—she waved at Marc's pictures on the wall—"are as beautiful as anything in ballet."

"How much better off a man would be if he went out and

played touch football on a Sunday afternoon instead of planting himself in front of a television set."

"Come on, Marc. Would you force people to fit your mold? What about people who aren't able to play games? Would you force everyone to play? Regardless of the situation? I'd say you'd make a good commissar, if I didn't know you better. What's really bothering you, Marc?"

Burr moodily dipped his spoon into the soup. Dahliah had put in some chili powder and lots of onion and garlic, but there was no meat. Any fat had to be safflower oil. But it was good. Delicious. Dahliah—God, what would he do if he didn't have her?—looked at him expectantly, patiently.

"I want to—does it really sound childish?—to do some good in the world, Dahliah, something really useful. Investigative reporting. Not whose ankle will be in good shape next Sunday, but which politician's been dipping into the till, who's been selling us out."

"Then quit, Marc. You can get another job with another paper."

"Where can I go? No one would hire me for anything but sports. I can't start over as an assistant copyboy."

"Can't you do investigative reporting in sports? Aren't there lots of shady things going on? I don't mean on the field, but in the front office."

"Oh, sure, there has to be. Big-time professional sports are too closely tied in with politics to be absolutely clean. But I can't get into that. How can I do the footslogging research when I'm trying to get two stories a day? What I really need is for someone to drop a nice juicy scandal in my lap."

"I have a little free time on some days, Marc. If you want me to check something . . . I'm good at research and I'm sure some of my students would let me check files not usually open to the public."

"Yeah, thanks, but I don't know where to start."

"What about the Gruber Dome? Aren't there lots of rumors about that?"

"There are lots of rumors about everything in pro sports. That doesn't mean they're true. Ninety percent of investigative reporting is checking records, sheet by sheet. Gus Gruber was too smart to do anything illegal. He just put a gun to the mayor's and the borough president's heads: Either build me a stadium to my specifications, with lots of seats and private boxes, or I'll go to Nassau County. The Brooklyn fans are so crazy, the mayor had to give in. So it was a steal. Gruber is making millions—he could sell the franchise right now for nine figures—and the taxpayer foots the bill. The funny part is, I'm not so sure the city didn't gain also, in spite of everything. The amount of business the Wizards bring in, and the amount of taxes . . . maybe the mayor is smarter than I think."

"Nothing, absolutely nothing for you to look into?"

"Yeah, sure, there are a few things that are always available in football, things like gambling and drugs, but every reporter has his eyes out for those. The trouble is, I spend so much time on routine crap. . . . My only pleasure is needling Julius Witter once in a while."

"Isn't the football season over Sunday? The Super Bowl?"

"So there'll be something else he'd send me on. Tiddlywinks or something like that, anything just to frustrate me, to keep from letting me have time. He's trying to get me to quit."

"Are you going paranoid on me, Marc?"

"No, really. He told me exactly that. Because I was forced on him."

"After fifteen years, he suddenly decides?"

"He's been trying for fifteen years, only I was too dumb to see it."

"To hell with him, Marc. Quit. If you're that frustrated, that unhappy. . . . It just isn't worth it. We can live on what I make for a while."

"An associate professor's salary? Two weeks. Why don't you go commercial, Dahliah? With your qualifications, you could be making double your salary in private industry. Or, better, in private practice."

"First of all, there isn't much call for psychologists in criminal cases, except where they're trying to prove some killer was not aware of what he did, and I won't do that. I just won't. I never told you, but I had a cousin who . . . The guy is now walking the streets; one year later he made a miraculous recovery. Someday, maybe, there'll be a verdict called '*guilty* by reason of insanity.' Until then. . . . Second, I can't set up an office in a loft building, and it costs over twenty thousand just to think of starting a private practice properly. If we start saving now, maybe in about ten years. . . ." She took the empty soup bowls off the table and stacked them in the sink. "Besides, I love teaching." She brought the big bowl of spicy sesame noodles to the table. "Your turn to cook tomorrow, Marc. I have my martial arts class at five."

"You could get a lot more exercise in ten minutes of gymnastics than in an hour of karate, and it's free."

"Freud once said, 'Never let anyone you love teach you to drive or to hang by your toes.' Besides, I'm too tall and too heavy for gymnastics."

"You're no taller than I am, and I'm ten pounds heavier than you."

"We're built differently, in case you haven't noticed. Women gymnasts have to be tiny and balanced."

"That still giving you trouble?"

"I have no trouble protecting my head, but there's one bitch who keeps hitting me where I stick out and claiming it's a lethal blow. I'm going to try taping myself flat tomorrow. Then we'll see what happens."

"Don't even think of it, love; it might stay that way. Tell you what, after supper I'll wrestle you on the mat, teach you a few things."

37

"You rat, if I find you've learned anything new, you'd better have an explanation ready." She got up, moved behind his chair, and put her arms around his shoulders, leaning her breasts against his back. "This is the way I like you, darling. The way you used to be. Forget about work and leave the noodles—they're fattening anyway. Come on, I'll pin you three out of three."

"Three? On a weekday?"

"Anytime. With one hand tied behind my back."

He put down his fork.

5

Marc Burr stuck his head timidly inside the door of the sports editor's office. "You rang, sire?"

Julius Witter didn't look up from the copy he was editing. "Sit. And see if you can shut up for two more minutes." His blue pencil was flying across the story, stopping every few seconds to make another correction. "Illiterates," he muttered. "If they made them pass first-grade remedial reading before they passed out the doctorates . . ." He raised his eyes to Marcus. "You know what one of them said to me the other day? When I told him if he didn't know how to spell a word, to look it up in the dictionary, he said, 'If I don't know how to spell it, how can I look it up in a dictionary?'"

"I guess you appreciate someone like me, then, Mr. Witter. Is that what you called me in for? To congratulate me on my command of the language?"

Witter stared at him in amazement. "Congratulate you? Me? Are you crazy? You're barely, just barely, adequate."

"Gee, Mr. Witter, that's the nicest thing you've said to me in fifteen years."

"That's the nicest thing I've said to *anyone* in fifteen years, Burr, but don't let it go to your head. It doesn't mean you're getting better, just that I'm getting soft in my old age. . . . I'm going to give you some added responsibility."

"You're resigning, sir? And recommending me to be the new editor of the whole toy department? Gee, I don't know what to say, sir."

Witter stared at him coldly. "Do you really think that's funny, Burr? Because if you do, if you really want to be a stand-up comedian, I'll be glad to give you a letter of recommendation to the nightclub of your choice. Attached to your letter of resignation, of course."

"No, sir, Mr. Witter, not a comic. I was only trying to ease your burdens, sir—lighten the atmosphere, bring forth that sunny smile."

"You want to see me smile, Burr? Really want to? I'll tell you when I'll smile, if you really want to know. All you have to do is—"

"No, sir. I'd rather not hear it. Things like that should be between you and your abnormal psychiatrist."

Witter took a deep breath. "Burr, I'm going to give you the opportunity of a lifetime, a chance to redeem yourself. You know how many reporters we have on the Super Bowl?"

"Twenty? Thirty?"

Witter looked at him, amazed. "What do you think we are, Burr, *The Times*? Full time, we have six, including you. The rest are doubling up in their specialties: fashion, food, Women's Page, science, finance, weather, and so forth, as these are affected by the big game. We did as well as we could with this limited staff because, with you covering the news and general color, I could assign the good reporters, the dependable ones, to strategic analysis, personal histories, past Bowl games, position-by-position comparisons, and all the other information our readers demand. However—"

"However, sir?"

"Yes, however. The Orcas flew in last night for the big official photography session at the Gruber Dome this afternoon."

"Don't worry, Mr. Witter. I'm up on all the latest news. I read *The Times* every day."

"Don't revert, Burr. I'm warning you. You got off to a good start this week. Don't louse it up."

"Yes, sir, Mr. Witter, sir."

"Now, much as our readers favor the Wizards, they still have some interest in the team that is going to wipe out the Wizards. So all my reliable reporters will have to do double duty, get all the background information from both the Wizards and the Orcas."

"The strain must be unbearable, Mr. Witter, having to get all those great big piles of handouts from *two* vice-presidents of public relations in one day. Then carrying these heavy loads to the press room and sending them verbatim to your computer. Cruel and unusual punishment, obviously. A word to the wise, Mr. Witter—the Guild will hear of this."

"So, Marcus, my boy, you are going to have a great opportunity: writing five hundred words of color and seven hundred words of news on the Orcas."

"I don't mind, sir," Marc said bravely. "In fact, it'll be a relief to get away from Verne Ketchel; he gives me a hard time if I even hint that Brooklyn is not heaven on earth and the Wizards are not the greatest team of all time. Who's going to cover them now?"

Witter stood up and put a fatherly hand on Marc's shoulder. "Do you really think, my boy, that I would take you off the job you're doing so magnificently? Where you have established your contacts and your spies? No, no, Marcus, I would not play such a low trick on a fellow toiler in the vineyards. The Wizards are your domain, as are the Orcas. Yours alone."

Marc brushed Witter's hand off his shoulder and stood up. "The Orcas are training at Yankee Stadium, Julius. In the Bronx. The Wizards are in the Gruber Dome. In Brooklyn. I can't do it, Julius. Physically impossible. My taxi could be held up in traffic for three hours."

"You're overwhelmed by my generosity, Marcus, but have no fear. I have arranged the logistics for you. You will take the subway; it will speed you to Yankee Stadium. Tokens will be provided," he added, beneficiently.

"I don't ride the subway," Marc said firmly, "especially in off hours. Muggers think I'm an easy mark because I'm small."

"Five eight isn't small, Marcus, just a bit below average. But I'll give you a tip: Wear a press pass in your hat; everybody respects a press pass. I saw a movie once where Roscoe Karns—or was it Frank McHugh? It was some time ago—had his life saved by his press pass."

"No, Julius. Absolutely, positively not."

"Four bylines, Marcus, think of that. I'll give you four bylines in each issue. A record. Pseudonyms, of course, but everyone on the staff will know. You'll be famous."

"I'll be dead. You can't do this, Julius. I'm going to take it to the Guild."

"Excellent idea, Burr. They're sure to rule in your favor. But you should also realize that other reporters on *The Sentry* do double duty. Betsy Malone puts out a column every day and still goes on assignments."

"I'll do a column every day too instead."

"Not right now, Burr, but do well on this simple little assignment and— Who knows? About your going to the Guild? Do it; you're sure to win. In fact, I will testify on your behalf that it is an exceptionally heavy assignment."

"You will?" Burr was suspicious.

"Of course, Burr. I am dedicated to the truth. But I would also point out that Mr. Heisenberg does not like reporters who go to the Guild; he prefers man-to-man bullying. Once he tells me that you are no longer his ideal. . . . How long can you live on unemployment, Burr?"

"You're a sadist."

"I am immune to flattery, Burr. However, I sense a certain reluctance on your part to take advantage of this sterling opportunity. As it happens, there is a possible opening which, if you really want it, I can make available to you. I'm sure I can find someone competent who will be glad to take your place, at a lower salary, of course, so that I can shift you to your new job. You, of course, will have to take a slight cut in salary too, but if that is your heart's desire. . . ."

"How much, Julius?"

"A mere sixteen percent. It has the additional advantage of putting you in a lower tax bracket."

"You're doing all this just to save money? My lousy few dollars is going to make you look good? Why don't you just put another man on, even temporarily?"

"That's not in the budget, Burr. Don't forget, unlike the very rich papers, *The Sentry* does not have one editor for sports news and one for sports administration and finance. I too am doing the work of two men. And yes, Mr. Heisenberg will be very happy to see our payroll cut, however slightly. It's the money with him, not just the principle."

"You're keeping both jobs because you want the power, Julius. Everybody knows that. Okay, it's worth it to get away from you. If it's the police beat or city hall, I'll take it."

"Unfortunately, my boy, my authority is limited to sports. One of our major favorites, very popular with a large segment of our readers, has taken on so many responsibilities of late that it is necessary to add a reporter/researcher to her staff."

"Her?"

"Nelda Shaver, whose 'The Sporting Woman' is one of the first-read features in *The Sentry*. You're ideal for the job."

"She's a moron, Julius. The name of her column . . . she doesn't even understand the connotations."

"True, but the average intelligence of a large segment of our readers is even lower than hers. That's what you fail to understand. She is well beloved by one and all."

"But she has nothing to do with sports, Julius; it's all

fashions and gossip. The latest in leotards, headbands, and jogging shoes; who's been seen with whom while hubby's been getting his brains beaten out on the field. She's sick, Julius, disgusting."

"I was very fortunate—actually it was quite a struggle—to keep her in sports. The features editor is dying to get her; she's a major profit center. She's getting another full column of space next week and needs help badly."

"She can't write three consecutive words in good English, Julius."

"That's another way you can help her, Marc. A few tutoring sessions after hours at her place? She's still considered an attractive woman, and I have the feeling she fancies you too. Shall I put you down as a volunteer?"

Marc sighed wearily. "All right, Julius, you win. I'll do both the Orcas and the Wizards."

Julius Witter reached into his desk and carefully counted out twelve subway tokens in front of Marc Burr. "A wise decision, my boy. I knew I could count on you."

6

The official photographer and his crew fussed the two teams closer together for one last shot and wrapped it up. At that signal, the reporters surged forward and surrounded their targets, the two head coaches. Marcus Burr held back a moment to take a quick one-handed snapshot of the rush for his Scrapbook of Infamy, then walked over to the group.

". . . lucky if we score at all," said Magic Madjeski. "The Orcas are so much bigger and stronger than we are, by all rights we should be allowed fifteen men on the field."

"Listen to the old faker"—Jimbo Tallifer grinned—"trying to con sympathy. Here we've just made a three-thousand-mile flight, some of the boys don't even know where the goalposts are, and we're in Brooklyn territory. You know what that means? Brooklyn fans are the most fanatic in the world. The psyching alone is worth two field goals. How would you like to try for a forty-yarder with ninety thousand witch doctors in the stands hating you and hexing you? You think you could be calm and relaxed under those conditions?"

"Do you think the home-team factor is going to play a major part in this contest?" a reporter asked Madjeski.

"There is a slight advantage, a psychological advantage only, in being the home team," Madjeski said. "But that only comes into play when the two teams are evenly matched. I consider it a moral victory just to be allowed on the same field as the Orcas. We'll be lucky if we end the game with no more than three of our regulars crippled for life."

Jimbo flushed at this. "You're quite a con man, Magic. We're the ones who are likely to be crippled. We're used to playing on grass at home—it has give—and this artificial turf at the Gruber Dome is new, two years old, and really tight. I expect at least three cases of turf toe, impacted big toes, just from our practice scrimmages. We could lose our best men from that alone, not to mention sprained ankles for our running backs."

"Won't the added speed and quickness that artificial turf permits be to the advantage of the Wizards?" another reporter asked Magic.

"If you're a halfback," Madjeski responded, "making an end sweep at full speed, and you're hit by a two-ninety-pound defensive end who is slightly slower than you, you think the turf makes any difference? Hell, my running backs and receivers will probably slow down unconsciously, just to reduce the impact with these monsters."

Jimbo laughed. "You'll never get the truth out of Magic Madjeski. If we're talking about the physics of the game, it takes a lot longer for a two-ninety-pounder to get moving, and a lot more power, than it does for a two-forty-pounder. Hell, the Wizards' offensive line will be into my defense before my fatsos know what hit them."

"Any time Mr. Tallifer wants to put his front four fatsos on waivers . . ." Madjeski said dryly. The crowd of reporters laughed.

"I wouldn't send my boys to the Gulag either," Jimbo said quickly. "Some of them are family men."

"You played under Madjeski for quite a few years, Tallifer," a reporter pointed out. "Was it really that bad? I've spoken to some of the Wizards players, and they didn't have any complaints."

"Let me hear you"—Jimbo zeroed in on that reporter—"say out loud, for the record, what a son of a bitch your editor is. No? Well, football players got to eat too. A young fellow isn't going to ruin his career by shooting off his mouth against the guy who holds his future in his hands. And the old-timers, the ones who are hoping to get in one more season before going back to the farm, they're too smart to tell the truth about the dictator."

"Does that go for your boys too, Jimbo?" Madjeski asked. "I don't remember reading where you were the softest coach in the league. And when you gave up playing and became a coach, did you ever thank me for teaching you all you knew?"

"Hey, yeah, Magic, that's right. I never did thank you for all you did just for me. I wonder why? Absentminded, I guess. One of these days, I'll pay you back for everything—you can bet your life on that. But I will admit that I learned a lot about coaching from you. Every time I came up against a new situation, I'd say to myself, 'I wonder what that old Magic would have done?' and then I'd do the exact opposite. Never failed. And look where we are today, both of us, you and me, Magic. You and me."

Madjeski flushed a deep red. "You always were a dumb jock, Jimbo, and you still think like one. A week ago I thought we didn't have a chance against the Orcas. Now that I see you haven't learned a damn thing since they made the mistake of letting you be the head coach, you're going to be in for a few surprises Sunday."

"Cool off, old man. I'd hate for you to have a heart attack before Sunday. You and your crazy collegiate stunts, the ones you steal from Carny and Boom-Boom, are the biggest factor in our favor. I'd hate to face those two without you to louse up their game plans."

"I run this team and I make my own plays, Tallifer, and you know it." The reporters were scribbling madly, overjoyed to have flushed out this open hatred with so little prodding.

"Sure you do, Grandpa." Tallifer needled. "Your mark is on everything. I hear you reamed out Crazy Al for getting you into the Super Bowl, and then fined your only experienced quarterback for celebrating a little. Real smart, that was."

"Who told you that?" Madjeski demanded. "Who? If it was Tilley, he's off the team as of right now."

"I hear it *was* Tilley," one reporter said, shoving in the knife. "Do you really intend to play the Orcas with a quarterback who has never played a full pro game?"

Madjeski just glared.

"It had to be Carny." Another reporter shoved the knife in deeper. "He hates your guts for the way you take credit for his plays."

"No, no," a third reporter corrected, "it was Boom-Boom Drogovitch. He once said your idea of defense is from the Middle Ages, and if he were head coach—"

"Are you really going into the Super Bowl," a fourth reporter yelled, "without your star quarterback and without your offensive and defensive coordinators? 'Cause if you are, excuse me, I've got to get a big bet down fast, before the word gets out."

"I have to confess," another reporter chimed in, "it was Herbert Lovell who told me. You going to put your general manager on waivers?"

"Actually, Gus Gruber leaked it," another wiseass yelled. "Fire the owner, Magic."

"Relax, fellows." Jimbo laughed. "Relax. Do you really think— Can't you see the old fox maneuvered the whole thing to this point so you guys would write there's dissension on the team. No coach with any sense would fire his only hope for the game, his starting quarterback. Especially one as unpredictable as Crazy Al. If Tilley thought this was for real . . . Forget it; it's all a big put-on. I don't know what's going on in Madjeski's head, nobody ever does, but the only thing I can think of that this kind of unprofessional display could accomplish is to increase the spread to the point where, even if the Orcas win by as much as, say, fourteen points, somebody is going to collect some very big bets. Is that what you're thinking of, Magic? Your retirement?"

Magic jumped for Jimbo before anybody could stop him, but the bigger man held him off easily, one hand against the old man's chest. "Take it easy, Grandpa," Jimbo said. "You're trying to get me to swing at you in public, but I'm too smart for that. We'll settle this on the field, right? On Sunday."

Madjeski pulled loose and faced the reporters. "You're a bunch of jackals, all of you. No more interviews." He stalked off toward the locker room.

"Do you really believe what you said, Jimbo?" a reporter asked. "About accusing Madjeski of betting against his own team?"

"Watch that putting words in my mouth, son." Jimbo Tallifer spoke very clearly and slowly, making sure he was understood. "First of all, I didn't accuse Mr. Madjeski of anything. I merely wondered why he took actions different from those I would have taken under the circumstances. Second, I never said he would bet against his own team. You've got it completely backward. It's just the opposite. If his words and actions lead you to print stories that will make it appear the Wizards must lose by a very big margin, the spread may rise to as much as fourteen or sixteen points, a huge spread for a single game between two conference champions. This means that Madjeski—no, not Mr. Madjeski, he wouldn't bet on a game, I'm sure—it means that if *someone* bet on the Wizards and we, the Orcas, won by thirteen points, the bettor would still win his bet. No way did I say, or even imply, that Mr. Madjeski would bet against his own team. That's not only criminal, it's morally repulsive."

"You've been bad-mouthing the Orcas all morning, *Mr.*

Tallifer," a reporter said, "and building up the Wizards. Are *you* trying to keep the spread *down*? For whatever reason?" he added sarcastically.

"I'm not trying to influence the spread," Jimbo answered, "but yes, what I said today might have that effect. What I'm trying to do is several things. I believe that we're the better team in every way, especially in the position of head coach, where we not only outweigh them but we outsmart them by as big a margin." Everyone laughed at this. "And therefore we should win. But I do want to avoid overconfidence. That could make us sloppy, lazy, ineffective. Then, you must remember, the Wizards just beat the three best teams in their conference, three weeks in a row. You think that's an accident? This team is fast and hungry; they're dangerous. The Super Bowl is going to be a lot closer, I'm sorry to say, than the Oregon fans think. Then there's Crazy Al. Everybody makes jokes about him. Very funny. But he's not crazy; he's very smart and very unpredictable. You've got to respect him. How do you defend against a wild card? If he breaks loose, who knows what will happen? And much as I hate to say it, Boom-Boom Drogovitch and Carny Quigley are in the same class as my Tank Chrysczyk and Scar Scorzetto; they're the best in the NFL. And last, keep in mind that this is a single game. One game. Anything could happen in one game; no way to predict it. Remember the '68 Super Bowl? The Baltimore Colts were going to wipe the floor with the New York Jets. Who won? Who? Right, the Jets, sixteen to seven. Under Joe Namath. Broadway Joe. Who some people accused of being a playboy.

"I'm not saying it's going to be that way. We should win and we *will* win, but nothing is a sure thing. Nothing. We'll just go in there and do our best from the moment the whistle blows. Now, I'm tired. I've had a hard week and a long flight, and my day has just begun. And if you think it's been easy, standing up here with Madjeski, watching my back—he's a tricky son of a gun—and fielding your perceptive questions, well it hasn't been easy. If you want more interviews, gentlemen, please wait until tomorrow. Until then, our PR guy, Sherm Katzenbacher, has a whole bunch of releases for you in front of the locker room. So long, gentlemen. See you tomorrow."

The crowd dispersed fast, headed for the press room, eager to get the latest feud on the wires. Marc Burr followed slowly, composing the story in his head as he walked, wondering how much of it was real.

7

Burr pulled the telephone out of the rubber cups and hung it on its cradle. He folded the computer into a neat little package and, carrying it by the handle, started to leave the press box, where he had gone instead of the press room on the lower level. It was a longer trip, but the quiet more than made up for that.

He sat down again in the empty area, the last reporter left in the stadium, he was sure, everyone else hurrying home early, for a change. Reporters know enough to take the break when they can get it; there is very little time off during Super Bowl week.

Marc's two news stories had been sent: the routine stuff about the official photography session and the good story about Magic Madjeski trying to slug his former star quarterback, Jimbo Tallifer. Marc had spent a long time thinking how to write that story. Well, not really. He had written the story quickly and easily, like an old pro, describing the peaks of emotion, the slow-burning blood feud, the hatred that Jimbo had brought into the open at, of all places, a simple formal ceremony where perfunctory handshakes, false smiles, and cliché responses were all that was required and all that was expected. The time, the extra time, had been pent by Marc on toning down the writing—to suit Julius Witter's requirements.

Marc wished that Dahliah had been there, had seen and heard everything. She would have sensed, maybe even understood, the deeper animosities beneath the surfaces. A rebellion against the old man by the young challenger? A rite of passage for the soon-to-be-crowned new king? But then, Jimbo Tallifer did not do things accidentally. One of the greatest quarterbacks of all time, on the field he had kept his cool, kept full command, in situations where tenths of a second counted, and made the right decisions an amazingly high percentage of the time. He was known for staying in his pocket of defenders, searching for a receiver, preparing to pass, all in the midst of a blitzing horde of brutes bent on destroying him, often passing as he was being dragged down. No, Jimbo had provoked Madjeski's outburst deliberately. But why?

There was the story; Marc was sure of it. The trouble was, if Jimbo had done it deliberately, there was no way Burr, or anyone else, would get that story out of him. But what the hell! It was still early. Why not give Madjeski a try? No other newspapermen around and no TV commentators sticking mikes into *your* interviewee's face and breaking the flow of a carefully set up series of questions.

Burr was alone in the elevator going down to the locker/office area. There was no sign of activity in the hall as he walked to the door at the far end. A sign read: HEAD COACH—PRIVATE. Marc knocked on the door. There was no answer. The echo had the feel of an empty house. He knocked again, louder, and waited. Still no response. As he turned away, he unconsciously tried the doorknob. It turned. Slowly, cautiously, he pushed the door open a crack and called through, "Mr. Madjeski? Are you there?" Silence.

He pushed open the door and looked in. The office was empty. Madjeski's desk was at the back of the room, a little

53

to the right of center, the famous green blackboard just t
the right of the desk. A line of trophy cases on the left wal
three sets of files on the right wall. On the front edge of th
desk, a set of bronze statuettes, a foot high, of football play
ers in action: kicking, running, blocking, tackling, center
ing, receiving. Compact, radiating strength and force an
energy. Idealized, exaggerated, slightly abstract. Beautiful i
the captured moment, Marc thought, just like my pictures a
home. Fundamental acts from the game.

Marc looked behind him. No one. He stepped inside an
closed the door softly. No reporter, no outsider, had eve
been in the inner sanctum before; Madjeski was a fanat
about security. Taking out his little autofocus camera, Mar
snapped the whole desk, then took shots as closely as h
could get of each of the little statues, for future blowups.
suddenly struck him one pose was missing: the passer—th
quarterback. Tilley must really be in the doghouse, h
thought, if Madjeski had taken his statue off the desk.

Marc took a series of shots all around the office—Witte
would be pleased to save the cost of a photographer—and
closer shot of the green blackboard. Maybe the chalked d
agram was one of Magic Madjeski's secret trick plays de
signed to be used in the Super Bowl.

It wasn't. It was just a plain old screen pass, from a sha
low shotgun formation, with a minor variation. The offensiv
linemen fake blocking the defense and let them throug
giving them a clear shot at the defenseless quarterback, wh
is dropping farther back. Meanwhile, the offensive lineme
run behind the line of scrimmage to form a protective wall i
front of the set back on the right. Just before the quarterbac
is killed by the charging defense, he lobs the ball to th
right, over the arms of the defensive end, into the hands o
the set back, who catches it on the run and follows his fou
blockers for a big gain around the end. With four blocke
leading the way, the play was good for ten yards—with
little bit of luck, maybe a touchdown. If the play was e:

ecuted with precision. If the defense was fooled. If the quarterback wasn't smeared first. If, if, if—always if.

But Madjeski had made the play even trickier. The weak-side halfback would be in motion to the right, crossing the quarterback as he dropped back, and the quarterback would take a handoff to him. The strong-side halfback would run left, in front of the quarterback and fake taking a handoff. The quarterback would fake a pass to the halfback going left, then lob a short one, laterally, almost backhanded, to the halfback who was now on the right side and who, with four men blocking for him, would take off for the goal line, leaving a thoroughly confused defense wondering which shell the pea was under.

If it worked. It couldn't work, of course. In college ball, maybe this kind of razzle-dazzle would play once in a decade, but in pro ball? With the quick reactions of the modern defensive linemen and linebackers? Ridiculous. The kind of precision needed to execute this play, the speed. . . . Madjeski had to be desperate, or crazy with anger at Jimbo Callifer, even to think of a play like this. To start a screen-pass play to the right, that was a normal maneuver. To have a halfback in motion going left and to fake a handoff to him, well, it took an extra tenth of a second or more, and a good lineman runs forty yards in less than five seconds, but it might work. But then to fake a pass left before lobbing a pass practically backhand, over the wildly waving arms of a giant defensive end, into the hands of a fast-moving running back while four huge gorillas are coming at you with murder in their hearts? Absolutely crazy. A good way to get a quarterback killed. If that was Madjeski's goal, a gun would have been quicker and cleaner.

Magic evidently knew this. He showed the quarterback taking one step forward as he faked the pass to his left, and then drew a very heavy line down the blackboard and to the left, where the quarterback would be running for his life. With good reason.

Although he was alone in the room, Marc looked around. He *was* alone; the wicked flee when no man pursueth. He took the eraser and carefully wiped the play off the green blackboard, and replaced a piece of chalk he found on the floor. Madjeski would never know who had done it—blame the cleaning crew, probably. Too bad, but this was Marc's break. He'd be the only one who had the diagramed secret play in advance. If it was used, of course. Whether it succeeded or failed, Marc would have the play *detailed* in his story. No way a TV commentator could follow it. Even a study of the game films later might not show clearly what had happened with such a wild play. Marc would have a scoop, a real old-fashioned scoop. Get Witter off his back for a while. He looked around again, then stopped.

There was a door on the far wall, behind Madjeski's desk. It had been a long day, and Marc hadn't had a chance to relieve himself all afternoon. And he had to take the subway home after he saw Boom-Boom, assuming the Wizards' defensive coordinator was still around. That door had to lead to Madjeski's private bathroom; no way was the head coach going to let down his dignity in front of the players, or even his closest assistant coaches.

Marc pushed open the door.

On the floor, his head in the toilet bowl, was Zachary "Magic" Madjeski. The back of his head was smashed in, a trace of drying blood on his gray hair. On the green tile floor, to Madjeski's right, was the missing bronze statuette—the quarterback, the ball clutched to his chest with both hands, preparing to pass. The hands were stained with blood.

8
- - - - -

Did I wipe everything I touched? Marc wondered, riding the elevator back up to the press box, the only place he could be sure was deserted. Only the two doorknobs, so that's okay. The blackboard eraser? The felt wouldn't take fingerprints. Sweat analysis? Dozens of people must have touched that eraser, or at least three. Besides, sweat analysis can't find you, it can only corroborate other evidence after the cops get you. Chalk dust? Marc slapped at his jacket. Nothing puffed off. Witnesses? He hadn't seen anyone and he was pretty sure no one had seen him. If he was wrong on that, he could always say—he hadn't been there more than a few minutes—that he had walked in, looked around, and walked right out again. No one could prove he had opened the bathroom door. Footprints? None. It was a short-pile, tightly woven carpet. Marc hadn't seen any indication of footprints but, for good luck, had scuffed over the path he had taken.

So it looked pretty safe. The photos? They would place him in Madjeski's office at a time no one was there, that's all; no way to tell when Madjeski had drawn the diagram. No, that was not all. The missing statuette on the desk, the quarterback. That would place Marc in Madjeski's office after the murder. Plus the three shots of Madjeski lying there, dead. Marc pressed the rewind button and popped the film cartridge out of the camera. He placed another cartridge in the camera, pressed the wind button, and snapped a few pictures of the empty playing field through the big sloped windows of the press box.

Marc sat in front of a telephone, rehearsed his lines for a minute, then dialed.

"Where the hell are you?" Julius Witter yelled. "Where are my two background stories? I'm keeping a thousand words open, and everybody and his brother has filed his assignment, everybody except you, my personal plague, Marcus Burr. Are you *trying* to get fired, Burr? Because if you are, this is the right way to do it." He paused for breath.

"Shut up, Julius," Burr said calmly. "Shut up and listen. I've wanted to do this all my life, ever since I was a little kid. Are you ready, Julius? *Stop the presses!*"

Witter hesitated for a moment, then said softly, "Okay, Marc, maybe I've been riding you a little the past day or two, but we're all under pressure this week. Or have you been drinking? I thought you never—"

"I'm not kidding, Julius," Marc interrupted, "and I'm perfectly sober. I have a story for the front page; nobody else has it yet. If you shut up and listen, you can be on the street before anybody even suspects—"

"Really, Marc? This isn't one of your stupid jokes? If you really . . . Hold on, I'll put a rewrite man on with us."

"No, Julius, just you. You can do the padding yourself. I don't want anybody to know about this but you and me; you'll understand why later."

"Okay, start talking, but this better be for real."

"The only problem is, Julius, I'm not sure I want to give you the story. I could call the *News* or the *Post* and get a permanent job on this alone."

"You ungrateful little punk. After all I've done for you? I taught you the business, everything you know."

"And I learned from you, Julius. Very well."

"What do you want?" Witter asked cautiously.

"Fifty bucks a week."

Marc could hear him sigh with relief. "I can promise you only twenty-five. But if the story is really good, and lasts for more than two days, I'll go to the managing editor and push for the rest."

"Next, I want complete anonymity. Nobody is to know that I broke the story until it's all packed up—not even the boss."

"That's easy. When you call about this, use my direct line. The by-line will be Mr. X, and I'll do all the rewrite . . . just get me the facts."

"One more thing, Julius. I'm to be the only one on this story."

"You're not thinking, Burr; you're letting it go to your head. If it's gambling or dope or sex or corruption, whatever it is, the city desk has to take over. The city editor will decide how many people to put on it and who. No way you can be the only one. Even if it involves sports. You've got to live with that, Marc. Sorry." He really sounded sorry. "I'd love to keep it in the sports section, you know that, but I can't."

"Okay, but I want a copy of all the notes and research the other guys hand in. Especially the police reports and the medical examiner's report."

"Murder? *Murder?* That's great, Marc. Fantastic. Start talking; I'm ready."

"You didn't answer me, Julius. Do I get the reports?"

"Of course, Marc. Anything I get, you get."

"Oh, and one last thing, Julius. No more two stories a day. I'm in the best position of anybody to get to the bottom of this, and I need the time to investigate further."

"Okay, Marc, I'll kiss your ass too, if you'll wash it first. Now will you *please* give me the story?"

"Ready? 'Dateline—Brooklyn. Zachary V. Madjeski, head coach of the conference champion Brooklyn Wizards, was found dead, on the green tile floor of his private bathroom, with his crushed head stuck in the toilet bowl. Next to him was the bloodied bronze statuette of a football player, the quarterback, taken from the set on Madjeski's desk. The police came to Madjeski's office on the ground floor of the beautiful new Gruber Dome as a result of a phone call from an anonymous male.' Take it from there, Julius."

"Holy mackerel, Marc, that's great. What do the police say? How much time do I have to get the Extra on the street?"

"The police don't know yet. Fifteen minutes after I hang up I'm going to call you from a pay phone downstairs and tell you the story, so if the police check your phone log, you can say that was when you got the call. When the police get there, I'll join the crowd. In fact, I'll probably be the only reporter in the stadium, so I'll get you the official news first too. *That* can be under my byline."

"Wait a minute, Burr. You didn't call the police? To report a crime? A murder? You were *in* that room, Burr, you had to be. You know how many crimes you've committed already? If the cops find out that you were in there and didn't call them right away, you'll never see daylight again. They'll have ten guys following you to pick you up every time you jaywalk. No wonder you wanted to remain anonymous."

"Yeah, well, I figured that out myself, Julius. Now write the story fast, get the biography ready—I want to check Madjeski's past. Hell, if you work it right, you'll have Madjeski's obit in the street before the *Post* has a headline."

"Yeah, okay, don't teach me what to do. But one more

thing, Burr. If you really want to stay anonymous, stay undercover. No one on the paper should know you're investigating the murder—not even our dear publisher. You have to keep doing everything the same way as before."

"I know that, Julius. I'll interview everybody in the case, the way I usually do, ask the usual questions. If they don't think I'm really an investigative reporter, they'll talk to me pretty openly. They'll even tell me things off the record, important things, that I won't print, but that will help me find the killer."

"Find the killer? That isn't what investigative reporters do, Marc. They expose things that—"

"Which in a murder case means find the killer."

"Okay, Burr, you have my permission to find the killer. You've got it in your head to play detective; enjoy yourself. But I don't think you caught my drift before, when I said you have to keep doing everything the same as before. I meant *exactly* the same."

"I know that, Julius. I'm going— Oh, no! I won't. I can't. You can't make me."

"Oh, yes. You will. You can. And I don't *have* to make you. We've got some pretty sharp reporters on the police beat. If they notice you're doing something different from what you've been doing before, they might put two and two together and figure something out. As it is, I'm going to have a tough time explaining how I got the story together before I got that call. And if you think any of them won't trade you to the cops for a very minor piece of inside information, you don't know how the police beat works. Or how happy any reporter would be to reduce the number of his competitors by one. Or how overjoyed the city editor would be to headline that a *Sentry* reporter broke the story. Or how ecstatic the Editorial Page would be to write editorials castigating the police for locking up a sports reporter who merely—"

"Okay, Julius, okay. I'll send my stories today." Though who, Marc wondered, would be around at this time to interview?

"And every day, Burr."

"And every day, Julius."

"On time, please, Burr."

"Yes, Mr. Witter. On time."

9

_ _ _ _ _

"So what's the story, Inspector?" Marc had his pencil poised over his notebook.

"Lieutenant. Danzig. Harvey Danzig." The detective looked like an accountant gone to fat, well dressed, gray haired, only a little taller than Marc, but his manner left no doubt as to who was running the show.

"Right, Lieutenant, I'll make sure they spell it right. Can I take a picture of you?" Danzig forced a smile. It was not a happy-face smile. Marc slipped the little camera out of his pocket and took a quick shot. The automatic flash went off, and Danzig frowned again.

"How come you're here already? What's your name?" Marc showed him his press pass. "Burr? Yeah, Burr. We just got the word a few minutes ago. So how come you're here so fast?"

"I was in the press room, Lieutenant, writing a background story. In advance sort of, in case I was too busy tomorrow. I wanted to see Verne Ketchel, he's the PR guy, get some handouts, and I saw . . . so what's the story?"

"It's Magic Madjeski," Danzig said reluctantly. "He's dead."

"You suspect foul play? Is that why they called the police?"

"Yeah, you can say we suspect foul play, Burr. You're not a regular police beat, are you?"

"No, sir. Sports. But I'll be accurate and I'll give credit where it's due."

Danzig stared at him suspiciously, then, as if he'd made a decision, said, "Okay. You play it right and we'll get along. Now we can't be sure until the M.E. comes, but it looks like Madjeski was killed by a blow on the back of the head by a hard object."

"You have a time, Lieutenant?"

"From the looks, about an hour, but don't quote that."

"Okay. Any clues?"

"Not yet. We have to wait until the technical crew gets done."

"Any idea who might have done it?" At Danzig's snort, Burr quickly explained. "I mean, was it a professional job? Like a guy surprised in a robbery?"

"Are you kidding? What's to steal in a coach's office, the crown jewels? Nah, this was strictly amateur stuff—spur of the moment."

"In a fight, you mean?"

"Nah, I don't think so."

"Deliberate? Murder?"

"Right now, all I can say is it's a case of homicide. That's all you can say too, Burr, understand?"

"Right. Have you questioned anybody yet?"

"Are you kidding? We just got here. Hey, Burr, you're assigned to the Wizards, right? Okay. Who had it in for Madjeski?"

"If I tell you everything I know, will you let me take a picture inside?"

Danzig looked at him as though he were crazy. "You're going to tell me anyway. *Then* I might be able to get you a print of the body."

"At the same time all the other reporters get one? Thanks a lot."

"Maybe a little sooner, if you cooperate. So who should I talk to first, Burr? Make it fast; I got competition too."

"Jimbo Tallifer. He's the head coach of the Orcas. James is his real name. He and Madjeski almost had a fist fight after the photo session today. Then, something is going on, I don't know what, with the assistant head coaches, the defensive and the offensive coordinators. Both teams, not just the Wizards. I'll write their names down for you." He tore a page out of his notebook. "Harold Drogovitch is the defensive coordinator for the Wizards; nickname is Boom-Boom. Edward Quigley is offensive coordinator. They call him Carny."

"Like in 'carnival'?"

"Yes, exactly. Because he's tricky and smart. Are you sure you don't know all this? It's been in the papers for a week."

"Keep talking, Burr. I'll tell you when to stop."

"Dino Scorzetto. Scar. He's the Orcas' offensive coordinator."

"Scar? He got a scar?"

"Not what you're thinking. I mean, everybody who ever played has some scars, but they're mainly from operations. No, this is just from his name."

"Everybody in football has a nickname?"

"Just about. Some of them are carryovers from when they were playing in high school. Don't you watch football? Even on TV?"

"Pool's my game. Anyone else?"

"The last one is Walter Chrysczyk. Tank. Defensive coordinator."

"And you don't know what's going on with these coordinators? How they could be involved with Madjeski? Killing him, I mean?"

"I'm not even sure they are involved, except for Jimbo. It looked to me like he deliberately provoked the fight with Madjeski. They really hate each other."

"Anybody else hate Madjeski?"

"Maybe Tilley, the quarterback. When they were arguing before, Jimbo said that Madjeski had fired Tilley, just before the Super Bowl game."

"The quarterback, huh?" Marc knew he was thinking of the little statue that killed Madjeski. "That's Crazy Al Tilley?"

"So you do follow football. If you know, Lieutenant, why do you ask me?"

"Here's how it works: I pick up a little here and there by asking. You get on my good side by answering. Right? Okay. Is he really crazy?"

"No. He's really very smart; maybe smarter than some coaches, even. Just a little, uh, wild. Uninhibited."

"Any other suspects, Burr?"

"I never said they were suspects, Lieutenant."

"Sure you did, Burr. Who else did you think did it, the cleaning lady? It had to be somebody close to Madjeski to want to kill him and to be able to kill him. Motive, means, and opportunity, you ever hear of that? Motive and opportunity means it was somebody he knew, somebody he would let get close to him. Means was right there in the office. That's three out of three, right, Burr?"

"I guess so, Lieutenant. What was the means?"

"No harm in telling you now. It was a statue, a metal statue he hit him on the head with." Marc noted that Danzig did not say what the metal was or that it was the statue of a quarterback. It was clear that Danzig was telling only what he wanted him to know.

"Was it big? Heavy? I mean, would it take a three-hundred-pounder to do that? A football player?"

"Nah, small. Even a little guy like you could handle it."

"Anything else you can tell me, Lieutenant, before I phone in the story?"

"You got it backward, Burr. You tell me everything you hear, *everything*, and I tell you what you can put into print and maybe a little bit more, off the record. But you double-cross me once, Burr, and . . . Understand?"

"Yes, Lieutenant, sir."

"Okay. Now once more, are there any more possible perpetrators?"

"No, sir, I can't think of any."

Danzig sighed. "That's why you're a sports reporter, Burr. Any guy on the police beat would have picked up on it right away." He shook his head. "Okay, so you're green, but I can still use you. The suspects will talk to a baby-faced innocent like you more than to the regular police reporters."

"Picked up on what, Lieutenant? What did I miss?"

Danzig looked at him with contempt for a moment, then relaxed. "Okay, maybe you didn't know. An anonymous caller tipped off *The Sentry*—that's your paper, right?—that Madjeski had been murdered in his office. How did he know that, Burr?"

"Well, I guess . . . maybe he opened the door by accident and saw—"

"Nobody opens the head coach's door by accident, Burr—it even says PRIVATE on it. And the body of the deceased was not in a position where it could be seen through the office door. Now what does that say to you?"

"The anonymous caller went into the office far enough to see the body of the deceased?"

"Damn right, he did. In fact, he went all the way in to where the deceased was deceased and—I might as well tell you now, it'll be in the papers tonight—he went into Madjeski's bathroom, at the back of the office, through another door. And he described—don't waste time writing this down, Burr, it'll all be in *The Sentry*—he described the color of the tile, the position of the body, the cause of death, and the murder weapon. That places him right at the scene of the crime, right?"

"Well, yes, Lieutenant, obviously. But maybe he came upon the body of the deceased later? After it was deceased?"

"If he did, it wasn't a hell of a lot later. I'm no medical examiner, but I would say the call was made a very short time after the crime was committed."

"Are you saying, Lieutenant, that the anonymous caller was . . . might have been the killer?"

"It wouldn't be the first time, Burr. This was a crime of passion, not a professional contract. The guy who did it, hell, he probably never killed nobody before. He's nice to his grandmother and he helps old ladies across the street. All of a sudden, he's provoked past the breaking point. He goes wild for a second—that's all it takes, Burr—and kills Madjeski. He goes out and sits someplace, maybe has a shot or two, thinks. His conscience is bothering him. He knows he should be punished for his crime. But he don't want to be caught, don't want to be punished. What does he do, Burr?"

"He calls the police, like a good citizen, and turns himself in?"

"Sometimes. And sometimes he calls his lawyer. Depends. Or he calls the papers or TV—might as well get famous, right? and confession is good for the soul. So even though it ain't exactly confession, he feels better, a little. And he gets a chance to tell his side of the story: Why the deceased was such a rat that he deserved to die, or that he just found out the deceased was screwing his wife and the deceased laughed at him, whatever the reason. Only this case, it's a little weird."

"Weird, Lieutenant?"

"Yeah. Let's say you was the anonymous caller, Burr. Who would you call?"

"Me? Why, nine-one-one of course. The police."

"Nah, not the police, Burr. On a paper. *The Sentry*. Who would you call?"

"Well, I'd ask the switchboard to put me on with whoever was in charge of murder. Crime."

"Exactly, Burr. Well, he didn't call the switchboard. He called an editor, would you believe it? On his direct line, not through the switchboard. And guess who? You'll never guess in a million years. Give up? The *sports* editor, that's who."

"Julius Witter? But he's my boss! Why would anyone . . . ?"

"That's what I want to know, Burr. And guess where the anonymous caller called from. Right here in the stadium. Third phone from the left in the bank near the east entrance."

"So the anonymous caller is a suspect too?"

"A suspect? Too? Hell, Burr, he's the *prime* suspect. What bothers me is, you're going to call somebody to report a crime. Why a sports editor?"

"That's a tough one, Lieutenant. So, let me get this straight: You're looking for a guy who Madjeski would let into his office, who had a strong motive to kill Madjeski, who reads *The Sentry*, and who is not a professional killer."

"Just about. But don't mention this to anyone. I'll question Witter myself about the voice and the accent and the mannerisms. What I want you to do, Burr, is to talk to the regular suspects. Not interrogate them, you understand, just a regular interview, and see what you can pick up. Anything you get, you tell me first, right? I'll give you my home phone too."

"Why me, Lieutenant?"

"Because you want to get on my good side, Burr. Because I just gave you exclusive information. Because I got a funny feeling about you, Burr, being the only reporter here so quick. Because if you talk to me enough, you might, you just barely might, remember something that you forgot to tell me before. So you're gonna help me, Burr, right?"

"I'll do my best," Marc said, trying to look enthusiastic.

10

"But he thinks *I'm* the killer, Mr. Witter," whispered Marc, looking desperately into his boss's eyes. "You've got to help me."

"There's no need to whisper, Burr," Julius Witter said. "No one in this place ever listens to me, even when I raise my voice slightly. And don't look so worried, my boy. Lieutenant Danzig does not think *you* are the killer, assuming you've reported your discussion with reasonable accuracy, he thinks the anonymous caller is the prime suspect."

"Yes, exactly. And when he finds out that I'm the anonymous caller, he'll arrest me."

"But he won't find out, Burr. I'm the only one who knows the voice, and I certainly won't tell him it was you. I'm shorthanded enough as it is until after the Super Bowl."

"Tell him it was a southern accent. A *black* southern accent. Deep voice, sounded like a real big guy. A defensive tackle."

"Do you want me to lie, Burr? Frame some innocent athlete? Do you really want some poor man accused of Madjeski's murder? I intend to tell Mr. Danzig the truth: that the voice that called me was a typical New York voice, a mixture of slight regional accents with a bit of a Brooklyn whine—colorless, dull, and uninteresting."

"Is that what I sound like?"

"I'm afraid so, Marc."

"You would turn me in, Mr. Witter?"

"Don't be silly, Marc. There are a million men in New York with voices like that. He'll never identify you."

"Suppose somebody saw me coming out of Madjeski's office? And tells Danzig? And he comes to you for verification?"

"Well, obviously, it would be my duty to tell him that it sounded like your voice, but I didn't tell him it was you before because the connection was bad and I wasn't sure."

"You *would* turn me in, Julius, wouldn't you?"

"Only to protect myself, Burr. After all, you're replaceable, I'm not."

"I'm not replaceable to me, Julius."

"A very narrow viewpoint. Selfish. But stop worrying, my boy. The odds are that Danzig will not identify you through my description of your voice. What other mistakes have you made?"

"Mistakes? My mistake was in not calling the *News*. They stand behind their reporters. I also took some pictures at the scene of the crime. What if Danzig finds them on me?"

"Pictures? Pictures! My dear boy, why haven't you mentioned them till now? You haven't given that film to a commercial photo processor, have you?"

"I do it all at home."

"The pictures are all clear and sharp? Slightly contrasty, ready for reproduction? How many?"

"Three. You want me to give you my pictures of Madjeski? To print in *The Sentry*?"

"What else are photographs of dead bodies for? It would help sell papers."

"It would help hang me."

"If they're found in your home, they will ensure a verdict of guilty. District attorneys are very fond of physical evidence; it's something juries understand. What if Lieutenant

71

Danzig decides to drop in to talk to you while you're out? From the way you described him, I don't think he would let a locked door stop him. No, my boy, the photographs will be a lot safer here."

"You're crazy, Julius. How would you explain your having them here?"

"The anonymous caller sent them, obviously."

"Why would he send them to you?"

"Same reason he called me instead of the police. . . . How about a little note with the pictures? Something like, 'I hope this helps you find who the murderer is.' The letters cut out of an old newspaper, of course. A *Sentry*. And don't embarrass me by leaving your fingerprints all over the envelope."

"Okay, I'll mail it tonight."

"No, no, Marc. Have you no idea of the time value of these photographs? Three, you said?"

"From different angles. The statuette is very clear."

"Good. Use a plain standard envelope and drop it through our mail slot downstairs. Mark it: TO JULIUS WITTER, SPORTS EDITOR. RUSH, URGENT, PERSONAL. In large letters. The three negatives only; we'll make proper prints here, and that will stop the police from searching your apartment. Destroy the rest of the roll."

"What about a raise, Julius?"

"I've already arranged it, as I promised. And if the story is hot for one more day, I'll try to get you another twenty-five."

"That was for the story, Julius. I'm talking about the pictures."

"Marc, you are fast becoming a greedy, grasping little opportunist. How much?"

"Fifty a week."

"My limit is twenty-five, as you well know, and I've already given you that."

"Twenty-five at a time, you said. This is a different time,

72

a new day, and a new twenty-five. And the rest of the new fifty if you put at least one of the pictures on the front page."

"These pictures are a danger to you, Burr. I thought you understood that."

"You're so right, Julius. I'd better go right home and burn the negatives."

Julius Witter glared. "Very well, then. You win. For the moment."

"Let me hear you say it, Julius."

"A twenty-five-dollar raise yesterday, for the story. A twenty-five-dollar raise today, for the pictures. Twenty-five more on Thursday if the story is still running, and I'm sure it will be, and twenty-five additional on Friday if any of these photographs are printed on the front page."

"Very good, Julius, and don't look at me that way; I'm only trying to get central heating for Dahliah."

"Well, let's see how you do when the real pinch comes."

"What real pinch, Mr. Witter?"

"Do you really think Danzig doesn't know you're the anonymous caller? Think about it, Burr. You're the only reporter in the whole stadium. Madjeski's door was unlocked. *The Sentry* was called. The sports editor was called on his direct line. You are a sports reporter for *The Sentry*. Danzig is no Sherlock Holmes. He doesn't analyze cigar ashes. If it looks like a duck and quacks like a duck and walks like a duck, in his book it's a duck. He must have been laughing like crazy inside while you were trying to con him. Then he tells you he wants *you* to find the anonymous caller for him. Think, Marc, if you're really just a simple sports reporter, how the hell are you going to find the mysterious caller? But if you're the caller, and he knows you are, you're going to fall all over yourself to try to give him evidence that you're not the guy he wants."

"Then why go through the whole rigmarole of my getting information for him? Why not arrest me right away?"

"He'll take everything you can give him, Marc. Why not?

You can get information he can't. But what does he gain by arresting you now? You're not going anyplace; you don't dare. He can arrest you anytime he wants, but why? He picks a fight with you, when you're on assignment, he picks a fight with *The Sentry*. We may not be *The Times*, but we have good lawyers and a tough publisher. You'd be out on bail in a few hours, but we'll be on his back, not just in this case, but forever. Don't forget, I did call the police. For being fifteen minutes late, nobody's going to fry. On the other hand, he can still make some trouble for you, and not much less for me. If he wants to. I can take it, can you?" The old man looked directly into Marc's eyes.

"If you can, Mr. Witter, I can. What do I do now?"

"Get me the pictures fast, then go out to the stadium. Go through your interviews, talk to the players, the coaches, everybody, but especially to the suspects—Danzig is right on that. I would trust his instincts—and see if you can put together a logical picture."

"Do I give Danzig the information I get?"

"Oh, yes, all of it; don't hold anything back. The sooner Danzig closes the case, the safer I'll feel. But send in the information to me too."

"Okay, I'll give Danzig— Wait a minute, Julius. You're telling me to be a detective? I thought you didn't want me to."

"Did I refuse you? Did I? Didn't I give you permission to find the murderer? Didn't you say that's what an investigative reporter does in a murder case? So, go find the killer."

"I thought Danzig was the detective."

"He thinks one way, you think another. You never know which way will work at any given moment. Just remember, there's a guy out there who will also be watching you—a guy who's already solved his problems by killing Madjeski. If he thinks you're getting too close, he may decide to try his luck again with another statuette. The blocker, maybe?"

"I'll be careful."

"I hope so, kid. I have a lot of hours invested in you. Now get going. Half the morning is gone already."

"On my way. Can I take a taxi?"

"The subway is faster. Go. And remember, four stories."

"What? After all we talked about? I have to check the suspects, find the killer, help Danzig, *and* write four stories?"

"All the same thing. The only difference is, half your mind will be concentrating on the story you're going to write, half your mind will be working on the game you're playing with Danzig, and the other half will be trying to fit what you learn into the murder jigsaw puzzle."

"That's three halves, Julius."

"You want to be an investigative reporter, Burr? That's how."

11

"Very nice of you to let me come up here so early in the morning, Al," Marc said. He was enjoying the view of the river from the big picture window of Tilley's East Side apartment. "This must be one of the most beautiful views in New York."

"It's not all that early," Tilley, wearing only shorts, grunted from the floor as the little old Japanese lady walked up and down his spine. "Ow," he groaned. "That one hurt. Take it easy, Miki."

"You have big tension there," the old lady said. "If you practice with this, you will hurt more. I will make relax."

"Okay, Miki, whatever you say, but I still think you're enjoying it." He looked back to Marc. "It's not all that early for me. Don't you start believing all that crap in the papers about how I stay up all night every night. I'm a pro. After a game, I celebrate. Before a game, I live like a monk. That view of the river . . . I look at it for hours. It changes all day long. And the ships? Very relaxing."

"Isn't this a condominium, Al?"

"What you're asking is, how does a player my age take a permanent place this expensive?" Miki pushed his head down with her foot, not too gently. "I'm not broke, Marc, just not liquid right now. I could sell this place today for almost twice what I paid for it, but I don't want to."

"You intend to stay in New York?"

"It's the place to be, Marc. One more year is all I need."

Marc hesitated, then said, "From what I hear, Madjeski wasn't going to give you that year."

"Is that what you came up here for, Marc?"

"Among other things. But if you don't want to talk about it . . ."

"No, it's okay. It'll be a change."

"A change? From what?"

"Aside from the police and the reporters, everybody treats me like I've got leprosy. The whole team. Even my receivers are wearing gloves. It might be catching."

"They think you killed the coach?"

"Think? Hell, they *know*. The story is, now, that I *threatened* beforehand to get Madjeski. I might have been a little hung over after the play-off game, but drunk or sober, I wouldn't be so stupid as to say something like that in front of witnesses."

"Did the witnesses say you threatened Madjeski?"

"I didn't threaten him, he threatened me. He said that unless I worked the big game his way, he'd put me on waivers right after the game and, at the same time, put out the word on how bad I was."

"What's wrong with working his way, Al? He's the head coach. Aren't you supposed to do what he wants?"

"Yeah, sure, normally. And it ain't that he was stupid—he was a no-good bastard but he wasn't stupid—just that . . . See, he's used to working with regular teams: one or two star players, real all-pros; a bunch of pretty good men; a few rookies; and a few old-timers on their way out. A normal mix. His plays were always tricky—they didn't call him Magic for nothing—and with a regular team, they'd work pretty good, most of the time. But we're not a regular team. I had to change the game plan a bit, when it was necessary, and some of the plays too, to suit our special conditions. It worked enough times so that here we are, going to play in the Super Bowl."

"And you were going to use your own game plan and your own plays instead of the head coach's? No wonder he was sore at you."

"Hell, no, I wasn't. All I was going to do was to vary things a little according to the situation. Like if the safety's pulled in a little too close, I'd throw a long one, even if it wasn't the play Magic sent in."

"But you're not supposed to be able to—"

"That's a crock. I can if I have to, and I've done it before. But Madjeski wanted me to use mostly short passes and running plays, the usual stuff, just fancied up a bit, that's all. What everybody expects us to do. Against the Orcas? Hah! We would lose big, for sure. Real big."

"You talk like the Wizards have a chance of winning, Al."

"Listen, it's one game; anything could happen in one game, if you got the right attitude. If you think you're going to lose, then you're sure as hell going to lose." Miki bowed and departed. Tilley got up and stretched in all directions for a full minute, then sat down and leaned forward to loosen his hamstrings. Another minute, and he took the lotus position easily.

"Let's get back to what you said before, Al. If the witnesses said you threatened Madjeski—"

"They didn't say it, that's just the point. Those dumb bastards on the team, my buddies—yeah, as long as I'm buying the drinks they're my buddies—they think they said it, but they didn't. They couldn't."

"Which they is they? Who's they?"

"Boom-Boom and Carny. They were sitting on each side of Madjeski when he threatened me. They did it too, threaten me, I mean."

"They were also angry with you, Al?"

"Oh, sure. First of all, anything Madjeski wanted, they'd

kiss his ass. Second, they just don't like a player, any player, who's smarter than them. No coach does."

"You consider yourself smarter than an experienced coach? Can I quote you on that?"

"Hell, no. You trying to get me in trouble for next year? I'll talk straight to you, Marc, but you've got to use your head on what you print. Otherwise, I'll deny everything and shut out your whole damn paper and tell them why."

"Okay, Al, you have no problem with me; you know that. Somebody else might not have asked." And another good story shot to hell. "Why are you so sure that Drogovitch and Quigley didn't tell the police you threatened Madjeski?"

"One good reason. I'm still walking around, right? If he thought I did it, Danzig would have had me locked away right now, wouldn't he?"

"Not necessarily," Marc said, not voicing his real thought that Danzig was playing cute, trying to lull Tilley into over-confidence. "Your boss, Gus Gruber, wants to see you in the Super Bowl, and he carries a lot of weight in Brooklyn."

"Not with a murder charge, he doesn't. Besides, Danzig could arrest me—I read him as one mean son of a bitch— and I could still quarterback the game. Gruber would get me out on bail."

"You still have the best motive, in Danzig's eyes."

"For what? How is it going to be different for me now? Boom-Boom and Carny still hate me, especially Carny. Why do you think they went with Madjeski in the first place, huh? 'Cause Madjeski's such a doll to work with? They're smart, the two of them. They could have stayed where they were for ten more years, right? No, they both were figuring that Madjeski would pack it in in two, three years, and Gruber would pick one of them to be head coach. By that time, the Wizards would have been a good team; Gruber was willing to spend the dough. We'd be the only team really *in* New York. In Brooklyn, which is even better. So what do I gain by killing Madjeski? Change one S.O.B. for another? Now where's my motive, huh?"

"Well, sometimes people do things in anger, Al."

"Not quarterbacks, Burr. We act fast, but we think first. Remember that."

"I'll remember it, Al. So who do you think will be the new head coach?"

"Could only be Boom-Boom or Carny, one of the two. My bet is Carny. Boom-Boom tells the truth most of the time; that kills him for head coach in my book."

"You say you didn't kill Madjeski—"

"What do you mean say? I didn't. Period. I know I didn't."

"You were in pretty bad shape last Monday. How can you be sure."

"'Cause I'm a quarterback, that's why. It's not the quarterbacks who pick fights in bars; we've got to protect our hands. It's not the quarterbacks who get called for unnecessary roughness; we're the ones it's used on. We're not fighters, we're lovers. You know who are the real killers? Defensive teams. All of them. Everybody, even the safeties. And the worst are the linebackers. You watch a middle linebacker someday. He's standing there ready to kill anybody he can catch, even his own team if they get in his way. He's like an animal. Wild."

"I don't know if that will cut any ice with Danzig."

"It would if he knew football. Why did I have to get the only detective in Brooklyn who doesn't know football?"

"Just lucky, I guess," Marc said, thinking of his own encounter with Harvey Danzig. "Boom-Boom Drogovitch was once a middle linebacker, the best of his time. Are you subtly hinting that Boom-Boom killed Madjeski?"

"If there were toothmarks on his neck, it was Boom-Boom," Tilley said positively. "Nah, Burr, I'm not pointing the finger at anybody; just trying to convince you that quarterbacks are not the type, that's all. What I don't want is big headlines in *The Sentry,* or in any other paper, that I'm a suspect or that I would even think of killing a guy under any conditions."

"Under any conditions?"

"You know what I mean, Burr. Come on, whose side are you on anyway?"

"Does that mean that Jimbo Tallifer couldn't have killed Madjeski? He used to be a quarterback."

"Jimbo's a different story. First of all, he *used* to be a quarterback, but even then, he was a mean son of a bitch. Once, when he thought a guy was banging him harder than was absolutely necessary, Jimbo called a pass play and told the line to let this guy through. When he came in reach, Jimbo put the point of the ball right in his face, with all his might, and he's a big one. Almost took the poor guy's eye out. Jimbo claimed it was a pass. No penalty, even. That's the kind of guy Jimbo Tallifer was. When he was a quarterback. Now he's a head coach; he gets paid to be a tough bastard. So you want to go after Jimbo, be my guest. But tell me something, why would an Orca want to kill Magic Madjeski?"

"Why, to make sure the Orcas win the Super Bowl. There's not only the difference between the winning and the losing purses, there's the reputation, next year's contract, endorsements, all sorts of material benefits. And some people don't like to lose."

"Nobody likes to lose, Marc, but the best way to make sure the Orcas won was to keep Madjeski alive and healthy. In a standard-type game, the Orcas would slaughter us."

"You're the only one who thinks that way, Al. Most other people, including your own teammates, think he's a great coach, professionally."

"I'm the only one on the team who's an experienced quarterback. We don't have the power to go toe-to-toe with the Orcas; we have to dazzle them with speed and fancy moves. We have to be Wizards."

"Wizards without Magic?"

"Fake magic, Burr, take my word for it. Whatever he used to have, he lost it."

"Some people say that about you, Al."

Tilley flushed. "Yeah, I know. Don't rub it in. But I stayed loose. I might have lost a little speed, yeah, the legs go first, but I gained an awful lot of experience. And I learned; I changed. In some ways, I'm better than I ever was. I can read a pattern now twice as fast as I used to. Hell, I can almost mind-read my receivers. Like ESP. And I've still got a damn-quick release."

"Everyone knows you're smart, Al. On the field. How are you fixed for dough?"

Tilley faced Marc. "What are you getting at, Burr? That I'm not loaded like some other quarterbacks I could name? Okay. I trusted people, my business manager, everybody. But I'm taking care of my own finances now. Another season and I'll be all right. What has that got to do with anything?"

"I don't know, Al—just fishing. There's talk in the press room about some rumors. There're rumors all over that some players are betting big on the Super Bowl."

"It's not just in the press room; it's in the locker room too. I'm sure some of the guys bet a few bucks secretly on a game where the spread warrants it. In my book, that's no crime. In fact, it gives the guy an incentive to play better. Most football players are not millionaires, you know, and the average playing life is very short. Very."

"I wasn't talking about you, Al, and I wasn't thinking about guys betting on their own team."

Tilley took a deep breath and let it out slowly. "Let me tell you something. I've been in pro football for fourteen years. I've seen guys play above their ability and play below it—nobody's great all the time. I've seen guys with desire and guys who just went through the motions. But I swear to you, in all this time I never had the slightest thought, the least little reason to think, that anybody I ever played with, or even played against, ever played to lose or to shave points. Never."

"Okay, Al, okay. Relax. I didn't mean to imply—"

"Yes, you did." Tilley no longer looked relaxed. "I don't want to discuss it any more today, especially when I'm this sore. I need my hands for Sunday, so it'll look good when I throw the game. And you can tell that to the other creeps in the press room." He took a deep breath, then another. His face returned to its normal color. "I'm going to the stadium now. If you want a lift, I'll take you, but no shop talk. Okay?"

Marc wondered how he had provoked this reaction. He was sure he had told Tilley that present company was excepted. Marc decided he would discuss this with Dahliah: what it would take to turn a mild-mannered quarterback into a fanged killer. Or a linebacker, same thing, if you believed Crazy Al. He also noted that Tilley had neglected to mention that he didn't know anyone who bet on his *own* team. Or deny that he did it too.

12

I've got the main story, Marc figured, big trouble between the quarterback and the head coach. But if I write it straight, it'll make Tilley the prime suspect for the murder. On the other hand, if I slant it too much in Tilley's favor, it'll look like a whitewash, and Witter will rewrite it his way. On the third hand—God, I'm beginning to think like Witter now—making Tilley the prime suspect might take some of the heat off the other prime suspect, the anonymous caller. Me. To hell with it, Marc decided. When I write it, I'll just let it flow and see what happens.

No way can I use the betting story. What do I write, CRAZY AL TILLEY SWEARS NO FOOTBALL PLAYER EVER BET AGAINST HIS OWN TEAM? That's like a politician swearing that he is not a crook. It brands you at once. No honest man goes around saying how honest he is; he just takes it for granted, like the color of his eyes.

Marc wandered through the locker room—thank God, Tilley was still showering—and into the trainer's area. The place smelled of liniment, alcohol, mineral oil, and antiseptic. Rubbing tables, heat lamps, diathermy machines, ice makers, banks of whirlpools and hydrotherapy tanks of different heights, sizes and types, cabinets full of bandages, slings, splints, and tape, tape all over, and bottles of all colors and sizes. In the back was the team doctor's office, the head trainer's office, and the massage cubicles. Vincent "Pusher" Rybek, short, sour, skinny, and wrinkled, was going through his inventory, making marks on his clipboard checklist.

"How's the injury list, Vinnie?" Marc asked.

"Officially? It's absolutely perfectly accurate and complete. Not one single B.S. report like 'Zoltan Szomodji has a hangnail and, since this might affect his kicking accuracy and may not be completely cured by Sunday, he is in the Doubtful category and may be placed on inactive reserve when the Thursday list comes out.'"

"Amazing. And unofficially?"

"Unofficially, we don't exaggerate any worse than any other team. Our Questionable group has a couple of Probables and a couple of Doubtfuls on it. The Probable list has a couple of Questionables and Sure Starters on it, and our Doubtful list has a few Questionables and Inactives on it. Otherwise, it's perfectly accurate. You think we want to tell the Orcas the *exact* truth?"

Marc grinned. "Any of the coaches around?"

"They're all in conference with the general manager, Marc. In his office."

"You know what it's about?"

"Sure. They're deciding the fate of the Middle East in there. What's the matter with you, Marc, you losing your grip? Madjeski is murdered yesterday, and you can't figure what they're trying to work out?"

"When do you think it will break up?"

"I shouldn't have said 'conference.' With Herb Lovell giving his usual monologue, figure about ten tonight. They already sent out for sandwiches for lunch."

"I need a color story, Vinnie. What've you got?"

"How about the tackle with two broken femurs that I pumped full of Novocain and sent back into the game? Nah, that was already in the papers. Then how about the line-

85

backer, who's selling free-base right out of his locker? No good; that's already been in the papers three times. Okay, the receiver who flies because he gulps ten amphetamines before each half? No, that's been used a couple of times too. Sorry, Marc, all the good stories been used up already by our fearless press."

"You forgot about the guys who work on your nickname."

"Yeah, them. Well, you're too old to be one of them." Rybek looked closely at Marc. "You look like you're under heavy stress, kid. Very tense. I got a mixture that's perfect for that; I'll give you a taste."

"Still pushing vitamins?"

"Not just vitamins, kid. Minerals, natural substances, amino acids, whatever the body needs. Here, look." He took off his Wizards' cap. "See? Remember ten years ago I was completely bald on top? Now I got hair growing."

"Not much, Vinnie, but, yeah, there's a few hairs up there."

"At my age, kid, even one hair is a miracle. When I get the formula down pat, I'll make millions."

"What about your Secret-Formula Super-Energy High-Intensity Power Potion? The one that turns wimps into savage beasts just before a game?"

"I improved it; added glutamine. Glutamine goes right through the blood-brain barrier and carries some of the other nutrients with it. I make everybody take a big swig just before each half. You think we'd be where we are without it? One of these days I'm going to sell it too. When I retire."

"Yeah. When you retire. How'd the new apparatus work out?"

"Pretty good, Marc; even better than I expected. You want to see? Come into the gym." He led Marc past the hydrotherapy tanks, along the corridor. "I gave it some thought—what you told me about gymnastics—and it sounded reasonable. Most of our apparatus was for muscle building, bulk, and strength. Contraction exercises. None of it was for flexibility, looseness, agility, relaxation."

The gym was unoccupied now, the weight racks neatly filled, the Nautilus and compressed-air machines, the Universal gyms, empty. The floor was carpeted, the walls mirrored. Scattered through the gym, where it could be fitted in, was some basic gymnastics equipment: parallel bars, still rings, and mats. The mats were relatively narrow, unlike the big square floor-exercise mats Marc was accustomed to. There were even two thick ropes hanging from the high ceiling.

"It's a little crowded," Rybek said, "but even in this past month, I've been getting results; definitely less sprains. And more looseness. Sometimes I've got three guys at once hanging from the bar. I told Madjeski, next year I want a separate room just for the gymnastics equipment. I'm going to have a rope-jumping area too, a punching bag to develop eye quickness, and a heavy bag for the defensive linemen. How'd you like to train my boys in gymnastics, Marc?"

"I'd love it, Vinnie, but I can't afford to." Marc apologized. He could see himself teaching three-hundred-pound guys to do a giant swing on the horizontal bar.

"Yeah, I know. Football is the worst-paying major sport in the United States. Well, anytime you want to, Marc, there's a place for you here."

"Yeah, thanks." Marc was touched. "But I still need a story."

"Use the gymnastics stuff, Marc. How many other teams do you think have anything like this?"

"You're right, Vinnie. Thanks. I was too close to see the story. This one will write itself." They started walking back to the trainer's area. "You know anything about the murder, Vinnie?"

"Nothing." Very curt.

"How about off the record?"

"I still don't know anything but what I read in the paper."

"You know who hated Magic Madjeski enough to kill him, don't you?"

"That? Sure. Everybody."

"Including you, Vinnie?"

Rybek looked straight at Marc. "He was a mean, spiteful, high-and-mighty bastard, Marc. He didn't care who he hurt or how much. The only thing he cared about was winning games. That and his publicity. There's many times I was icing a guy's knee—ice is a real miracle drug in sports; works wonders fast and does no harm—when he tells me to shoot in Novocain and send the poor guy back in. I never did it, Marc, and I never will. Pain is the signal, not the cause. I used to tell him to put it in writing, so if the guy was crippled permanently, he'd know who to sue. Madjeski never did."

"Why didn't he fire you, Vinnie?"

"He was afraid to. There's nobody on a team knows more secrets than the trainer. I could take one look and tell you who's using anabolic steroids, who's popping amphetamines. Anything at all. I don't need blood tests. I could give you a better diagnosis than most doctors, in ten seconds. I could retire on one book, just one book."

"You'll never retire, Vinnie, you know that."

"I would if Madjeski fired me. I'd get a smart young writer like you and I'd dictate it all to him. We'd both make a million. What do you say, Marc?"

"Anytime you're ready, Pusher."

"I'll let you know." He looked off into the distance.

Marc brought him back. "Were you serious about everybody hating Madjeski? Enough to kill him, I mean?"

"Dead serious. But hating enough doesn't mean doing it."

"Somebody did it. You got any ideas who, Vinnie?"

"Yep."

"You want to tell me about your ideas, Vinnie?"

"Nope."

"Come on, Vinnie. Could it have been any of the players? Some of them are pretty touchy just before a game. Some of them, it's like if you said hello, they'd tear your throat out."

"Madjeski was killed *after* a game. And they *won* the game."

"So none of the players is a likely suspect?"

"Didn't say that."

"Oh, yeah, everybody thinks Crazy Al did it. Leaving him out, did any of the players do it?"

"Very doubtful."

"Not the equipment guys or your assistants?"

"Never."

"The front-office guys?"

"Them? Hah!"

"That leaves the coaches, right? Which ones?"

"What do you think, Marc? Which ones would gain the most?"

"So it's Tilley, Boom-Boom, and Carny?"

"You said it, not me. Couple of other guys hanging around yesterday. From the Orcas. One of them had a bit of a do with Madjeski."

"Jimbo Tallifer? He was in this side of the Dome?"

"Him and a few others. This is a modern stadium, Marc. Everything is connected. You can go around the whole inside on this level and never see daylight."

"What were they here for, Vinnie? Who were they?"

"Head coach, defensive coordinator, and trainer."

"Jimbo Tallifer, Tank Chrysczyk, and Needles Corvus? What about Scar Scorzetto?"

"Didn't see him."

"Isn't that unusual? If the top brass comes to visit, shouldn't all of them be there?"

"I don't think it was an official visit; just like they dropped over."

"What were they doing here? When were they here?"

"Snooping. Jimbo said it was to pay their respects, but they were looking around. Needles especially. I locked up all my special mixtures; people are always trying to steal a bottle. To analyze. Won't work; it's been tried before."

"You showed them around?"

"A bit. Then took them to Herb Lovell's office and left them there."

"When was this?"

"After everybody had left."

"Then they, one of them, could have . . ."

"That's what I've been trying to tell you, kid. You're not too fast today, Marc."

"Which one do you think . . . ?"

"Needles Corvus. He's a sneaky one."

"I didn't even know he knew Madjeski."

"Somebody's been around as long as Madjeski, he's bound to cross paths with everybody in the NFL."

"Oh, God, two more suspects."

"Three."

"Oh, come on, Vinnie. Needles isn't the type."

"You don't want to listen to me, why do you ask?"

"Okay." Marc sighed. "Three."

Rybek looked at him shrewdly. "So it's true, eh? You're trying to find the murderer. Just be careful, kid; that's all."

"Me? No. Hey, well, yes, like a reporter, you know. Trying to get the news."

"Don't bullshit me, Marc. I've been around a lot longer than you. Just this morning the word went around that you're playing detective, trying to hunt down the killer."

"When? Who said it?"

"First thing this morning. Don't know who."

Marc knew. Harvey Danzig. Making Marc the sacrificial goat, the lure. Paying Marc back for the anonymous phone call to the sports editor. Cracking the whip. Why sweat trying to find the killer? thinks Danzig. Put out the bait and let the murderer find Marcus Aurelius Burr. And while the murderer is busy murdering poor, stupid, innocent Marc Burr, that no-good bastard Harvey Danzig, expert detective and pride of Brooklyn Homicide, will be reading the Miranda rights, slowly, to the busy killer. Perfect. Just what Marc needed to think about on the way to the Bronx instead of watching out for muggers.

"Here's a bottle of my Secret-Formula Super-Energy High-Intensity Power Potion," Rybec said. "I don't usually give bottles of this one out, but I trust you. A swig before any stress will do it. Make that two swigs; the way you look, you'll need it."

13

_ _ _ _ _

"So it's the boy detective himself," Jimbo Tallifer jeered. "Okay. Burr, you've got me. I killed Madjeski because he wouldn't give me his secret code ring to decipher his fantastically tricky playbook." He roared with laughter and slapped his hand hard on his desk.

"Come on, Jimbo," Marc protested, "I need a story about that fight you and Madjeski had."

"You can read it in the *Post;* they had a good write-up. Where were you this morning when I had the press conference? Why do I have to go over it twice?"

"Don't go over it; give me a new slant."

"First of all, it wasn't a fight. Madjeski started to take a swing at me, and I just held him off. Gently."

"He was that mad?"

"Well, I must have struck a nerve."

"You're supposed to be cold, calculating, controlled, Jimbo. The coolest quarterback ever. Would Jimbo Tallifer lose *his* temper?"

"I might. Or I might just stay cool and do what I had to do the smart way."

"From what I understand, Madjeski was killed on the spur of the moment. By someone who suddenly got sore at him."

"Still going to deny you're playing detective, Burr?"

"If I've got the name. . . . Actually, I wouldn't really mind figuring out who did it; I need a raise."

"I wish I could help you get that raise, Burr, but you're looking the wrong way. Nobody suddenly got sore at Madjeski. He was the kind of slave driver you could learn to hate in five minutes. He got his kicks making his players sweat and squirm. If he had to let a man go—that's the hardest thing for a coach to do, you know, especially if the poor guy's been with you for ten years—if Madjeski had to let a man go, he'd do it at the worst possible time in the worst possible way. Hell, I remember one time when I was a player. . . . This guy, no names, he'd been with the team for four years, and his wife was tired of living in apartments six months a year with two kids, so he asked Madjeski if he should buy a house. Madjeski encouraged him, told him he was going to get a five-year contract and a big raise. One week after the guy bought the house, Madjeski cut him. Right after a scrimmage, not the night before. Right in front of everybody Madjeski told him, and then he told the poor guy that he had decided to cut him a month ago."

"That took guts."

"That took shit. Madjeski was surrounded by his assistant coaches; he always liked to have big men around him that he could bully. The guy he cut was so crushed, he didn't even say a word; he just broke down and cried. In front of everybody. Did Madjeski even say he was sorry? Make some excuse? He laughed, said it would improve discipline. Guts? Madjeski was a yellow-bellied coward all the way through."

"He swung at you, and you're a head taller than him."

"It was fake. He knew I wouldn't let him hit me—I haven't slowed down that much—and he knew I wouldn't hit him, not in public. Hell, one swing and I'd have killed him. It was all put on."

"Somebody did kill him with one swing. On the spur of the moment."

"What I've been trying to tell you, Burr. . . . You're just not listening to me. Madjeski might have said something or done something that triggered the killing at just that moment, but it had its roots way back. Whoever it was, he must have hated Madjeski for a long time, and Madjeski must have kept rubbing salt in the wound. It probably kept building up and building up so that the guy was on the brink of killing Madjeski a hundred times, but something kept him back. This time they were alone, and Madjeski must have said something, done something. . . . The guy is sitting there trying to control himself, to keep his mind calm, when all of a sudden it can't be controlled anymore, just too much for a man to stand. He picks up the statue and bang. Finally, Madjeski gets what's coming to him."

"What's the story, Jimbo, behind your hatred of Madjeski? The whole story?"

"You looking to get me in trouble, Burr?"

"Everbody knows you hated him. All I'm looking for is a story. I'd rather have it from your lips, Jimbo. And I do respect you. It'll be a straight story, I promise you. Fair."

Jimbo Tallifer looked suspiciously at Marc for a moment, then said, "Let's go for a walk. I can't stand being cooped up in the office anymore."

Jimbo didn't say a word until they were out on the field. The grass was beautifully cared for, even and green; the Yankee Stadium groundkeepers had done a magnificent job. Jimbo put on his aviator sunglasses and just stood there for a while, clearly enjoying the sight and the feel of the natural turf. Marc too felt a bit more relaxed, almost calm and at peace.

"It was in my last year as a player," Jimbo said, looking at the bleacher seats. "I'd gotten used to Madjeski's nasty tricks and his cheap shots. Never really gotten used to them, but I sort of circumvented them. I paid no attention to his crap and his lies, and my agent took care of the business. I was a big star, on my way to cracking all the records a quarterback could have. I was making good money and was going to make a lot more in the next few years. This game was the last game of the regular season, and it would decide whether we'd be in the play-offs or not.

"It was third and seven on their forty, we were behind by six, and Madjeski had sent in a pass play, a hook-and-go. I would have called a hook and picked up the first down. I didn't like Madjeski's play. It would take at least a second more to run a hook-and-go than a simple hook, and their defense was cutting through my pocket like a knife. That was an extra second I'd have to stand there—exposed—before I could pass. When I got to the line of scrimmage, I could tell they were going to blitz. I should have called an audible, changed to a hook or to a draw play, but Madjeski would have skinned me alive, that's how brainwashed I was.

"I dropped back to pass, and just as I was ready to throw, I was hit on my blind side by the defensive end, a real big guy, hit hard. I've got no complaints, it was a clean hit, but I felt something go in my right leg, burn. I passed out and, of course, I dropped the ball.

"I was sitting on the bench with the trainers working on my leg, lots of ice all around. Madjeski was screaming at me, calling me all sorts of names, acting like it was all my fault. Then he went off to watch our opponents march down the field to a touchdown. Just before the kickoff, Madjeski comes back to me. Doesn't say a word to me; doesn't ask how I feel. He tells the trainer to tape it up stiff, then inject Novocain. The trainer objects; he doesn't know what's wrong. Madjeski tells him to do it—it's only for one play—to do it or get off the team. Madjeski doesn't let the doctor near me. The trainer pumps me full of Novocain, slips a couple of plastic splints around my lower leg, and tapes me up good.

"Madjeski wants a bomb, a long bomb. First play, from our twenty. I limp out, right leg stiff as a board. I can't feel a thing, like I have no leg. It doesn't matter. I'm still the longest passer in the league. We'll go into a shotgun; no way can I back up or even move. I tell the guys to protect me, but good. They swear no one is going to even breathe on me.

"I get a good snap and I pump left to fool the defense, then look back to my receiver. I twist right, take a crossover step with my left foot, and I fall down. No pain, just no right leg. Nobody touched me either.

"This time they carry me off. I found out later that the first tackle had broken, a big crack, the head of my right fibula, the smaller lower leg bone. The force of the twist, my weight, and the shifting to throw had completed the damage. The styloid process and part of the fibula had split off completely. The external lateral ligament was badly torn, and the long external lateral ligament was ripped in half.

"Two operations, three months on crutches, and a year with a cane. I still have a slight limp. Playing football was out. Maybe I was lucky. There was an opening for a quarterback-receiver coach next season. I grabbed it. Maybe if I hadn't been hurt, I'd never have gotten to where I am today. Maybe. But if I'd had the choice, I wouldn't have volunteered to do it this way."

"I understand," Marc said sympathetically. "But aren't there other tough coaches?"

"Tough, yes. Hell, we're all tough. But none of us would sacrifice players like meat. He never even came to see me in the hospital. Lucky for him he didn't."

"An injury isn't enough reason to—"

"It isn't one thing. I keep telling you, Marc, but you don't listen. It's a buildup, over and over, until you're ready to kill the next guy who steps on your toe. Then the guy who's torturing you does one more thing, just one more bad thing, no worse than what he's done before, deliberately, and you'd kill. Even you, Marc, even you. Anybody would."

"Did you, Jimbo? Was it you?"

Jimbo Tallifer looked at Marc sadly. "Would I tell you all

this if I had? You know, many times that first year, I thought, if I just could get that bastard near me, if I could just put my hands around his neck and squeeze, slowly, slowly. . . . But as the time passed, I realized that would be too easy. I wanted to hurt him where it would hurt him the most. I wanted to show the world what a lousy coach he was, wanted to make him go out a loser. And I would take his money away too. The three things that meant the most to him: winning, respect, and money. I would take these away, all at one time. Then make him live with nothing.

"I put together a good team, a great team. Not just to wipe him out—I never figured the Wizards would get to play us—but because that's the way football should be. When the Wizards won the conference title, I figured out how to do it. I'd beat him by the biggest score in history. I'd break every one of his fancy plays. I'd show him up for the lousy coach he is. And I'd make him lose money, a lot of money."

"Madjeski bet on his games?"

"You didn't know? Hell, it was common talk in those days. Why do you think he made me go in with a broken leg? To beat the spread, Marc—so he'd win his bet. Some coaches want to win so badly they'd do almost anything. Almost. With Madjeski, the money was just as important as the winning. More important. Much more."

"The way you told it, he didn't necessarily know you had a broken leg."

"He didn't care; that's the point. He didn't give a damn for us. I once saw him send in a guard who had been laid out twice in the game already. The poor kid must have had a concussion, didn't even know which way to face. Another concussion could have finished off his brain for good. Did Madjeski care? Like hell he did."

"Then why did you go to visit him, Jimbo? To steal his playbook?"

"How long have you been in this business, Marc? I

wouldn't take Madjeski's playbook if you handed it to me. What for? You ever watch a game? You ever see that ninety percent of every game is the same plays everybody uses in the same way? Every team? If you put my playbook next to any coach's in the league, you'd have trouble telling which is which. The difference in coaches is in the selection of the players, in the training, the practice, the method of execution, in the inspiration—that's right, inspiration—and in the game plan. The adjustments you make to take maximum advantage of the capabilities of your team, the physical advantages you have available to you, the awareness of your weaknesses, and the style and weaknesses of your opponent. Plus some real-time decisions. Plus your philosophy—the way you see the game. Do you send in every play, some plays, or no plays? Do you play a situation safe or take a risk? Do you listen to your coordinators, your spotters? Are you able to analyze your work coldly, honestly, from the game films, or does your ego get in the way? Can you plan the strategy and tactics properly, or do you kowtow to the owner and the press? A million things like that, Burr; that's what coaching is. The plays? Hell, they're like chess pieces—more or less the same for everybody. It's how you handle those pieces that makes you a good coach or a bum."

"Then why did you go to the Wizards' side of the stadium?"

"For pleasure. Madjeski couldn't take being humiliated, especially in front of his subordinates. Then too I wanted to see their training facilities, get some idea of how Pusher Rybek works. Our stadium is pretty new, but it still has some faults that I want to correct next year. Then I hoped to maybe have a chance to see Boom-Boom or Carny; even with the others around, I'd let them each know, one way or another, they could talk to me privately if they wanted."

"Oh yeah? You didn't make that crack about their being as good as Tank and Scar accidentally, did you?"

"I never say anything accidentally to the press."

"You were hinting to your coordinators that they shouldn't ask for too big a raise next year? That they were replaceable?"

"A bit of that, yes. They're going to get good raises next year anyway; they deserve it. But I don't want them to go crazy either about how much they're worth. Then too one or both of them are going to get an offer to be head coach someplace; it's almost automatic when a team has a record like ours. I wanted to feel out if Boom-Boom or Carny might consider coming with me if I had a vacancy."

"Why didn't Scar come with you? Where was he at the time you went over?"

"Scar's mother had a big homecoming party set up; she hadn't seen him for months. All his relatives from miles around. Scar took off the minute the photographer snapped the last picture. Otherwise I would have taken him with us too."

Marc thought for a moment, then asked, "Can you be sure that Tank didn't have a chance to drop in to Madjeski's office when no one could see him?"

"You're as subtle as an elephant, Marc." Jimbo smiled widely. "What you're really asking is, Can anyone swear *I* didn't go into Madjeski's office yesterday afternoon?"

"Yeah, well, same thing, I guess."

"I spent some time with Carny, sort of reminiscing, but I wasn't looking at my watch."

"When was this, exactly?"

"I don't know, *exactly*. From the way Danzig was acting, it had to be about the time Madjeski was killed, but whether it was before, during, or after, I have no idea."

"So you and Carny are alibis for each other?"

"Yeah, and we could also be covering for each other, if you want to put it that way. Even if I knew exactly when I met with Carny, you can't fix the time Madjeski was killed that close. Hell, the way I understand what happened, the whole thing could have taken thirty seconds."

"Or the killer could have been with Madjeski for a half hour."

"Or anything in between. I guess we're all still prime suspects. We were out of sight of each other for quite a bit of time. You want to get out the cuffs?"

"What about Scar? Could he have come back after he said he was leaving?"

"Very doubtful, Marc. If anyone had seen him in the stadium, doing anything, he'd be the automatic prime suspect. Besides, his Momma would've killed him if he was one second late; I've met her."

"What you said before, Jimbo, that you never say anything accidentally to the press. Does that go for me too?"

"You're the press, ain't you? Relax, Marc, I don't tell lies too often either; I just watch what I say."

"I still have to get a couple of stories in today, Jimbo, but you said you were talking off the record. What words do you have for the great American public?"

"Oh, lots of stuff. You can recite the history of what Madjeski did to me and why I hated him. But be sure to put in, now that he's dead, and with that incentive gone, the score could be very close."

"You betting on the Orcas, Jimbo? Really?"

"I'm not saying I do, Burr, but if I did bet, it would always be on the Orcas. But I have nothing against the Wizards now, so if we're far enough ahead that I could feel safe, why should I humiliate them? Don't put in," he added, "that it's within my power to humiliate them, Marc. That's strictly off the record. The patrons like an even game."

"What about a color story? Background?"

"You might try one on teams and their coaches who are successful for a lot of years and make a lot of money for everybody."

"Gee, thanks, Jimbo. I can see now why you don't have to budget too much for personal PR."

"Yeah, well, I do what I can. And don't forget, shamus, I

don't give personal private interviews too often. You got yourself a real scoop there."

Yeah, Marc thought, Jimbo Tallifer came off holier than the pope and you pointed an arrow at Tank, Boom-Boom, and Carny. But not at Crazy Al. Why? I guess Tilley's got enough arrows pointed at him already; some in his back.

14

"Are you sure it was Lieutenant Danzig who did it?" Dahliah asked after Marc had filled her in on the events of the day. She ladled the steaming mushroom-barley soup into her plate and passed the pot to Marc.

"Who else?" Marc asked reasonably. "He's sore at me because I phoned *The Sentry* first and, in addition, he wants a decoy to attract the killer. I don't think he'd mind very much if the murderer got me just before he got the murderer. In fact, I think he'd prefer it that way."

"How about your boss? Julius Witter? Couldn't he have told somebody you were looking for the killer."

"What would Julius gain if I were killed?"

"Big headlines. And the same if you actually caught the killer. Either way he wins. In any conflict situation, you have to look for who gains by a specific action."

"Well, I suppose it's true, but I don't think Witter did it. He likes to kill his reporters himself. What I was hoping was . . . would you analyze the case for me? The suspects? After all, you're a psychologist and you specialize in crime."

"That's very flattering, Marc," Dahliah said, "but I'm a teacher not a police officer. I don't know if I . . . I mean, I'll be glad to help in any way I can, but wouldn't it be easier to just drop the whole thing? That way, the murderer would have no reason to be afraid of you, and you don't really care who killed Madjeski, do you?"

"Well, it's a big story, and I would like to get an exclusive. Besides, I can't drop the case. Whatever I do from now on, they'll still think that I'm trying to find the murderer. If I go to the toilet, somebody's bound to think I'm looking for clues."

"And you're worried, afraid, the murderer will think you're closing in on him and—and attack you?"

"I might not even know what I'm doing, and he'd feel he had to kill me to protect himself."

"Eat the bread *with* the soup, Marc; it's whole grain. . . . Do you really think you have a chance to solve the case?"

Marc moodily tore off a piece of the hard dark bread. "I better have a chance. If I don't turn up something soon, *Danzig* will kill me."

Dahliah put her hand over Marc's. "All right, darling. Let's try to analyze the situation. Start with Zachary Madjeski."

"Why him? He's the victim."

"When you figure out why Madjeski was murdered, you'll be close to knowing who done it. From what you tell me, Madjeski was a thoroughly nasty character."

"No pro football coach is an angel during business hours, but yes, everybody agrees that Madjeski was the world's worst."

"Compensation for being so small?"

Marc flushed. "Come on, Dolly, he wasn't much shorter than I am."

"Yes, darling, but it doesn't bother you because you were a world-class gymnast. Whatever the reason, you don't have to keep proving yourself the way Madjeski did. You're sweet, and everyone who knows you loves you."

"Except Julius Witter."

"Socially, I mean. But Madjeski, he worked in a world of

giants. It was important to him to dominate, to control his world."

"At press conferences, he was always polite, restrained, aloof even, like a king. The only time I saw him lose his temper was yesterday, when he swung at Jimbo Tallifer."

"Do you think Tallifer was right? When he said that Madjeski had the whole thing planned?"

"The trouble is, I'm not a mind reader. It was certainly out of character for Madjeski."

"Mr. Tallifer sounds like a very competent judge of character to me. The way he described the buildup of tension until a minor incident triggers an explosion of violence—that's a well-known pattern in assaults and murders between people in close contact with each other."

"You can't be both a great quarterback and a great coach and be stupid, not know human nature. But Jimbo is also a great manipulator. He never tells anyone everything he's really thinking, especially the press."

"Do you think he made this analysis for a reason, Marc? That he doesn't really believe it?"

"Oh, I'm sure he believes it, but I'm also sure there are other explanations for how Madjeski was murdered that are just as reasonable. You'll notice that, if you believe Jimbo's slow buildup idea, it puts him and his two top assistants out of the picture." Marc picked up the empty bowls and put them into the sink.

"What's next?" Dahliah asked.

"Spinach pies," Marc said. "Also bought in the deli. My head was too full to even think of cooking. They're very good; we've had them before." He brought the tray to the table. Dahliah served them both. Marc refilled both glasses with cranberry-apple juice.

"Crazy Al Tilley," Dahliah said. "He still seems to be the most likely suspect. What's he really like, Marc?"

"Very smart, quick thinking, quick reactions. Lots of guts. He's the smallest quarterback in the NFL. The present ideal is a guy six three, big enough to throw over the hands of the defense, weighing about two ten and able to take some hard licks. Tilley is a scrambler. If he can't find a receiver open, he leaves the pocket, his protective blockers, and runs until a receiver is free or until he sees a chance to gain some yardage. He's the leading ground gainer among quarterbacks and he's scored more touchdowns in his career than some fullbacks. But he's also been hit hard when he wasn't able to get out of bounds in time or to fall down before being hit."

"You're saying he has courage," Dahliah said. "He's willing to take risks and he does unconventional things. Doesn't this describe the murderer too?"

"It doesn't take courage to hit an old man on the head from behind. And if a guy was ready to kill Madjeski, he didn't have to suddenly realize it was the perfect time. Since it had to be someone close to Madjeski, or at least someone who knew him well, the killer must have had a hundred opportunities that were just as good as this time."

"There was no other time before Tuesday when Tallifer and his associates were in the vicinity. If the killer wanted to have additional suspects to blur the picture, that was the ideal time."

"Sure, Dahliah, but the killer had no way of knowing whether Tallifer and his crew were all together or separated. If they were all together, they'd be ruled out as suspects. And you're assuming that the killer was Crazy Al, Boom-Boom, or Carny. It could just as easily have been Jimbo or Tank. And the reason any one of them waited till now was that he didn't have a chance to be alone with Madjeski all year long at a time when no one saw the two together."

"If it was one of the Orcas, Jimbo or Tank—my God, the nicknames these characters have; right out of Damon Runyon—there was no slow buildup of hatred. This would have to be a planned murder."

"Who's a better planner than a head coach or a defensive coordinator?"

"The spinach pie was delicious, Marc. What's for dessert?"

"That I cooked. Cut a ripe papaya in half, scoop out the seeds, add heather honey and lemon juice, and slide into the oven. It was easy." He gathered the plates and brought the hot dessert to the table.

Dahliah took a spoonful and sighed. "Absolutely delicious. You'd make some girl a terrific husband."

"Anytime you're ready," Marc said seriously. "I'm not the one stepping on the brakes."

"When I'm ready, Marc, it will be you; you know that. Now let's get back to Madjeski."

"I'd rather—"

"Later. Tell me about the other three suspects."

"Well, I haven't interviewed them yet about the murder, but I know Boom-Boom and Carny pretty well, and I've spoken to Tank several times."

"Are the defensive players really as fierce as Crazy Al said they were? I once read an analysis of the various positions on a football team. The researcher said that the defensive linemen and linebackers are big, tough, aggressive, independent, and reckless. They would do anything to get their hands on the ballcarrier, like blood-crazed sharks."

"It's not quite that bad, Dahliah. Defenses are planned today, just like offenses, and very often one defenseman will sacrifice his chances in order to let a teammate get at the quarterback or the ballcarrier. Defenses are also very fluid today, shifting before the ball is snapped, to confuse the offense. But yes, you've got the defense personality down pat."

"Both Boom-Boom Drogovitch and Tank Chrysczyk played defense, you said. Are they like that today?"

"Somewhat. You've got to realize that, as players, they were all keyed up, their entire being focused on stopping the play, getting the ballcarrier, making him fumble, or even stripping him of the ball. In a game, they'd be at a very high emotional pitch. As coaches, as defensive coordinators, essentially assistant head coaches, they have to be more thoughtful, more mature, more rational."

"But the same characteristics that made them great football players are still there, aren't they? The personality is essentially unchanged?"

"Oh, sure, Dahliah. I'd hate to be standing anywhere near Boom-Boom when he lost his temper. Or Tank, for that matter."

"So either one could have killed Madjeski? . . . Who'd be more likely to successfully plan a crime?"

"From what I've observed, offensive linemen are more programmed. Every move has to be exactly in accord with the play as diagramed. The slightest deviation can cause the play to fail, or worse, cause a fumble that turns the ball over to your opponents. Everything must be timed to the split second. A tenth of a second's mistake on anyone's part, and it will look like comedy night at the demolition derby."

"Is that why in football they say that such and such a team is like a well-oiled machine?"

"A precision chronometer is more like it. An offensive player is carrying out a carefully designed plan, and he had better do exactly what the plan says. Exactly."

"And these plans are made by the offensive coordinators? Carny and Scar?"

"With the head coaches. And, while all plays are very similar, each coach designs his plays so they will fit the physical and mental capabilities of the players he actually has, not some theoretical ideal. And these plays are practiced, rehearsed, over and over, until everything is automatic and the execution is perfect."

"So if you were going to plan a murder, an offensive coordinator would be the ideal planner?"

"Sure. So would a head coach. Like Jimbo Tallifer. And

so would a quarterback—the guy who leads the play, the guy who executes the plan with precision."

"Crazy Al Tilley, for example?"

"He's still my first choice, Dahliah."

"But any one of the five could have done it, couldn't he? Or any of a hundred others, for that matter?"

"Any of a million others, if you look at it that way. But it had to be done by someone who could get into Madjeski's office, someone close to Madjeski or someone Madjeski knew, someone who Madjeski would turn his back on. So for all practical purposes, it's one of those five. On the other hand, if it were that sure Al had done it, Danzig would have taken Tilley downtown and sweated him already."

"Can you really sweat a famous personality, such as the star quarterback of the Brooklyn Wizards, in *Brooklyn*, just before the Super Bowl? Wouldn't Danzig need a stronger case than a quarterback's personality profile?"

"Of course. That's what he's got me for. He wants me to irritate somebody, one of them, the killer, to the point where he'll try to kill me. And maybe even succeed."

"How will that help Danzig?"

"I don't know. Maybe he hopes that I'll scrawl, next to my body, in my own blood, the name of the killer."

"Now you're being morbid, Marc."

"But I'll fix him. If that happens, I'm going to write, very legibly, HARVEY DANZIG IS THE MURDERER. That'll fix him good."

"You're under too much stress, Marc. Come to bed."

Stress. That reminded him. He took the bottle of Pusher Rybek's Secret-Formula Super-Energy High-Intensity Power Potion out of his jacket pocket, opened it, and took a big swig. Then he took a second drink. If Rybek said two, two it would be.

15

The phone woke Marc. "Still in bed, Burr?" Witter asked. "No wonder I don't get your stories on time."

"For God's sake, Julius." Marc protested. "It's six o'clock in the morning. What's so important that— There's been another murder?"

"Worse. Mr. Heisenberg—he's the guy who pays my salary, remember? He phoned me. Woke me up. Late last night. Out of sheer kindness I didn't wake you up too, although I should have, since it was all your fault."

"Julius, I can't do any more than I'm doing now. Tell Mr. Heisenberg that."

"I don't tell Mr. Heisenberg anything, Burr. He tells me. And you can do a good deal more than you are presently doing, but we will discuss that at another time. I'm calling to tell you, to *order* you, to do less."

"You are?" Marc was fully awake now. He got out of bed and took the phone as far away as he could to avoid waking Dahliah. "What's the catch?"

"No catch, Burr. With your usual clumsiness, you created additional difficulties for me. I permitted you the pleasure of quietly finding the murderer of Mr. Madjeski. Discreetly. And what did you do? You told everybody in the world that you're a big-shot Sherlock and that you'll have the killer behind bars in forty-eight hours."

"Me? I never—"

"And that the killer has to be either the Wizards' star quarterback or their sterling offensive coordinator or else their peerless defensive coordinator."

"But I didn't, Julius. I—"

"Mr. Heisenberg, who signs my paychecks, got a very angry call from Gus Gruber, who complained that you have been harassing his star employees and asking questions that show that you're trying to frame one of them before the big game."

"I haven't, Mr. Witter. I talked to Tilley and Rybek, that's all. I asked some others a few questions about various things, including the murder, naturally. Nothing else, Mr. Witter, I swear it."

"That's not what Mr. Gruber thinks, and he pulls a lot of weight with Mr. Heisenberg."

"It's the truth, Mr. Witter. I never accused anybody."

"Mr. Augustus Gruber does not wish to have his three most important employees, who are leading the triumphant march of the conquering Wizards toward their rightful and certain acquisition of the NFL championship, annoyed any more than they have to be by the authorities because of the half-baked, malicious accusations of a totally irrelevant reporter. He demanded that you be fired forthwith."

"I'm fired?"

"Certainly not. When it is time for you to be fired, would I deny myself the pleasure of watching an unrepentant sinner get his just desserts by firing you over the phone? No, you are not fired. As of now, at least. Mr. Heisenberg stood up to the forces of censorship and promised Mr. Gruber that you would not call nine-one-one even if you saw Mr. Tilley, Mr. Drogovitch, and Mr. Quigley, in concert, burning down the orphanage."

"I'm off the case? Is that what you're telling me?"

"I doubt that you've ever been on it, Burr, but yes. You are to expend no time or effort—repeat, zero time and effort—on attempting to determine who the killer is. Do I make myself clear?"

"But Harvey Danzig—"

"Would you rather depend on Lieutenant Danzig to support you in your present undeservedly extravagent life-style than Mr. Heisenberg?"

"No, but—"

"No buts. Yes or no."

"Yes. I mean no. I mean yes, I won't try to find the murderer. But if I talk to anyone, on either team, the subject of Madjeski's murder is bound to come up."

"If it does, you will listen politely, then forget all you have heard. Even if, *especially* if, one of the three favored gentlemen should decide to confess all to you."

"What if one of the Orcas confesses?"

"Then, of course, you will do your best to see that justice triumphs, the duty of every red-blooded American citizen. And that *The Sentry* gets an exclusive. In fact, it would not be amiss if you were to slant your stories, ever so slightly, but unmistakably, so as to indicate that the killer was almost certainly a member of the Oregon branch of the forces of evil. We're still putting out a newspaper, you know."

"That could even be true, Julius. How will you handle the truth?"

"I have no interest in the truth, Burr; I only want the news." He hung up. Marc immediately called Harvey Danzig and made an appointment to see him at his office at eight-thirty.

"Jesus, Burr," Danzig complained, "can't you do anything right? I asked you to bring me a cheese Danish; I hate prune." Danzig's desk was piled high with papers; he moved them aside to make room for his coffee. He did not make room for Marc. "Madjeski's not the only case I got," Danzig explained.

"I'll give you my bran muffin," Marc offered.

"Okay," Danzig grudged. "Better than nothing. I'll save the prune for later." He carefully rewrapped the Danish, put it into his top drawer, and took a big bite of Marc's muffin. "You didn't report to me yesterday. Didn't I tell you I wanted to know everything? You trying to get me mad at you?"

"No, Lieutenant"—Marc apologized—"but I didn't learn anything important."

"You're deciding now what's important, Burr? Not me?"

"No, no. What I mean is, I didn't learn anything that isn't common knowledge—stuff you know already."

"You're a mind reader now? That's good. I could use a good mind reader. I'm holding a guy now, I *know* he killed three people, but I can't find the bodies or the knife."

"It doesn't matter anymore; I've been ordered to stop detecting."

"Ordered? Who ordered that?"

"Mr. Witter did. Mr. Gruber told Mr. Heisenberg, he owns *The Sentry*, and Mr. Heisenberg told Mr. Witter and Mr. Witter told me."

"And you're going to stop looking for the murderer?"

"Well, of course. I have to. I work for Mr. Witter; he pays my salary."

"He pays your salary, okay, but you don't work for him."

"I don't? But—"

"You don't. Period. You work for me." Danzig took off his gold-rimmed glasses. "You still don't understand, Burr?" he asked patiently. "I'll explain it to you. What can Witter do to you? Fire you? That's the worst, right? So you get another job, right? You'll live. Now, what can I do to you? I can put you in a cell with a real nut case. He's suspected of raping and strangling a whole string of derelicts. You don't look all that good to me, Burr, but compared to the bums he's been raping, you gotta look like the Queen of Sheba to him. So who do you work for, Burr?"

"For how long, Danzig?"

"Just till the case is closed, Burr. I'm a fair guy, ask anybody. But you don't want to be in this position too much longer, do you, Burr? And I've got a lot of other cases too, right? So let's clean it up in a hurry; what do you say? Apply a little pressure and sooner or later somebody cracks. Right, Burr?"

"What will you do if I get fired, Danzig?"

"You win a few, you lose a few." Danzig shrugged philosophically. "I lose you, I find another reporter who screwed up. Nah, that'd take too long. I'm betting on you, Burr. You're my man; you can do it. The right questions in the right way, got it?"

"If I start putting on more pressure, I'm going to get fired. Guaranteed."

"Sure you will, Burr, but not right away. It takes time for news to filter up all the way to the big shots. By that time we'll have the killer and I'll be a hero."

"And I'll be dead."

"Not necessarily, Burr. It would be a real stupid thing for someone to do. Because then I got the killer cold."

"Great. And what do I do, Danzig? Pray that he misses?"

"Nah, he won't use a gun. His M.O. is clubs. Just don't let anybody suspicious get behind you."

"Terrific."

"You don't understand, Burr. If the case isn't closed by Monday morning, it'll never be closed. The big game is Sunday afternoon. The big parties are Sunday night. That, by the way, is when you'll nab him. The tension is relaxed, everybody's stewed, nobody's watching what he's saying. That's when you keep your eyes and your ears open; that's when you'll find out. And as soon as you do, you call me. Got it? Because Monday, the Orcas go home. Everybody goes home. It's a dead issue on Monday, right? So actually, the case is closed, one way or another, Sunday. Midnight. No later. Right?"

"Suppose I don't turn up anything by Sunday midnight, Danzig."

"Then I'll have to cuff you to one of the weight machines, where the murderer can easily find something heavy to part your hair with."

"You're setting me up to get killed, Danzig."

"Why should I do that, Burr? You're not thinking again. I don't want you killed; I need you to find me the killer. Or if you can't, to find me the guy who made the anonymous phone call, right? Don't think negative, Burr; you'll just make yourself miserable. Smile, kid. You'll catch the killer. I got confidence in you."

Sure, Marc thought. Confidence.

16

The full impact of his predicament hit Marc when he left the police station. He was hogtied in a double bind inside a dilemma at the dead end of a blind alley.

If I keep looking for the murderer, Marc calculated, I'll lose my job a lot faster than Danzig thinks—both Gruber and Heisenberg are very fast with their phones—and Danzig will have nothing to gain by not arresting me for murder. Then Julius Witter will have to testify that I made the phone call, the first call, to him at just about the time of the murder, and I will be indicted for murder. In order to avoid trial, where they'd *have* to find me guilty, I would have to admit that I did not call the police at all, that I left the scene of the crime, that I erased the blackboard and moved the chalk and the eraser and maybe messed up other possible clues, and that I took the pictures that I did not turn over to the police but sold to my boss for a fifty-dollar raise. None of which will show me in the best possible light.

On the other hand, if I stop looking for the murderer, Danzig will arrest me immediately, and the whole scenario will be repeated. The only difference would be that Julius Witter would keep me on the payroll for a few more hours, just until Julius himself was arrested as my accomplice, as accessory to my crimes.

Maybe if I just *fake* looking for the killer, that would hold off Danzig for a while. Maybe if I stay away from the stadium, the killer can't get at me. A guy like Tank, for instance . . . no way is he going to be able to follow me unseen. No, the sensible thing for the killer to do, whoever he is, is to hire someone—you can get a junkie to kill for the price of a fix, can't you?—hire someone who fits into the neighborhood, like the two teenagers who've been following me for the past block.

Following . . . ? Yes, definitely following. Looking casual, but positively following. Marc stopped and looked into a store window. The two stopped too. When Marc started walking again, they started walking too, in no hurry. Two big teenagers, grown men, actually.

They were obviously not drug addicts, they looked too strong and healthy for that, but hired thugs. Killers. Wait, don't panic. How could the murderer know where I would be at this time? If I hadn't been so preoccupied with my problems, I'd have become aware of them long ago, in time to do something.

Marc took another quick look. The men were wearing expensive sneakers and had their hands in the pockets of their black jackets. Menacingly. The jackets were emblazoned with big red Day-Glo emblems: a gorilla, arms upstretched and teeth bared, ready to attack. Under the gorilla, in big letters, the legend KING KONG KILLERS.

No point in running: Bring on an attack all that much sooner, and there was no doubt they could outrun him easily. Marc started walking down the subway stairs, slowly, casually. As soon as his head was below street level, he bounded down the steps, heart racing. As soon as he got to the bottom, he'd run to the other side and up the stairs, back to where he'd come from, toward the police station. At the bottom of the steps Marc stopped dead. There, in front of him, was a barred turnstile, with a NO CLERK ON DUTY sign. Probably the two muggers had trapped victims here before. No need to hurry; no place to go.

Marc felt around in his pockets and found a token—good old thoughtful Julius Witter—and prayed that no one had stuffed the coin slot. The token worked, the turnstile turned, and Marc ran onto the station platform.

A train was just pulling in. Marc sprinted to the left, out of sight of the subway entrance. He reached the end door of the last car just as the doors opened. He dashed in, praying, "Close, *close*," and stood, at the door, watching, keeping an eye on the subway entrance in the distance. Maybe the two thugs, counting on their intended victim's lack of tokens, had forgotten to bring tokens themselves. That hope died. The two appeared just as the train's doors closed. They ran to the train, but it was too late. The train started moving. Marc sat down in the car and settled back in his seat. Safe.

Marc's breathing and heartbeat started to return to normal. He noted, absentmindedly, that the subway car was entirely empty except for him. A loud ratchet noise made him glance toward the end of the car just in time to see the two men open the door at the front of the car. *How?* Oh, God, Marc realized, they had simply climbed on between the cars. Still in no hurry, they walked slowly toward him. Marc tried to pull back in his seat, but there was no place to go.

The two stood, slightly separated, in front of Marc, and turned slightly toward each other to cut off escape. Neither spoke for several seconds, just stood there. Then the one on the left said, "Got the time, mister?"

Without thinking, Marc slammed his right foot forward, hard, into the side of the knee of the man on his right. The knee cracked sideways audibly; the man screamed and fell to Marc's right. Marc jumped up and over the fallen man and ran forward in the car. The second man, taken by surprise, was far behind him, running, now with a sharpened screwdriver in his right hand. Marc pulled open the heavy door at

117

the end of the car and stood on the platform between the cars. He pushed open the door to the next car and ran forward again. This car was empty too. His pursuer had gained ten feet and was closing; there would be no time to open the door at the end of the car. Instinctively, Marc grabbed vertical post at full speed, swung around it horizontally, and kicked both feet, full force, into his attacker's head. The man's head snapped sideways, hard, all the way. He dropped, limp, to the floor.

Marc swung his feet to the floor, ready to attack again. He watched the man, who did not move. Marc walked slowly through the sliding doors into the next car and continued on until he was in the car with the conductor. Most of the people on the train were in that car.

That was stupid, Marc thought. I should have given them my money. Did I kill that guy? I know I didn't kill the first one, though he'll never walk straight again. But the second one. . . . His head went all the way back, sideways. A hard two-legged kick and the whole swing of my body with it. He was very limp when he dropped. But I've seen guys knocked out in the ring who dropped limply and got up a minute later. Maybe . . . But why should I care? He was going to kill me. Self-defense. Self-preservation. One killer less. I might have saved a dozen lives today, who knows? Still I've never killed anyone before. How can I be so calm? If I killed him. If.

Marc saw he was at the right station for the Grube Dome and got off the subway. Mustn't tell Dahliah; she'd get upset. Very upset. That was the last thing he wanted to do make Dahliah feel bad. He'd never ride that subway again; the guy who lived, he might be waiting with a big gang, or even if they met accidentally. . . . And the police? Would they be looking for the subway killer? If they were, no one would suspect a mild-mannered reporter. But something still bothered him: Who were those two thugs? Ordinary muggers—or hired killers?

17
- - - - -

There were too many reporters and too much TV equipment
to fit into the Dome's briefing room, so the press conference
was held at the north end of the football field. No chairs had
been set up for the press, Marc noted, so it was going to be a
short conference. Pudgy Verne Ketchel, the vice-president
in charge of public relations, had arranged a lectern on a
small platform, and five chairs: for Herbert Lovell, the general manager; for Augustus Gruber, the owner of the franchise; for Harold Drogovitch, Edward Quigley, and himself.

Verne introduced Herb Lovell. Herb called for a minute
of silence in memory of the great, the beloved, the sorely
missed and soon-to-be-beatified grand old man of football,
the supreme coach of all time, Zachary "Magic" Madjeski.
Heads were bowed for thirty seconds.

Herb then took the opportunity to say a few words about
how rapidly, how decisively, how firmly the statesmanlike
Mr. Augustus Z. Gruber took command in this hour of crisis
and, with his masterful hand on the tiller and his eagle eye
on the goalposts, had evaluated the problems, considered
the alternatives, and determined the course that would control the destinies of the Brooklyn Wizards and, indeed, of
the entire National Football League for millennia to come, if
not of this whole great nation as well. Without further ado,

Mr. Augustus Gruber, philanthropist, industrialist, and owner of the Wizards.

Gus Gruber was short, slim, gray, and big-nosed. His clothes were expensive, his hair was expensive, his nails were expensive, and his tan was expensive. His voice, Old Brooklyn, had not cost him a penny. He liked it that way and, had he been able to change it, would not have bothered. "I know how to make beer," Gruber announced. "Learned it from my father and my grandfather. And I know how to run a business. There has to be one boss in a business, any kind of business. Just one. One guy to make the decisions and to take the heat. On the Wizards, that was Magic Madjeski, may God rest his soul. Madjeski is gone, the business must go on, and there has to be a boss, a new head coach, to take his place.

"But you can't bring in a new head coach from outside at this time, even if there was one available, which there isn't. He wouldn't know the team, he wouldn't know the way we play, he wouldn't know what Madjeski had in his head.

"So the smart thing to do is to use the existing staff. We've got two really fine seconds-in-command here, Boom-Boom Drogovitch and Carny Quigley. Top coaches. In their own way. Quigley's been concentrating on offense and Drogovitch's been concentrating on defense. To have one of them making decisions in the other man's specialty, it could be a disaster. Maybe, by next season, yes, maybe one of them could possibly be designated head coach. But not right now. Let's see what happens in the big game on Sunday; that could help me make up my mind one way or the other.

"Football is a game with three teams: the offensive team, the defensive team, and the special teams—what you press call the suicide squad. When the offensive team is on the field, the defensive team is on the bench, and vice versa. So what I have decided is this: When the offensive team is on the field, Mr. Edward Quigley will be the acting head coach. And when the defensive team is on the field, Mr. Harold

Drogovitch will be the acting head coach. The two will get together to set up the game plan in accordance with what Coach Madjeski laid out, which I understand was pretty complete already. When there's a kicking situation, both men will consult with the special-teams coach and make a majority decision.

"Now this may seem pretty unusual to you, members of the media. Maybe it is. But under the present circumstances, it's the best solution for this disaster situation. And it's going to work; I feel it in my bones. We're out to win the Super Bowl, and I know my two leaders, Quigley and Drogovitch, will do a terrific job to beat the Orcas and to show me which one deserves a shot at being head coach next year. And I'll be watching. Thank you. That's all. No questions. Verne and his boys will be passing out today's handouts. And in the press room, there's beer and peanuts for everybody. 'Goobers Go with Gruber's,' remember? The beer, you will be pleased to know, is the new Improved Gruber's Lite, the 'Litest Lite of all the Lites.' Go ahead, now, enjoy all you want."

The crowd of reporters broke up, most going to the press room to send in their stories, the rest clustering around Quigley, Drogovitch, Ketchel, and Lovell. Marc walked slowly toward the press room. He'd send in the story cold and then, when the crowd thinned out, he'd grab either Boom-Boom or Carny in private for a color story. And a not-so-subtle interrogation about the murder of Magic Madjeski. As Danzig had ordered this morning—only this morning? My, how time flies when you've maybe killed someone—the right questions in the right way. Enough pressure and, sooner or later, somebody cracks, right? Right. Me.

18

"Of all the stupid, idiotic— You're sure this is off the record, Burr?" Carny Quigley asked. They were standing on the sidelines watching the players in a warm-up workout. "If this gets out, Gruber will bounce me tomorrow, and I'll know whose head to tear off."

"Absolutely off the record, Carny," Marc said reassuringly. "All I'll write is that, while the coaching staff unanimously approved Mr. Gruber's decision, the man in the street had different feelings."

"Okay." Quigley cooled off a little. "It's the stupidest thing Gruber ever did, and he's pulled some lulus in his day. You can't have a summit conference in a game; you've got to have a decision fast. Even with a time-out, you have only ninety seconds."

"Would you rather have had him pick Boom-Boom?"

"It'd be better than this jackass arrangement, but Gruber should've picked me. I'm the logical choice. Not that Boom-Boom isn't qualified; he's one of the best. But he's been defense all his life; he thinks defense. Defense is loose, flexible, changeable. You shift around, you use stunts and games to confuse the offense. It's a lot of individual initiative; you're pretty free on defense to do what's got to be done. Sure, sometimes a couple of guys team up to make a hole for a linebacker to blitz through, or a cornerback passes a receiver on to safety, but you practically never see a whole team on defense acting like a unit. It's improvisation, practically."

"You think an offensive specialist would be a better choice for head coach?"

"Hell, yes, it's obvious. Offense is planning, precision, the whole team moving like the fingers of one hand. Every lineman doing his exact part at the exact right instant. A well-oiled machine, right? Offense takes in the whole team; defense is three separate and distinct layers, each with a different function."

"Boom-Boom wouldn't necessarily agree with that, would he?"

"Now don't you go quoting me to Boom-Boom either, you hear? I've got to live with him, work with him, in the Super Bowl. Maybe next season too."

"Maybe? Did you get any firm offers?"

"People are always sending out feelers to me; it's only natural. Any time a team wins the conference championship, especially with the physical equipment we've got, what we *don't* have, to tell the truth, the coordinators always get feelers."

"Boom-Boom got them too?"

"We don't discuss it all that much in detail, but him too, of course. He's good, damn good."

"Did you accept any of the feelers?"

"My answer always is to make me a firm offer, and then I'll let you know."

"But you don't want to leave the Wizards, do you?"

"It's my team. I built it up to this point. All we need is a little more muscle and we could be in the play-offs next year too. I've got some young guys, full of piss and vinegar, they'll be starters next year for sure. But I don't want to be offensive coordinator anymore. I've got enough years under my belt, and enough smarts, to run a team all the way. It's

123

time I was head coach. And if I can't be head coach with the Wizards, if I've got to go someplace else, then that's just what I'll do."

"Is that off the record too, Carny?"

"Yes. No. You could do me a favor, Burr, in return for this exclusive. Slip in, very subtly, you understand, that it's well known that some teams are offering me the job, head coach, for next year. That'll get Gruber off his ass."

"Okay, Carny. It'll be a pleasure. Tell me something. Didn't Al Tilley contribute something to the season you just had?"

"That crazy bastard?" Quigley got red. "Yeah, he contributed all right. Headaches. Every time one of his wild tricks works, you guys put out big headlines about how Tilley won the game all by himself. But when he screws up, it's the lousy plays and the incompetent coaches. Why don't you guys wise up?"

"You sound jealous of him."

"Damn right I am. Publicity is just as important in this business as ability. Ninety-nine percent of what we do, the coaches, is invisible, and we get paid accordingly. If a play is set up so perfectly that there's a hole a Girl Scout could walk through backward, the guy who waltzes the ball across the line gets all the cameras pointed at him. And next year, he gets a whopper of a raise. But if some fancy glamour boy gets sacked, it's because I don't know how to set up a good pocket right."

"Cheer up, Carny. If the Wizards do well in the Super Bowl, you may be head coach next year."

"Yeah? That's another of Gruber's stupid tricks. If he had named me head coach today, I'd be at the head coach level no matter how we did Sunday. Now, we don't know if it's me or Boom-Boom; see what I mean? My whole future depends on what happens Sunday. If one or two of those animals screw up, I'll be out on my ass. And even if we do real good, what's to stop Gruber from bringing in an outsider?"

"Nothing, I guess, but what makes you think—"

"What makes me think? Did you get that part in his speech where he hinted an outside coach was not available?"

"Sure I did, but that doesn't mean anything. It could just be his clumsy way of warning you not to ask for too much next year."

"That makes me feel real good, Burr, you know? After all these years I'm still at the mercy of a jerk like Gruber, or a nut like Tilley. What do I do if Tilley stays up all night before the game? It won't be the first time he's done it."

"But what if Tilley does a great job?"

"That's just what I mean. I got to sweat out my future on what Crazy Al does. And even then, if we make a good showing, and Gruber decides to use one of us, he's still got to decide: Did defense do better than offense or vice versa? In one game. Damn, that jerk don't know the difference between a shoulder pad and a hockey puck, and he's going to analyze the fine points? It depends more on which TV announcer he listens to than on anything else."

"You really don't like Tilley, do you?"

"Listen. You can't have a quarterback who's a disruptive influence and who rides roughshod over the coach. A little bitching? Hell, that goes with the game. A few audibles when it's necessary? Fine. But we spend a lot of time thinking up a game plan—it's like planning a war, you know—and then to have the guy in charge of the field forces change everything? Hell, you might as well play by guesswork."

"Still, the Wizards are in the Super Bowl. Is that an accident?"

"Partly it's luck. The three top teams in the conference were so good that they clobbered the rest. We just didn't have as bad an average as the others. Eight and eight, and we're in the Super Bowl." He shook his head in amazement. "But the rest of it was good coaching, good game plans, new tricky variations of plays to take advantage of our assets:

speed and artificial turf. And good conditioning, good training in the fundamentals."

"Didn't Tilley help too?"

"Yeah," Carny said grudgingly, "at times. He's real smart, you know; you can't take that away from him."

"He hated Madjeski, didn't he?"

"He hated all of us, and we didn't exactly like him too much either. What are you getting at, Burr?"

"Do you think he killed Madjeski?"

Carny thought for a moment. "It's possible; I wouldn't want to say no for sure. But how're you going to prove it? There's no way to prove anybody did it, is there, from what I understand? I mean, if somebody saw anybody going into Madjeski's office, in or out, Lieutenant Danzig would have had him in the clink by now, wouldn't he?"

"Well, there are no witnesses, you have to be right about that. But maybe some other kind of evidence? Background information? Circumstantial evidence? Were you around when the Orcas came over on Tuesday afternoon?"

"Yeah, sure. I even spent some time talking to Jimbo."

"Trade secrets?"

"We didn't give anything away to each other, if that's what you mean; we're both pros. But it's always good to talk to another guy who understands your work, your problems. We go back a long way, and we know a lot of the old-timers, a lot of stories."

"Do you think any one of the Orcas could have done it?"

"Could have? Sure, anybody *could* have. But did? What for? Maybe Jimbo, I don't know; he really hated Madjeski's guts."

"Enough to kill him?"

"Look, Burr, you've been asking around for two days now. You know that everybody hated Madjeski. What are you getting at?"

"Did Boom-Boom hate Madjeski? Enough to kill him?"

"Boom-Boom hated Madjeski, I hated Madjeski, and the

guy who swept out the locker room hated Madjeski. So what? Enough to kill him? Who knows what's enough for anybody? What I might just pass over would drive Boom-Boom crazy, and vice versa. It also depends on the situation. Some days you could spit in my face, and I'd wipe it off and smile. Another day you could mispronounce my name, and I'd knock your teeth down your throat. It all depends on how I feel, what happened that morning or the night before, my relationship with you, a million things. Look, here you are, asking me if I killed Madjeski. Don't deny it, Burr, that's just what you're doing. Am I sore at you? No. Well, maybe just a little. There are some other guys, one columnist especially who's been riding me, could ask the same questions, and I'd break his arm. It all depends, see?"

"Yes, I see, Carny. Without getting you more sore, who do you think killed Madjeski?"

"Anybody who was here that afternoon could have done it."

"You and Boom-Boom? Jimbo, Tank, and Needles?"

Quigley wrinkled his brow. "You can leave Needles out of it. He ain't the type."

"The rest of you are?"

"We're all ex-players. We're big and strong, fast reactions, tough, independent. And none of us liked Madjeski."

"Did you see anyone near Madjeski's office?"

"Sure. All of us, myself included."

"Was there a connection between Tank and Madjeski?"

"Don't you do your homework, Burr? Sure there was; all of us. Jimbo and I spent half our talking on what a bastard Madjeski was, who he treated the worst. Madjeski started off bad when he first got into football, and he got worse, much worse, as he got experienced. I got the last two years, when he was a real expert."

"Then why did you stay? You could have gotten a good job elsewhere."

"I knew what I was getting into before I left Boise; I'd

heard the stories. But he promised me—not in so many words, you understand, but it was clearly understood—that at the end of that year he was going to step down and I'd be head coach in his place."

"You believed this?"

"Not completely; Madjeski wasn't famous for keeping his promises. But I figured I could take all his crap for a year or two. How much longer could Madjeski stay active? Or alive, for that matter, if you want to know the truth."

Marc shifted gears. "Listen. Carny, if I wanted to bet on the Wizards, what's the right spread? This is completely off the record; I happen to need money very badly right now."

"Completely off?" Marc nodded. "Okay. Well, if they give us twelve points, bet on the Orcas; no way we're going to be that close. If they give you twenty-four points, bet on us. We've got some surprises up our sleeves; no team's going to spot us twenty-four, I don't care what they say."

"What if it's halfway in between? Eighteen points, say?"

"That's a toss-up. You can bet on either team; it's a gamble. I can't do that though. If I were to bet, it would have to be the Wizards or not at all."

"You ever bet on a game you're playing?"

"Are you looking for trouble, Burr? You know we're not supposed to bet. I didn't say I *did* bet, only that *if* I were to bet, how I'd do it."

"Yeah, but still. . . . I've heard that lots of players and coaches bet, and I was wondering if Madjeski ever did."

"How the hell would I know that? You think he'd ever tell me anything like that if he did? Or about anything he did that might give me a hold over him? Why're you asking?"

"I thought there might be a connection with his murder."

"Connection? That I would know about? Listen, Burr, I've got enough problems as it is. Go bother the Orcas for a change."

"What about my story, Carny?"

"You've got your story, Burr. 'Acting Half-Assed Head Coach Edward Quigley is of the opinion that the innovative solution put forth by Mr. Augustus Gruber is the greatest thing since jock straps. It is bound to confuse the Orcas, the hidebound traditional Orcas, to the point where the Wizards will walk all over them.' And don't forget to put in how you heard I got some good firm offers already." He stalked off.

19

Marc had taken a taxi to Yankee Stadium; no way would he use the subway in the foreseeable future. The receipt was in his wallet, although there was very little doubt that Julius Witter would disapprove payment for such luxury, especially if it was to save Marc's life.

Marc caught sight of Tank Chrysczyk at the far end of the field and ran to intercept him. There was no mistaking Tank's silhouette; even in civilian clothes, he was broader than most of the players who were wearing shoulder pads.

"What the hell do you want?" Tank growled. The afternoon sun beaming off his thick glasses struck Marc's face like twin spotlights.

"I need a story," Marc said. "Anything."

"You don't have enough with that dumbjohn Gruber? The moron!"

"You disagree with his solution?"

"Yes, I disagree with his solution." Tank mimicked Marc. "Who ever heard of two head coaches? One for offense and one for defense? Hah! Hell, next they'll make a head coach for left-handed receivers and one for right guards."

"But doesn't that help you? The Orcas? The lack of decisiveness, I mean? Maybe even dissension?"

"I don't want any help. I don't *need* any help, especially

from a jerk like Gruber. You know what this makes us look like, huh? Like we're big guys ganging up on a crippled little old lady. If we do good, it's not because we *are* good, but because Gruber messed up his team. And if they do something right, even like complete one short pass, they're geniuses and we're bums."

"Can I print that?" Marc asked.

"Hell, no," Tank said.

"Well, if I can't have that, at least give me a news story."

"How about how we're handicapped because we're practicing on natural grass but we have to play the game on artificial turf?"

"Yeah, that's okay for background, I guess. But aren't you going to have two practice sessions in the Gruber Dome?"

"Snake Bloodworth was complaining to me just today. He can't make his moves on artificial turf the way he's used to. He's afraid to sprain an ankle."

"The turf is faster. Bloodworth will run away from tacklers. They'll never touch him."

"He'll be slower because he can't twist. The turf's got no give, like grass."

"It's the same for both teams."

"It ain't. They're used to it, we're not."

"All right, you've convinced me. You want me to take up a collection for the poor Orcas who only lost one game last season?"

"That ain't funny, Burr. The game we lost was on artificial turf. We should've won it."

"And what about your blitz, Tank? The Orcas have the best blitz in the league. When you catch a quarterback and slam him down on artificial turf, he's going to be a little shook up for a while."

"We don't purposely slam quarterbacks down, Burr. Don't you go printing garbage like that. We make clean tackles. We tackle hard, sure, that's how I teach them, but we don't purposely go out to cripple the guy."

"Maybe not purposely, Tank, but I've seen some quarterbacks lie down very fast when they see the Killer Whales coming at them."

"They're yellow, Burr, that's why. Just because my front four is a little bigger than most, it doesn't mean they're out to break knees."

"Yeah? Two quarterbacks who played against you are still on crutches."

"Accidents happen, Burr. That could have happened to anybody. Now get off the subject, will you? We got a good record on penalties, don't we? Better than average? Facts are facts. We got nothing against anybody."

"That's not how Madjeski saw it."

"That was Madjeski. He's dead now, burning in hell."

"I heard you had something against Madjeski. What's your side of the story, Tank?"

"It's not just my side, Burr; it's the truth. He broke up my marriage."

"How could he do that, Tank? I don't see him as the type to fool around with anybody's wife, and I certainly can't imagine any woman in the world who would find him attractive."

"Nah, it was nothing like that. If it was, he'd have been dead long ago, right in front of everybody. Like that." The giant twisted his hands as though he were wringing out a towel. "This was when I was with Tacoma. My first coaching job, and it had to be with Madjeski."

"How did he do it, then?"

"He gave me work, extra work, overloaded me with work. Work where I'd have to be off alone by myself. Watching films. Analyzing. Alone, no phone, nothing. Unreachable. Times I wouldn't get home till two, three in the morning, night after night, seven days a week. None of the other coaches had to, but he said he was grooming me. For bigger and better things. There were times when my wife had to reach me, important things. He never told me. She used to think . . . A couple of times Madjeski, when she phoned, he used to tell her I had left hours ago. After a while . . . You know how women are. She got the kids. And she blames me. To this day, she blames me. Says it's all my fault. Won't listen to a word. Won't even talk to me. She hates me and she taught the kids to hate me. Told them I'm no good. She's one hour from here, that close, but she won't see me and the kids, my kids, they don't want to see me."

"You're divorced?"

"We can't get divorced. Separated. It's a lousy life, Burr, without a family. A man should have a family."

"But with the separation agreement . . . ? Don't you have the right to . . ."

"Rights? Sure. I got rights. What good are rights when your kids hate you? Your own kids? Madjeski did this to me. Purposely."

"Why should Madjeski do a thing like that?"

"Because he's— He was the lousiest, meanest bastard who ever lived, that's why."

"Yes, I know, but what reason?"

"Because I wouldn't— It was when we were with Tacoma. I was defensive line coach. Madjeski calls me into his office one day. He wants me to place a bet for him on this week's game with a bookie."

"Why you? Couldn't he do it himself?"

"He must've just lost his bookie. Probably welshed on a bet, that's the kind of guy he was, and no other bookie in the area would take him on. The word goes around very fast in that world."

"Did you know any bookies? Then?"

"Sure I did; everybody does. You do too, even if you don't think you do. Not that I did any betting myself, you understand, but I knew where to go and how to do it. Madjeski thought everybody bet on the games because he did. That's how he thought."

"So why didn't you accommodate Madjeski? Or at least recommend him to someone you knew?"

"Are you kidding? First of all, you don't recommend anybody to anybody unless you know the guy is a man of his word. If Madjeski had lost his regular bookie, there had to be a reason. Second, if you're in football, you can't bet direct, you've got to get somebody to do it for you. Look what happened to some real good guys not too long ago. And last, Madjeski didn't want to do his own betting, he wanted me to do it for him."

"From what I've learned about Madjeski, that wouldn't be a smart thing to do."

"Not smart? Are you kidding? It would be dangerous as hell. As I said, he'd probably already welshed on one bookie. What do I do if . . . ? You see, you go to a place to bet, you don't run down some dark alley with a sack of cash. You pick up the phone, you say something to identify yourself, you ask for the odds on the teams, then you agree with the guy on the other end of the phone that you're playing so and so much on this and that team at a spread of such and such. This guy, maybe you've never seen him but his word is good and your word is good. Every once in a while you settle accounts; either you send him or he sends you, depending on who's ahead. It's all trust, credit. What do I do if Madjeski welshes? Or says, no, he didn't tell me to lay a bet on *this* team, he told me *that* team?"

"You refused him?"

"I told him to shove it and walked out."

"Wasn't that risky? He was the head coach, after all."

"A lot less risky that betting for him would have been. That's when he started his campaign to destroy me. He was too smart to do it openly; he knew if he tried anything blatant, I'd bust his head wide open. Hey, wait, Marc, I didn't mean that the way it sounded; just a way of talking, that's all."

"I know you didn't, Tank. Don't worry."

"I was so green, I believed him when he said he was grooming me. It was only after my wife saw the lawyer . . . but by then it was too late."

"What did you do?"

"It was the end of the season. My contract was up. I got a job with Wyoming, and my wife moved to Long Island, to be as far away from me as possible, to cut down my chances of seeing her and the kids."

"You know, Tank, there's a story there, a real human-interest story. If you'll let me write it."

"Are you kidding? That's private, personal."

"Maybe it's time, then. Show your wife that it wasn't your fault."

"I don't know." The big man took off his thick glasses and polished them slowly, uncomfortably. "You know, Marc, it might help; nothing else has before. It just might help. Okay, you go to my wife—it's only an hour—and tell her. I'll give you her phone and address. You tell her what I told you; it's the truth. If she'll talk to me after, just talk to me, that's all, in the house, you can use the story. But not if she don't; only if she does."

"I don't know if I can convince her, Tank. I'll do my best."

"You're a good talker, Marc. Talk good."

"I'll try, Tank. I'll really try."

"I want my kids, Marc. I want them to . . ." He let the words trail off, stared into the distance.

"You really hated Madjeski, didn't you?"

"The guy who killed him deserves a medal, whoever did it."

"Who do you think did it, Tank? Could it have been one of the Orcas?"

"Not a chance."

"Okay. Who on the Wizards did it?"

"Had to be a coach. Madjeski wouldn't call in a player for a private talk; he'd make one of the coaches handle that."

"Which coach would Madjeski call in?"

"Well, most likely—I'm figuring the odds now, you understand, not the facts—it would be Boom-Boom or Carny."

"Which one?"

"Not Boom-Boom. You know why? Because in all the years he played, Boom-Boom never clipped a guy from behind. He always hit a guy face-to-face. Boom-Boom would never hit a guy, even Madjeski, when his back was turned."

"So your choice is Carny?"

"Of the coaches? Yes."

"Who else is there? You said Madjeski wouldn't call a player in for a private session."

"There's one player he'd call in."

"Tilley? Crazy Al?"

"He really had it in for Madjeski, everybody knew that. And he's sort of wild. Very unpredictable."

"So you think Tilley did it?"

"No, I'm pretty sure he didn't."

"Carny, then?"

"Not him, either."

"One of the minor coaches? Kicking, maybe?"

"Nah. If it was a coach, it had to be one of the two coordinators. But it wasn't."

"What makes you so sure?"

"They're too big."

"I don't get it. What does size have to do with it?"

"When I was on my way to Boom-Boom's office, I saw a guy come out of Madjeski's office, just about the time Lieutenant Danzig said Madjeski was killed. It couldn't have been Boom-Boom or Carny; they're too big. It couldn't even have been Tilley. It was a little guy. About your size."

Marc's heart jumped. "Did you—did you recognize him?"

"How could I? I was cleaning my glasses and the lights were sort of dim and I was too far away. By the time I put my glasses back on, he was gone."

"Did you follow him?"

"What for? I didn't know Madjeski was dead at the time. I realized only later, when Danzig asked me."

"You told Danzig about this?"

"Sure. Why not? But don't tell Danzig I told you. He made me promise not to tell anybody."

"Don't worry. How did you describe him to Danzig?"

"Like I said, a little guy. Short. His clothes were dark. Blue or black, something like that. I don't see so good without my glasses, especially far away, and it was sort of dark." He turned away abruptly. "You finished now? I got to go inside; lots of things to do." He walked away.

Yeah, I'm finished. Marc knew that for sure. No wonder Danzig is cracking the whip. He *knows* it's me; he just can't prove it. Yet. So if he puts on enough pressure, he thinks I'll crack. He's right. In fact—Marc had a sudden flash—it's worse than that. What Danzig doesn't know for sure is that I'm only the guy who called in the story, who took the pictures. From the evidence Danzig has, I could just as easily be the murderer.

20

"You want the real truth about Walter?" Joanne Chrysczyk poured boiling water into the instant coffee and pushed the cup across the kitchen table to Marc. She was wearing high heels and patterned stockings, with a long string of pearls across an expensive-looking tight black knit dress. Her nails were shiny red and quite long. Her bright blond hair was lacquered neatly in place; makeup was complete and not overdone. She was almost as tall as Marc and still slim, though what once must have been a trim, girlish figure was, at forty-five, verging on hardness. The kitchen was spotless, ready for the critical eye of any wandering poll taker. If it weren't for the anger in her eyes, Joanne Chrysczyk could have stepped, unchanged, into a floor-polish commercial. "Sugar? Milk?"

"Black is just fine, Mrs. Chrysczyk." Marc took a sip. It was weak; Dahliah would be pleased. "This is delicious." He lied.

She accepted the compliment with a brief smile. "Yes, I was always a good cook. My mother brought us up . . . The kids today, the young girls, they don't know what's important. A good home—that's where you learn proper upbringing."

"Yes, I can see that you're a very good homemaker, Mrs. Chrysczyk."

"Call me Joanne, as long as we're going to talk. I prefer it that way."

"Thank you, Joanne. And you can call me Marc. You were about to tell me, when I interrupted, what it's like to be a football wife. I'm sure most women don't understand the difficulties."

"Marc, they have no idea. They think it's all glamour, being famous, lots of money, six months' vacation every year, a big strong husband. . . . Sounds like heaven, doesn't it? Well, they're wrong, completely wrong. If they knew what it's really like, they'd never marry a football player. Nobody would. Ever."

"Aren't there many good things about the life of a football player, Joanne?"

"Maybe there are, but not for the wife. Before there are children, some parts of it can be fun. Half the time you're in a new place, a different place, every week. But the trouble is, Marc, it's the same new place every time. And it's all the same new place every other place is. You think it's very different, one hotel from another? Not even the shopping's different, just the names of the stores."

"But you're together, with lots of free time. Football isn't a nine-to-five job, exactly."

"It's worse. Much worse. He used to get up early, real early, because he had to have a big breakfast—you have no idea how much that man could eat—and you can't practice on a full stomach. I had to get up with him, to make breakfast, no matter what. Then he drove to the stadium and was gone all day, exercising and practicing. When he came home—and it wasn't early—he stank of beer, and I knew that he'd been sitting in a bar with his buddies instead of coming home to me. Then I got to give him supper—a hot supper, even though I never knew when he was coming

139

home—and then he sat with the playbook until the middle of the night. Dancing? *Anything?* We didn't even watch TV together. That's *when* he came home. What about the time he had to watch the movies? The same movies of the same game, over and over, that he'd seen a million times? On those nights, he didn't even say hello, his head was so full of who did this and who did that and what to do *if*."

"I never realized—"

"Nobody does. Nobody understands what I went through. Would you believe that the night before a game, a player can't even sleep with his own wife? The coach says it drains your strength, would you believe it? He has to sleep in a hotel near the stadium and the coach checks to see he's in bed at ten? A big healthy man like that can't sleep with his own wife on a Saturday night? Or go to church with her on Sunday morning? Two hours of workout and four hours of practice don't sap your strength, but just barely touching your own wife does? And on Sunday after the game? It's like not being married at all. It's even worse than not being married. He's so beat up, he can hardly move. He's the strongest man in the world, and for one lousy hour-a-week's work he got to soak in a hot bath for two hours? And limp?"

"Well, football is a rough game, Joanne. There are many players almost as big and strong as Tank . . . Walter. They used to double-team him regularly. He took a good beating every game."

"He took a beating? What about his wife? Whatever he got, I got more."

"He beat you?"

"Walter? He wouldn't dare."

Marc wondered how that worked, but put it aside. He didn't want to know. One thing about Dahliah . . . "I guess it's even worse after the children come," he murmured sympathetically.

"Is it ever. You have the first one just when you least expect it and, all right, it's God's blessing. That's what you got married for, to have children. So you figure you might as well have the other one now, both together, get it over with, and then, in a few years, you're pretty free again. Only it doesn't happen that way. Now you're stuck at home and you can't even go with your husband at all. All year long, you can't go anyplace or do anything. Like being chained."

"Well, doesn't the off-season . . . ? It's six months long, Joanne. That's a *good* vacation."

"For other men, sure. I talked with the other wives. They went away together, they did things; some of them even went to Europe. Not Walter. He had to keep in perfect shape, work out every day, hard workouts. He had to have good food; we hardly ever went out to a restaurant. He had to go to bed early. He had to study, study, study. Everything. Not just his own position, not just his own team, but everything."

"Well, that's part of the job—the weekly game, that's just the tip of the iceberg."

"Are you telling me something I don't know? Let me tell you some things. People think, you're a football player, you've got to be making a million dollars. Baloney. Football is the worst sport, when it comes to money, in America, especially if you're just beginning. You have to go around all summer making speeches, posing for pictures, showing how equipment works, even opening supermarkets, just to make a living. A *living*, that's all, a *bare* living, in those days. And when you finally start making a good living, it's over. You're too old. How many thirty-five-year-old football players do you know? Maybe some kickers, but not defensive tackles. So you have to make it while you're young, or else. There are plenty of ex-football players selling used cars now, players who used to be stars. Plenty."

"So you had very little time with your husband, even then. That was the worst part?" Marc was trying to keep the flood going. He didn't have to try very hard; this had been dammed up for years.

141

"Oh, no. The worst part—ask any player's wife—the worst part is not knowing if your husband is going to come back crippled or not. Every game, practically—it doesn't matter how big you are, how strong, how good—every game, somebody gets hurt. Sometimes it's bad, real bad. You could be crippled for life, paralyzed, even. . . . And if you can't play anymore, you think the owner's going to support you for life? Who's going to feed the kids, cover the mortgage, pay the bills? You know how much it costs to maintain a home and raise two kids?"

"You stuck with Walter through all of the hard times, Joanne. What made you finally leave him?"

"I started to talk to the other wives. I learned plenty. Sure their husbands worked all day long, long hours, but not like Walter. He was gone twice as much as any of them. And they came home at night, at a reasonable time. Late, maybe, but not too late. And you could call them if you had to, but I could never reach Walter. One night, when our daughter Valerie fell out of bed and cut her chin—right where you could see it—I had to take her to the hospital all by myself and I had to find a doctor who could stitch her up so it wouldn't show. In the middle of the night. Where was Walter? Watching films, he said. Hah! Fooling around with a chippy is more like it."

"I heard that Walter was a very conscientious coach, Joanne, and he never even looked at another woman."

"Well, you heard wrong, Marc. I know different. Mr. Madjeski, God rest his soul, explained it to me. When it got to be too much for me, I asked him. . . . He came right over; really tried to help. He explained it all to me. Football coaches, anyone who has anything to do with football, especially if they were big stars like Walter, are very attractive to a certain type of woman, women of rather low moral standards. They hang out near the stadium, or near the hotel where the team is staying, and they wear very revealing, low-cut clothes"—she unconsciously ran her hands over the front of her dress, smoothing and tightening the jersey—"and they act very forward, extremely forward, and it's very hard for a man who hasn't seen his wife for several days to resist the temptation."

"Well, that may be true in some cases, but most of the players I know—"

"Walter was the worst. Mr. Madjeski explained to me that with men like Walter, it doesn't mean a thing. Of all the hundreds of girls . . . He was sure Walter didn't care for any of them a single bit, probably couldn't even remember their names, and that I shouldn't take it to heart as long as Walter came home on time regularly and was warm and loving with his family. Which he didn't and he wasn't. That's when I finally made up my mind."

"I was talking with Walter just today, Joanne, and he told me how much he missed you and the children. Still, after all these years."

"Yeah? He should have thought of that before he started fooling around."

"Well, if it happened, it was a long, long time ago. He said he really misses you and would like to talk with you."

"I don't want to talk to him," she said, tired. "There's nothing new he can tell me. He'll just tell me he never did anything, and that I'm crazy for suspecting him. Same old lies."

"Maybe he can tell you what's in his heart in a different way, Joanne. Maybe if he confesses, and says how sorry he is . . . I'm sure he really loves you. Would it hurt to just talk to him? Let him come over?"

"Well, maybe once. To see if he's really changed. All right, but tell him you talked me into it. Tomorrow, at eight."

"Uh, Joanne, he can't come tomorrow. The Super Bowl. He can't go anywhere or do anything until Sunday night."

"Football comes before me, again?"

"It's the *Super Bowl*, Joanne. Everybody, myself included, is working double and triple times normal. He's doing it for the money, for you. I'm sure"—Marc took a blind stab—"that he's been very generous with money, far more than the separation agreement called for."

"That way—yes, he's always been good that way."

"I'll tell him Sunday, then. Okay?" Marc looked pleadingly into her eyes. "He's really been knocking himself out the past month, and I'm sure he'd love to have a quiet evening at home with you on Sunday. And a good home-cooked meal."

"Well"—Joanne thought hard—"I guess it wouldn't hurt."

"That's fine, Joanne; just great." He took her hand in his, warmly. "You'll never regret it." Marc looked at his watch. "It's getting late. Would you mind driving me to the train station?"

If anyone had a reason to kill Magic Madjeski, Tank Chrysczyk had a lulu.

Joanne appraised him, up and down, slowly. "You look a little tired too, Marc. Why don't you relax, take your shoes off, stay for supper. I'll get you a drink while I change. It's been a long time, and with the kids at school, I get a little tired of eating alone."

"I'd love to," Marc said, very earnestly, "but my wife expects me for supper."

"I see." Joanne glanced at his bare left hand.

"Perhaps you'll come to dinner at our place some night—maybe with Walter."

Joanne Chrysczyk gingerly touched her lacquered blond hair, as if to smoothe down some imaginary stray wisp. "Anything is possible," she said tartly.

21

"Why are we meeting here?" Marc asked as Lieutenant Danzig led him into the diner for breakfast the next day.

"It's the best diner in Brooklyn," Danzig answered, eyes searching the room.

"Yes, fine, looks very nice, but why not in your office?"

"You're not reliable, Burr. I ask you to bring me cheese, you bring me prune. Here, the waitress brings me what I want."

"Come on, Danzig."

"Besides, the first time you come to my office, you're a suspect. The second time, you're a stoolie. Some of the guys around the house are real creeps, you know? Always sniffing after promotions, looking to break a major case. One of them gets the idea you know something, he could start following you around, and when the killer gets you, he gets the killer. That way, he gets all the credit on what I set up, and I'm out in the cold. There's a good place." He led the way to a just-vacated corner booth. "You wouldn't want that to happen now, would you?"

"I wouldn't mind having a cop following me around, watching over me."

"Yeah? And if this creep shows himself and scares off the

killer? There goes the case, all my time and work for nothing."

"I wouldn't mind a bit having the killer scared away from me."

"Sure you would, Burr, believe me. 'Cause then you've got to give me the anonymous phone guy."

The waitress came over, put a menu down in front of each of them, and waited, pencil poised. Danzig waved away the menu. "I'll have a large orange juice, fresh squeezed, not out of the pitcher; three eggs, jumbo, over light, in butter; a double order of home fries on the side, crisp; three slices real Jewish rye, with lots of seeds, warmed, not toasted, and plenty of butter. A mug, not a cup, a mug of fresh-brewed filter coffee and a cheese Danish. Each time you see the mug empty, you bring another mug and another cheese Danish until I tell you to stop. And a little bowl of strawberry jam, the imported, none of them little plastic cups." He turned to Marc. "What'll you have, Burr?"

Marc hesitated.

"Tell her what you want, Burr." Danzig was impatient. "I ain't got all day. Don't worry, everything here is fresh, homemade." Marc was looking at the right side of the menu. "They even bake their own Danish."

"Well, then," Marc said, "I'll have a small orange juice, an order of pancakes, and a glass of skim milk."

"Make that buckwheat pancakes," Danzig told the waitress. "Blueberry buckwheat pancakes; he'll love them. Bring extra butter for the pancakes, melted butter. That way the butter don't cool off the pancakes, Burr. And bring him plenty of maple syrup. They got real maple syrup here, Burr, not the supermarket crap. You could also bring him a prune Danish; he likes prune." As the waitress slid away, Danzig explained. "In case you don't want to eat the prune, I could wrap it up for later."

"The prices here," Marc said. "It's very expensive."

"I told you," Danzig said patiently, "it's the best diner in

Brooklyn. What're you worried about? It all goes on the expense account, don't it? You don't have enough cash on you, they take credit cards."

"Mr. Witter won't approve buying you breakfast; he ordered me off the case."

"Bury it some other place. Now tell me what you found out yesterday."

"So you got good reactions out of Carny and Tank? See? I told you, you gotta ask the right questions in the right way."

"Yeah, suppose one of them—they're all very touchy; it's two days before the Super Bowl—one of them gets annoyed, thinks I'm bothering him too much, and takes a swing at me?"

"Great. Then I take him downtown and sweat him for a couple of hours and see what falls out."

"While I have a broken arm? And what if he isn't the killer?"

"You can get a broken arm fixed real fast these days and be back on the job in two hours, so that's all right. And the odds are that the guy who slugs you ain't the killer, so we learned something already. The killer's got to be more under control, know what I mean? He ain't gonna take chances on being picked up for assault while he's worried about being fingered as a murderer, right?"

"Gee, that's great, Danzig. But suppose he breaks my jaw? Then I can't go around asking the right questions in the right way, right?"

"Yeah, well, you've got to learn to move fast, Burr. Keep your head protected. You exercise?" Danzig asked as the waitress brought their orders to the table.

"Regularly. Every day."

"You gotta watch your diet too, Burr. Too much weight'll slow you down. You better leave the prune Danish." Danzig moved Burr's pastry to his side of the table. "So both Carny and Tank got good motives, huh?"

"Tank hated Madjeski because he broke up his marriage. Carny hated Madjeski on general principles and also wanted to inherit his job as head coach."

"Which one do you figure as being the perpetrator? I mean, figuring the odds."

"Tank is probably more direct and more violent. He was a tackle, after all, while Carny was a receiver. But Carny is shrewder, sneakier, a planner. It's a toss-up. But don't forget Crazy Al and Jimbo. Jimbo—I got the impression he hated Madjeski more than anybody. He's a head coach too, a really good planner, and the smartest of the lot. On the other hand, Crazy Al is the most unpredictable. Very volatile."

"Okay, okay. So which one of them is the killer?"

"How do I know, Danzig? I haven't seen any real evidence yet. Have you found any clues you haven't told me about?"

"Clues? What the hell do you think this is, Burr? TV? Clues is for books; this is real life. In real life, you don't look for clues. Nine times outta ten you know who the killer is right away. You know who's been screwing who's wife; you know who's been robbing the company blind; you know who hates the victim like poison. That *who*, he's the one; he's the perpetrator. So you apply pressure, and he cracks. Then you take him downtown, and you sweat him a little. Then you let him sign a confession. Then you put him on TV, read him Miranda, make him sign the confession all over again for the TV. Then you explain things to him; the facts of life. You tell him if he tells his lawyer you read him Miranda after he signed, you're gonna put him in with the animals for a night or two before he calls his lawyer. When you're sure he understands what the score is, then you let him call his lawyer. That's how to crack a case, Burr. In real life."

"What about the tenth case, Danzig? When you don't know who the killer is right away?"

"You know what the trouble with you is, Burr? The trouble with you is you're trying to make things complicated.

148

You probably even *like* things complicated. TV is complicated; books is complicated; real life is simple. Plain. Not fancy. If I don't know who the perpetrator is right away, and it's an amateur case where I don't have a stoolie, I take all the guys who *could* have, and I take all the guys who *should* have, and who's on both lists, one of them is the killer. Then I apply pressure to everybody, each one. The killer cracks. Then I take him downtown and I sweat him a little. Then I—"

"Wait a minute, Danzig. What if, when you apply your pressure, he doesn't crack?"

"What's the matter with you, Burr? You don't understand English? I said you apply pressure, right? I didn't say *how much* pressure, did I? I apply pressure, nobody cracks. I apply more pressure. Nobody still cracks? So I apply still more pressure, right? Still nobody cracks? Okay, now I put on *much* more pressure, *big* pressure. He cracks. Sooner or later, he cracks, right? I got plenty of time and plenty of pressure and nothing else to do; he's got to go to work, lots of things. Who's gonna win, huh? Right. Lieutenant Danzig, that's who. He cracks. Then I take him downtown and sweat him a little and then—"

"Okay, okay, Danzig; I get the picture." And I'm going to get, Marc thought, *still* more pressure, right? And after that, the *big* pressure? Save yourself the trouble, Danzig. I'm ready to crack right now.

"So all I want from you, Burr," Danzig said, "is to give me the name of the killer. I'll do the rest. And do it fast, huh, Burr. I got lots of other cases on my mind."

"Take it easy, Danzig. I haven't finished yet. I still have to talk to Boom-Boom."

"Yeah, I forgot how slow you move. Okay, you're gonna interrogate him right? The right questions in the right way?"

"Definitely. Today and Saturday both teams are using the Gruber Dome for practice. So the Orcas can get the feel of the stadium, the artificial turf."

"Don't that mean the other guys'll be watching their secret plays?"

"Sure, but neither team is going to be practicing any secret plays these last two days. Each coach has been studying the other team's game films of the last season, and especially the play-offs, for the past two weeks. There's very little one team doesn't know about the other."

"Who's gonna win?"

"Are you thinking of betting on the game, Danzig?"

"Never you mind, Burr. Just answer the question."

Marc stared at the lieutenant suspiciously, wondering what would happen if he touted Danzig onto the wrong team. "Well, everybody's agreed that the Orcas are the . . . the more powerful team, and they have a much better record than the Wizards. The Orcas lost only one game in the entire season and shut out their opponents seven times. The Wizards won only half their games and, when they did win, it was only by a few points."

"So if a guy wanted to bet, let's say, he should bet on the Orcas, right?"

"It's not that easy, Danzig. In football, you don't bet on who wins; you bet on the spread. That's the handicap that the expert line makers in Las Vegas, where gambling is legal, figure out to equalize the strength of the teams. For example, if they believe that the Orcas will win by fifteen points, they will add fifteen points to the Wizards' score. It doesn't have to be a whole number either; it could be sixteen and a half points or thirteen and a half points, like that."

"So even if a team lost, you could still win money betting on it?"

"Certainly. If the score ends up twenty-four to nine in favor of the Orcas, and the spread is fifteen and a half, you add the spread to the Wizards' score and get twenty-four and a half. Even though the Wizards got clobbered in the game, you win your bet."

"Okay. Sounds simple. So which way would you bet, Burr?"

"Well, if you believe Carny, for twelve points take the Orcas and for twenty-four points take the Wizards."

"And in between?"

"It's a gamble."

"Are you going to bet, Burr?"

"I don't think so; I don't have much money."

"If you was gonna bet, how would you bet?"

"I'd follow Carny's advice. At either twelve or twenty-four points, I'd put everything I've got on it. At thirteen, fourteen, or twenty-three, twenty-two, I'd bet as much as I could afford to lose. At fifteen, sixteen, or twenty-one, twenty, I'd risk a hundred bucks."

"And at seventeen to nineteen?"

"Nothing. I'm not a gambler. I like the odds in my favor."

"So what's the spread now, Burr?"

"Still at eighteen. But it could change Saturday, or even Sunday, if any drastic developments take place."

"You mean like if Tilley got arrested for murder?"

"Or if Jimbo got his head bashed in too—anything like that. I'm sure that Madjeski's murder affected the spread."

"Yeah, well, that's one of the things I want you to think about, Burr." He abruptly changed the subject. "You know any good bookies?"

"No, but I could find out: My steady knows a lot of cops. You could find out even easier, Danzig."

"I don't want any of the guys to know, if I decide to do it. Let me know how to get in touch with a good bookie tomorrow morning, just in case, and what the spread is. That is, if you think Carny is right."

"I'm not taking any responsibility for what Carny says, Danzig. If you win, you win on your own, and if you lose, it's not my fault."

"Okay, okay, don't be so touchy. You think Carny is betting on the game?"

"If the spread is right, I'm sure of it."

"And the other guys? The suspects, I mean?"

"Them too."

"For or against their own team?"

So this is what Danzig is getting at, Marc thought; nibbling at the perimeter and finally sinking his teeth into the center. "I would be very surprised if any of them even *thought* of betting against their own teams. That goes against everything that's been drilled into them from the day they first saw a football at the age of four. Besides, it's very hard to throw a football game and get away with it. I mean, I suppose it could be done, but your loss in income over the next few years would far outweigh any winnings you could reasonably expect, unless you were very rich and could bet very high. That is, if you were a player, and your actions caused your team to lose a Super Bowl game, you might be waived out of football altogether. You'd lose endorsements, speaking engagements; it could cost you hundreds of thousands of dollars. And it's very hard for a single player to affect a game. The key play may never come up, or if it does, it may not come your way."

"It's not hard if you're a quarterback, Burr."

"Tilley? Come on, Danzig. He risks injury to win every time he leaves the pocket to scramble."

"He's on his way out anyway, from what you told me."

"Yes, but . . . I just don't believe it. I've gotten to know him over the past two years. He's not the type."

"Everybody's the type, Burr, if there's enough dough on the table. And it don't have to be a player. A head coach could throw the game even easier, right? Send in the wrong play, maybe?"

"Jimbo Tallifer? You're crazy, Danzig. He wants to win more than anyone."

"Sure, Burr, but win what? And by how much? Couldn't

he still win the game—right?—and keep inside the spread and win lots of dough too? Much more of a sure thing than beating the spread, right? But I wasn't thinking just of Tallifer. Aren't there *two* head coaches on the Wizards?"

"Boom-Boom and Carny? The two of them working together to lose? Impossible. They're in competition with each other to make head coach."

"I didn't say together, Burr. Separately. And if the defense or the offense screws up once, just at a crucial moment, does that mean the coach is a lemon? That it's his fault? Or was it the players who made the mistake? Everybody makes mistakes, Burr."

"Then you might as well suspect Tank, too."

"Now you get the picture, Burr. When you talk to any of these guys again, see how they feel about betting."

"You think Madjeski's murder had to do with betting?"

"I don't think anything yet, but I've got to check out everything, you understand? Okay. Meet you here tomorrow, same time."

"On Saturday? Here?"

"Yeah, here. What's the matter, you didn't like the food? Oh, I get it. You want to sleep late 'cause it's Saturday." He frowned at this evidence of Marc's self-indulgence, then his face relaxed. "Okay, if it bothers you that much, make it nine o'clock." Danzig got up from the table, heavily. "Leave the waitress a good tip, Burr; she did good." He lumbered out.

Marc called Dahliah from a phone in the diner's lobby. Luckily, she had not yet left for school. She promised to ask her students for the name of a cooperative bookmaker who would be willing to talk to Marc. He couldn't believe that Danzig didn't know all the bookmakers in Brooklyn and wondered what new trap Danzig had set for him.

22

Harold "Boom-Boom" Drogovitch was not in a good mood. "How in hell," he asked heaven rather than Marc, "can I hold a line against an offense that's twice as big?" Boom-Boom had not been in his office when Marc arrived; Marc had found him leaning against the stands, watching the Orcas practice.

"Not quite twice," Marc corrected. "Just a little heavier."

"Not quite?" Boom-Boom glowered. "Their *receivers* weigh as much as my ends. Almost."

"Yeah, but your guys are really quick, Boom-Boom. They get off the mark as fast as the offense, even though the offense knows when the snap is coming."

"Yeah, and then they hit a stone wall. You're quick, Burr, right? Especially at your size. You want to try bouncing off me? See how far you get? I won't even use my hands."

"No thanks, Boom-Boom; I value my neck. But your guys aren't going to go charging into any stone walls either. You're going to go heavy into stunting, aren't you? Around, across, and behind the enemy?"

"I've got no choice, do I? If I can't go through them, I've got to go around them. But I'd rather have the muscle; that way I can choose what to do."

"Your men are also faster. Your linebackers will be in their backfield before the quarterback takes three steps."

"Yeah, sure, if they can find a hole to go through. But when you have seven big whales in front of you, practically shoulder to shoulder, where you going to find a hole?"

"Stop moaning, Boom-Boom. The Longhorns were almost as big as the Orcas, and you held them down pretty well."

"You think that's going to work twice, Burr? Hell, Scar's been studying the films of that game for two weeks. He knows every move I made there. I've been going crazy trying to figure out stunts and games he's never seen before."

"He's seen them all, Boom-Boom, just like you. The trick is to make new combinations of old moves to confuse them."

"Gee, thanks, Burr. I never thought of that. What would I do without you?" He put his big horn-rimmed glasses into his pocket.

"Have you and Carny worked out how you'll handle the situation?"

"More or less. We're in general agreement on the game plan, and it'll be like Gruber said, what else can we do? On defense, he'll advise me, and I'll listen, but I'll make all the decisions. On offense, I'll do what I can to help him, but I wouldn't interfere. We'll manage okay, but it would've been better if we had a real head coach with full authority."

"Madjeski?"

Boom-Boom stood in thought for a moment, then spoke. "Look, with all his faults, he still knew football. He wasn't afraid to try different things and he made decisions fast."

"You didn't agree with him, did you?"

"Lots of times I didn't, but he had the authority, and I did what I had to do."

"He didn't like Tilley's new ideas, did he?"

"None of us does, but it isn't that they are new ideas, it's that Tilley doesn't do what he's supposed to do. He's unde-

155

pendable; you just can't count on him. He's a disruptive influence too, always making wisecracks about the coaching staff to the other players. I don't care what you think about the coach, you've got to respect his decisions, follow orders on the field, otherwise you don't have a team."

"When you left Georgia, Boom-Boom, when you were hired here, you knew what kind of reputation Madjeski had in the trade, didn't you?"

"I was an all-pro middle linebacker. You think I couldn't handle a little pressure?"

"It was the opportunity that decided you?"

"Damn right. I could have stayed another ten years in Georgia with no chance to move up. Here I had a good shot at head coach in a year."

"Madjeski promised you the job?"

"In plain English. I made him say it, but he wouldn't say it in front of witnesses and he didn't put it in writing, so I knew the score."

"You'd have to wait for him to retire to become head coach?"

"Yeah, and even then it wouldn't be a sure thing, but I had a shot at it, which was more than what I had where I was."

"Or wait for Madjeski to die?"

"To die, yeah. I thought about that too. What have you got on your mind, Burr?" Boom-Boom didn't look any more menacing than before, but his voice had lowered and he was speaking more slowly, more distinctly.

"I'm trying to get information that will lead to finding out something about Madjeski's death, Boom-Boom. Got any ideas?"

"I didn't benefit, Burr, as you might have notice, if that's what you're thinking about. As a matter of fact, I'm worse off than before. Gruber, it's as plain as the nose on his face, is thinking about getting an outsider in."

"What will you do if he does, Boom-Boom?"

"I'll decide that when it happens. If it happens. Why? You know something I don't know?"

"No, Boom-Boom, not even rumors. What are your present plans?"

"Try to figure out a defense to keep the Orcas from walking all over us. I make a good showing, maybe I'll get a good offer."

"If I were an owner, I'd be making offers to all four of you: Tank, Scar, and Carny too."

"Yeah, they're all good. Trouble is, there'll be, at most, one spot open next season. Two, if Gruber don't pick Carny or me."

"You never know what will happen, Boom-Boom. You really think you can stop the Orcas?"

"It's one game, Burr. I held the Longhorns to fourteen, and they were damn big. Maybe I can do the same for the Orcas."

"What do you think the score will be?"

"What's the matter with you, Burr? You think I'm a fortune-teller? If I could answer that, I'd spend my time at the track instead of here."

"Okay, wrong question. What do you think the spread should be?"

"Thursday's spread was plus eighteen for us. Sounds about right to me. Why? You betting?"

"I'm considering it. You?"

"Hell, no. Gambling is for suckers. I've got a family, and I spend my time figuring out defenses so maybe, if God is good to me, I can get the winner's end of the Super Bowl bonus."

"Something you said before doesn't figure. You held the Longhorns to fourteen, but you think a spread of eighteen is okay?"

"The Orcas are bigger than the Longhorns; Jimbo is the best coach in the business; Tank and Scar are better than the

Longhorns' coordinators; we've got this stupid double-head-coach business instead of the right way; I don't think Tilley learned his lesson yet; their defensive line is twice as big as our offense. . . . You want me to go on? Believe me, Burr, the line makers know their business; bookies ain't in the business to lose money."

"Speaking of bookies, do you know if Madjeski used to bet?"

"Madjeski was not the kind of guy to tell anybody anything like that, especially me."

"Why especially you?"

"Because I say what I got to say, and I say it straight."

"That must have annoyed Madjeski a little."

"Maybe it did, sometimes, but tough shit. That's the way I am. You want me, you take me that way."

"Tank paid you a compliment, Boom-Boom. He said you never hit a guy from behind."

"He did? That's nice. Tank's a good guy, but what he said ain't strictly true. If I was chasing a ballcarrier or a receiver, hell, you got to tackle the guy from behind. Or on a blitz, you hit the quarterback any way you can, including the blind side, as long as he's got the ball. What Tank meant, I never blocked a guy from behind, clipped him, that's all."

"He said it to prove you couldn't have killed Madjeski."

"Yeah, well, Tank's trying to help when I don't need it. You're going to kill a guy, you don't play by the rules. Football's a game; it has rules. You play football, you play by the rules. Life ain't a game. If a guy deserves to be killed, you don't follow any rules."

"Did Madjeski deserve to be killed, Boom-Boom?"

"For what he did to some guys, probably. But I could take what he dished out to me; I'm tough."

"You're saying you still want to be considered a suspect?"

"No, I ain't, Burr. Don't start getting any stupid ideas. I was with Tank when Madjeski was killed."

"Not necessarily, Boom-Boom. It only took a few seconds

to kill Madjeski, or maybe a few minutes, that's all. Both you and Tank had time to do it before you got together."

"Neither of us did. I know I didn't and Tank . . . he wouldn't hit a guy with a statue. You know how big he is, how strong? He could pick *me* up with one hand. If he was going to kill Madjeski . . . Hell, Madjeski was smaller than you. Tank would just twist his head off if Madjeski got him mad enough. Believe me, whoever it was, it wasn't Tank."

"Who do you think it was, Boom-Boom?"

"That's all, Burr. We've got a tough enough row to hoe, even if everybody's in top condition, without your coming around making trouble, upsetting everybody, and the cops putting one of my people away. No hard feelings, Burr, okay? But if you want to be a big-deal detective, do it after the game." He strode away toward the other end of the field.

Marc watched Boom-Boom's back for a while, then walked slowly into one of the tunnels leading to the office area under the stadium. He went into the downstairs press room, opened his little computer terminal case, and sat for several minutes at the keyboard. Nothing.

He still didn't have a story, news or color, about the Wizards today. Julius Witter would roast him alive. After he skinned him.

Marc folded up the computer terminal and decided to visit Pusher Rybek. Rybek was always a good source of news and always happy to talk; maybe Marc could pick up something and turn it into news. If that failed, well there was always Verne Ketchel's handouts. All the papers would have the same story but, what the hell, no reporter could get an exclusive every day. If he wrote it up properly, it would sound different.

For once, Rybek wasn't in the trainer's area; it was completely deserted. Marc sat down in one of the chairs behind the line of hydrotherapy tanks. Everyone was so goddamned touchy today, and it wasn't only the normal tension of two days before the Super Bowl. Marc was sure that Boom-Boom would have gotten angry, might even have hit him, if he had pushed one inch more. From the front, of course, but Marc wasn't so sure it would have been any better for his health. No, in spite of what Tank had said, Boom-Boom was still a prime suspect.

There was the story: the feeling of tension in the air, the stress due to the coming game combined with the stress due to the murder of the head coach, of wondering who the killer was, who the police would arrest. Yes, definitely a story, a good story. Marc got up and started to head down the dimly lit corridor leading back to the press room. He passed two of the tunnels leading to the field, then, as he entered the third one, something whizzed past his head, very close, and struck the concrete wall on his left with a tremendous ringing bang. Instinctively Marc dived headfirst for the area past the tunnel from which the missile had come. As his hands touched the floor, he bent his elbows to take up the shock, tucked his head under, and went into a fast forward roll, bouncing upright with a half twist as soon as he was past the exposed tunnel opening. He immediately fell forward again, silently cushioning the fall with his arms. Moving very slowly, he inched his head forward at floor level until he could see into the tunnel. No one was there.

Marc stood up behind the protection of the corridor wall. He peeked out into the tunnel again. Still empty. Slowly, watchfully, he walked over to where the missile had struck the inner wall of the corridor. A big chunk of concrete had spalled off, showing gray against the light green paint. Whatever had sailed past him, if it had hit him, would have taken his head off. Completely. His body would be lying there, dead. His body. A shiver passed through him. Like Madjeski's body, but it would be *his* body. Dead. He kept looking at the tunnel entrance.

On the floor, about ten feet away, was the weapon. A disc, steel, painted red, about four inches in diameter, with a hole in the middle. Cast in one side were the figures "1¼." Marc recognized it at once. A weight, a one-and-a-quarter-pound weight, for the adjustable dumbbells from Rybek's gymnasium. Small enough to fit into anyone's pocket; big enough to kill. The killer had a long throw to make—over sixty feet. To throw, or to scale the weight accurately, that distance one needed the arm of a quarterback. Or an ex-quarterback. Or a big ex-football player. Any ex-football player; they were all big.

Marc walked slowly, carefully—eyes fixed on the entrance to the field—along the tunnel, hugging the wall, ready to dive again. When he got outside, everything looked normal, perfectly normal. No one knew or cared that he almost had been killed. Normal. Why not? How long would it take to go quickly into the gym, maybe even the day before, and slip the little weight into a pocket? How hard would it be to watch for an opportunity to kill Marc from a position of comparative safety? How hard would it be to time Marc's passing the other two tunnels, to walk ahead fast and, as soon as Marc entered the area at the third tunnel, to throw the little weight at Marc's head? The throw itself? One second. Less, if you had a quick release. Then to return to what you were doing before? Another two seconds? Who would notice?

Danzig was right. You ask the right questions in the right way, the pressure increases, and someone cracks. The murderer cracks. Not *cracks;* cracked. Like the wall. Or, by only six inches, Marc's head. Don't let anyone get behind you, Danzig had said. Or alongside of you either? Or in front of you? You'd need eyes all around your head. The next two days were not going to be fun, Marc decided.

23

Mr. Silver was dressed in soft gray. He was small, plump, and gray-haired, and wore bifocals with silver frames. He was seated facing the door at a table for two and signaled slightly to Marc as he entered the restaurant. Dahliah had arranged the appointment through one of her students. Dear Dahliah! What would he do without her?

"Thank you for taking the trouble," Marc said. "I really appreciate it."

"Not at all, Mr. Burr," Silver said graciously. "Please sit down. Mutual friends assured me you were an unbiased reporter and quite trustworthy."

"I try, Mr. Silver, but actually, all I want is some technical information. Please call me Marc."

"What is your purpose, Marc? Do you intend to write an exposé of gambling, sports gambling, in New York?"

"Not in the foreseeable future. If I ever do, I will check with you on quoting any specific information you give me that I don't get from another source."

"Will you present all sides of the story, Marc?"

"If I ever do an analysis of gambling, yes I will. But my interest in betting is limited to football right now."

"As applied to the murder of Zachary Madjeski?"

"Yes, Mr. Silver. You've been checking up on me, I see."

"It's always useful to know the person you're talking to. Or about. Do you believe there's a connection between Madjeski's death and betting on football games?"

"I don't know, Mr. Silver, but I have to check this out."

"As requested by Lieutenant Danzig?"

"As *pressured* by Lieutenant Danzig. You know him too?"

"An odd individual, Marc. Very low level, but somehow, he often gets his man. Possibly because he thinks like— You know the story of the lost horse? No? It bears repeating. In the village a horse had disappeared. The villagers looked everywhere, but the horse could not be found. Finally, the village idiot appeared, leading the horse. When asked how he had known where the horse was, the idiot said, 'I thought where would I go if I was a horse and I went there and there he was.'"

"Sometimes I think Lieutenant Danzig is a lot smarter than I think."

"Well put, Marc; he is not a fool. Treat him with caution. One final matter, Marc. Are you recording this conversation? In any way, even by transmitter?"

"No, Mr. Silver. I'm not even going to take notes. All I want is background. You can search me if you want."

"Unnecessary, Marc. Have you decided what to order? Would it make you uncomfortable if I ordered creamed herring?"

"Not a bit, but I can't join you. I'm going to have the chopped eggplant appetizer, split-pea soup, spinach with boiled potato and sour cream, and a macaroon with tea."

"That sounds good; I think I'll have the same." Silver signaled for the waiter. "Do you mind if we talk while we eat?"

"I'd prefer it. I have to go to the stadium and interview some people, and it's after one already."

"I'll drop you off; saves time. One more thing: In order to simplify our talk, I'm going to use first person, as though I were a bookmaker myself. This does not mean that I am. I am knowledgeable, but not necessarily involved."

"I understand. How did you get . . . become knowledgeable about bookmakers, Mr. Silver? Is that really your name?"

"I'd like you to address me that way, please." He paused for a moment. "I was a mathematics student, a long time ago, majoring in probability—a fascinating subject. By the way, if you're interested, read *Probability, Statistics and Truth*, by Von Mises. Not the famous Von Mises—Ludwig, the economist—it's by Richard Von Mises, the mathematician."

"Is it easily available? Will I be able to understand it?"

"Most of it, I'm sure. You can skip the difficult parts. It's been out of print for some time, but you'll be able to find a copy in a university library. You'll learn a great deal about probability and about the strengths and weaknesses of statistics, both of which are almost universally misunderstood, even by some professionals. Now, as to how did I . . . ? After I got my master's, I had to go to work full time; I couldn't afford to go for a doctorate. I took a job as an actuary for a big insurance company. It was a boring job, highly repetitive, with little chance for advancement. One of my colleagues, I noted, was very interested in sports. He confided he had been betting on various games. I was shocked. Gambling? This was as far from my upbringing as stealing."

"You started gambling too?"

"My colleague showed me that there were occasionally anomalies in the odds; that sometimes the probability of one team's winning was significantly greater than the odds on that game. If you played such games consistently, the probability was quite good that, over a period of time, you would end up winning some money. Everyone thinks that, of course—that his choice is better than the odds warrant, otherwise why bet at all—but careful study of the situation will often provide a small edge that will lead to consistent winning. For a year I studied sports and betting; for a mind trained as mine was, it was child's play. For three months I made paper bets, to test my ideas. On paper, my winnings were considerable. I decided to try with real money—not very much, I was quite poor in those days. I won with some regularity. After six months I increased the size of my bets and still won much of the time. At the end of that year I had saved a sum greater than my year's salary."

"It was then that you quit your job?"

"Oh, no. I was, I still am, of a rather conservative set of mind. The bookmaker I had been working with had a talk with me. He was disturbed that I won so consistently, and wanted to know why."

"I can imagine. He would have preferred that you lost consistently."

"No, he wouldn't. You don't understand, Marc. The last thing a bookmaker wants is someone who always loses. This kind of person can end up stealing money from his employer, depriving his family of necessities, committing suicide, even killing a relative for an inheritance. There even have been cases where the client comes in to the bookmaker's office and shoots some poor clerk because he blames the bookmaker for his own stupidity. The bookmaker gets blamed for his client's insanity, the police are ordered to crack down; all sorts of hardship. People suffer, the client's family most of all. Bookmakers don't want that; they don't want trouble of any kind, they really don't. No, the ideal client is one who, over the course of the year, ends up about even on his betting. Whether it's a small amount won or a small amount lost doesn't matter, as long as it's well within the client's budget for recreation."

"Recreation? Losing money is recreation?"

"If you can ask that question, Marc, no, for you it cannot be recreation. But for many it is. Man was not made to sit at a desk and push paper; we are not that far removed from the jungle. You can't fight tigers in Times Square or bring back the bacon you yourself hunted on Wall Street. There must be, for many men, substitutes for the thrill of the hunt and the excitement of the battle. Football is the new moral equivalent of war, but watching often isn't enough. There is no direct participation, no risk and no trophy; no laurel wreath for the watcher. Betting is one way of getting involved, of risking part of yourself, and of tasting triumph. Your lady is a psychologist; ask her."

"I don't have to, Mr. Silver. What you say makes perfect sense. But to get back to what you said before, about bookmakers wanting clients who break even, I don't understand that. How can a bookmaker make a living if nobody wins or loses?"

"Let me finish my story and you'll understand. I explained to my bookmaker that I understood the mathematics of probability and that I had studied the sporting events carefully, recorded what I considered pertinent information, and organized this information properly. When the odds were out of line with the probability of winning, I bet appropriately. He liked that, I suspect, because he was afraid I had inside information he didn't have access to. He offered me a job at a considerable increase in salary."

"So that's how you got started?"

"No, I refused, of course. I told him I would consult for him on the side, exclusively, for a year, and give him my analyses for a lump-sum payment of double my net winnings of the past year. Then, after the year was up, we would talk again. I also got him to let me continue my own betting, provided I did it out of state and divided my bets among a number of bookies, so as not to establish a consistent pattern of significant size with any of them. That year, having a considerable bank account to work with, I made more than twice as much betting as I had the previous year."

"You went to work for him then?"

"No. I have always led a simple life. Mathematics was my pleasure—it still is—and math comes cheap. By that time I had a sizable bank account, many accounts—no sense catching anybody's attention, since all my winnings were tax free—and I felt I was ready. Instead of accepting employment, I proposed that I buy, for cash, a small piece of his business and that every year I buy another small piece so that—he was not a young man and was beginning to think of retirement—when he retired, he would have his money already invested and be able to live happily ever after. Further, my presence would relieve him of a good deal of administrative work and, as a bonus, I would continue my analyses, which I enjoyed, and bring the odds his establishment offered more into line with reality. Everyone gained, no one lost; an ideal situation for us both."

"So that's how you became a gambler, Mr. Silver. Fascinating."

Silver sighed. "I'm sorry, Marc, you have it completely wrong. You'll have to sit still for another lecture. Bookmakers are not gamblers. The last thing a bookmaker wants to be is a gambler. Bookmakers are agents of their clients, actually, businessmen who happen to be, in this state, in an illegal business. Do you know Latin, Marc?"

"No. Sorry."

"Crime can be divided into two parts: *malum in se* and *malum prohibitum.* Crimes in and of themselves, such as armed robbery, and crimes defined by the government in charge of wherever you are, such as cutting hair without a license. Everyone agrees on the first kind of crime, but there is a good deal of disagreement on the second. Bookmaking, for instance, is perfectly legal in some states. In some countries, in fact, bookmaking is a respected, and even an honored, profession."

"Such as England."

"Great Britain, yes, for one. The bookmaker serves a useful, often necessary, function. Suppose you have a disagreement with a friend as to the comparative merits of your softball team as against his. One way, a pleasurable way, to

settle the argument is to have the two teams play each othe
a series of games. Sometimes you and your friend will wage
something on the outcome, especially if you are not activ
players, for various reasons: to show support for your home
team or for your opinions, to increase interest in the game
to vent emotions, or even to make money, if you really be
lieve your heroes will win. Often the bet will be for even
money, which does not represent the actual probabilities o
the game. But you may not wish to bet at even money, you
may not have someone to bet with, or even to argue with
you. You may feel you have knowledge, insight, a certaint
that your team will win, but everyone in your village feel
the same way and no one you know will bet against you
What do you do?"

"You go to a bookie?"

"If there is one, Marc. Often there is. At your book
maker's office you will always find someone willing to be
with you on either side. There you will always find the ap
propriate odds, or very close to the appropriate odds. There
you can be assured that if you win, you will be paid, unlike
what happens all too often between friends, who are now ex
friends. At your bookmaker's you can be sure there will be
no misunderstandings, no 'When I said six-to-five, I mean
you give *me* the six.' No 'You picked the champ? Are you
crazy? *I* picked the champ.' In short, you will find the idea
betting situation. If you want to bet, that is. Nobody twists
your arm. If you're a stable client and have a good record,
you will even get credit, at no interest, sometimes for a
month or more. And you don't pay taxes on your winnings
What could be better?"

"It sounds ideal. But I've also heard that some bookies
have tough guys who'll break your legs if you don't pay."

"That's the trouble with all illegal business; you can't sue
for your rightful money in court. Suppose you're a bookie
and a guy comes to you to bet on a fight. The boxer he picks
loses, and the agreement is that the payoff is the next day.

This guy comes in—you're in the middle of paying off the winners and collecting from the losers—and says he's sorry but he doesn't have the money to pay you. He can't get the money from a bank, he can't get the money from friends or relatives, and he has no assets. Would you please carry him for another week? He swears he'll pay you then. You agree; what choice do you have? But you have to charge him interest, just as you have to pay interest on the money you borrow."

"I've heard of that. Six for five for a week."

"With credit card interest at nineteen percent a month today, and with a person who has no money, no credit, and no assets, what would you charge? He could skip town, a guy like that. So sometimes, because you can't go to court, you have to resort to force. Not because the hundred dollars is so important, but to keep the rest of your clients honest."

"I take it, Mr. Silver, you're not in that situation."

"I'm lucky. We're a high-class operation. If one of our clients did not pay his bill on time, he would be called and politely asked when he felt he would be able to pay. No interest, if the time is reasonable, but no bets would be accepted in the interim period either. If he broke his word a second time, we'd cut him off and tell everyone about it too. He'd be unable to place a bet anywhere; not even in Alaska, Hawaii, or Puerto Rico."

"That's all?"

"It's enough. For a compulsive or a chronic gambler, this is the worst punishment of all. Often it's sufficient to bring forth payment very rapidly. And apologies. But from that time on, the client leaves a sizable good-faith deposit with us." Silver paused for a moment. "I'm sorry for the digression, but you brought it up."

"I don't consider it a digression, Mr. Silver; I find it very interesting."

"Let's get back to the point I made: Bookmakers are not gamblers or, at least, don't want to be gamblers. You see, gambling means just that, taking a risk. If you, as a book-maker, gamble, with the amount of money you handle in a week, or in case of the Super Bowl, in a day, you could get very rich if you covered all the bets on one team only and won. You could also get very broke in that same day if you lost. If you're a gambler, you might even enjoy, momentarily, the thrill of possibly losing in one day everything you built up over the years. You might not enjoy seeing loyal employees lose their jobs, and loyal clients with no place to go, but what the hell, that's the breaks of the game, isn't it? And if you suddenly made a million, or ten million, would that make you any happier? If you were a gambler, yes, it would, momentarily. But if you were a gambler, you might very well blow the whole ten million in the next weekend too. In fact, if you were a gambler, you probably would never have ended up as a bookmaker."

"You were a gambler, once, Mr. Silver."

"Not quite, Marc. I bet relatively small amounts of money, money I could afford to lose, systematically and with a good deal of knowledge, only in situations where the odds were significantly in my favor. Not for the pleasure of gam-bling, but only to make money. According to the laws of probability, over a fairly long run, I would have ended up winning significantly—not quite breaking the bank, but win-ning significantly. But I gave that up as soon as I could; that is not the mark of a gambler. Now, my ideal is that on any sporting event the total amount that is bet on one side ex-actly balances the total amount that is bet on the other side."

"How do you make any money, then? Don't you have overhead?"

"The overhead is a very small percentage of the total handle. I make money on my commission. For using my ser-vices, the bettor—let's confine this to football, since that's your present interest—wages eleven dollars for every ten dollars he can win."

"You collect a ten percent commission?"

"No, no, Marc, much less. If a bettor wins exactly half of his bets, he ends up paying me a little over four and a half percent for my services. A very reasonable charge, I would say."

"Oh, I get it now. The bettors are not betting against you, they're betting against each other. And if you get the same amount bet on each team at the prevailing odds—spread—you have a guaranteed four and a half percent of the total money bet."

"With no risk, Marc. If it works out that way. Now do you see why I don't bother to gamble?"

"What do you do if the spread changes, to balance your books?"

"We can easily work out the mathematics of that."

"What do you do if you don't get exactly the same amount bet on each team at exactly the same odds? After adjustment?"

"There are several things we can do. Easiest is to change the spread."

"How can you change the spread? Isn't that set in Las Vegas after they analyze the record, the comparative strengths of the teams, and all the other factors?"

"There is a popular misconception that the Las Vegas line is an exactly accurate representation of the relative strengths of each team. It isn't, although the comparative strength is a major consideration. The spread is designed to equalize the *betting* on each team, and the people who set the spread are very careful, very competent professionals."

"Then how can you avoid getting unbalanced betting in Brooklyn, where everybody is going crazy over the Wizards?"

"You change the spread. For example, the Wizards came down at plus eighteen, a perfectly reasonable number. I set my spread at seventeen, and still got a huge imbalance. So I dropped it to sixteen, and that still didn't stop the Brooklyn fans. I am now at fifteen, and there I stay. Under no conditions will I deviate more than three points from Las Vegas. And the bets still keep pouring in, all on the Wizards."

"If the Wizards win, or come within fourteen points of the Orcas, you stand to lose a lot of money, don't you?"

"Yes, I could, on this game, and I'm prepared to lose if it happens. But if I stick to my principles, stick with the proper odds, or close to them, *all* the time, I may lose occasionally, or win occasionally, in special situations, but at the end of the year, I will do well. On the other hand, if I deviate too far from the line maker's spreads, I become a gambler, and get into an area of uncertainty. Then I do not know what will happen at the end of the year." He looked piercingly at Marc. "You sound as though you know something I should know. Have you picked up anything in hanging around the two teams?"

"There's general agreement, both teams, that if the spread goes up to twenty-four, the Wizards are a lock; if it goes down to twelve, bet the mortgage on the Orcas."

Silver nodded. "Daydreams. No bookie in his right mind would deviate six points from Las Vegas. Unless he's already bought a ticket to Rio."

"Why do you limit yourself to three points, Mr. Silver?"

"I have a great deal of faith in the ability of the Las Vegas line makers; even at three points I am concerned. But more important, even at fifteen, I'm starting to get outside money coming in heavily on the Orcas. Very heavily. That's good, but it's also dangerous. Imagine what would happen if I went to fourteen, or even lower. Half the country would be betting with me. Brooklyn alone, or even New York, can't balance the rest of the world. There's no way I can balance more than a certain amount."

"Can't you just refuse the bets? From strangers, I mean?"

"I don't take any bets from strangers, but I can't refuse a good customer. What do I do if a regular calls up and wants to bet three, four, five times his usual money on the Orcas?

And he does this several times a day, every day? I know that some of his customers from Oregon called him and requested that he bet twenty thousand in Brooklyn at fifteen, because some books in Oregon are going as high as twenty-one to cool down the crazy Orcas' fans."

"Can't you and the Oregon bookies lay off some money on each other?"

"We do, to a certain extent, but it's not easy. It takes time; you have to use a pay phone; and there's always a last-minute rush just before game time because some bettors think that way they'll get the latest information on who's going to win. There's also the problem of some books running scared; a couple of little guys in Brooklyn who take only local money are already at fourteen. My clients are pretty loyal, but they're not chained to me, and there are some gamblers who'd kill for a half point more."

"Then with a six-point difference between Brooklyn and Portland, a full touchdown, why doesn't every gambler in Oregon come to New York and every Wizard fan run to Oregon?"

"It's not that easy, Marc. If you're a Brooklyn fan and you want the Oregon spread, are you going to fly out twice, once to bet and once to collect, for a thousand-dollar bet? The airfare and the expenses would more than eat up your winnings even if you were sure you would win. Assume you want to bet fifty thousand and you've always wanted to see Portland. You pack a suitcase full of cash—no checks, even if the Oregon bookie would accept it; why give the IRS half your winnings?—and fly out. You check into a hotel and then what? Look in the Yellow Pages under BOOKIES? Ask the bellhop which bookie is reliable? Or a guy in a bar? Are you going to go to a strange place with fifty thousand in cash?

"Let's pass this. Your second cousin-in-law knows a guy who knows a guy. You give him fifty thousand in cash and he gives you a slip of paper. I hate to say it, Marc, but if you go back to collect your winnings plus your own fifty, you may not find anybody home. Not all people who call themselves bookmakers are legit. There are some people, I'm sorry to say, who would rather relocate in Seattle or Boise than give a stranger from New York one hundred thousand dollars. And if there are ten New Yorkers like that, the bookie and your second cousin could go to Rio for a long, long time."

Marc digested this. "You've been very helpful, Mr. Silver, and it's been very interesting, but my real concern is still the Madjeski murder. I'd like to ask you some questions; you don't have to answer."

"Just keep them general, Marc, and we'll see."

"Do many football players bet on games? Their own games, I mean?"

"I don't know what *many* means, and I have no accurate way of knowing with absolute certainty if even one of them bets if it's small amounts, but I can give you a considered opinion, provided you understand that I don't have any firm evidence to back it up. Yes, I believe some football players bet, through proxies, of course. Some do it out of pride, loyalty to their own team; some do it only when they feel the spread is exceptionally favorable or with what they think is insider's knowledge. The money involved is not very much and, in toto, has no statistical significance."

"Have you noticed any unusual betting patterns for this Super Bowl game?"

Silver considered this for a full minute. "I hope you're not leading up to . . . I don't have full information; bookies don't publish their daily handle. But yes, from the limited information I have available to me, mostly through analysis of my own operation and some discussions with others, I have noticed a ripple. It's a very small ripple, true, but I'm very sensitive to these things. There have been some unusually high bets locally on the Orcas from a small number of people whose credit rating, statistically speaking, does not support that kind of money. Also statistically speaking, it does not affect my operations at all, but it's an annoyance, an itch. On the other hand, I'm not the only book in New York."

"Have you identified the source? I don't mean the proxies; I mean the people behind the proxies."

"I think I have. These proxies, from their betting patterns in the past, and from other evidence, are probably affiliated with some of the Orcas. I've spoken with my colleagues, and they agree. The consensus is that some of the Orcas are *very* confident that they will win and want to ensure their winning the betting as well as the game. I see nothing to be concerned about in this."

"Have there been any similar ripples in Oregon that you know of?"

"To a smaller extent, from people whose previous betting patterns indicated they might be representing some of the Wizards."

"Players or coaches?"

"No easy way to find out. Possibly both."

"Again, betting on their own team?"

"Yes. If you felt the Wizards had a chance to win, wouldn't you rather get a twenty-one-point handicap than the fifteen now available in Brooklyn? Even if you had to pay a little extra, win or lose, to the proxy?"

"Of course, I would. Now I have to ask the question. Do you believe anyone from the Wizards is betting on the Orcas?"

"No." It was firm, strong, unequivocal. "I can't prove this, but I firmly believe that I'm right. If such a thing had happened, was happening now, I think I would have seen or heard, or felt something. Maybe not much, but *something*. I'm *very* sensitive to anything like that. The one thing we in the profession hate and fear is instability, unpredictability, deviations from the expected patterns. It throws all calculations off. It turns us into gamblers, playing against a crooked wheel. If any of us, or anyone in the NFL, even *suspected* something like that, very rapid, decisive action would be taken. Now *you* must answer this, Marc. Do you have any reason to believe that anyone on either the Orcas or the Wizards has bet, or intends to bet, against his own team?"

"No, Mr. Silver, no reason at all. Not the slightest. I had a feeling that betting might have been connected with Madjeski's murder and I was exploring the idea."

"I want your promise, Marc, that if you have any evidence, the *slightest* evidence of such a thing, that you will call me immediately. I'll give you a number; someone will be there who will always know where to reach me."

Marc promised. At the same time, he remembered what Mr. Silver had said about how a businessman in an illegal business was unable to use the courts. Marc decided to drop the matter very quickly. "One more thing, Mr. Silver. Lieutenant Danzig asked me for the name of a bookie. I believe he wants to bet on the game himself."

Silver's face was grave. "Stay out of it, Marc. This could lead to a very bad situation for you."

"I'll tell him I just couldn't find one."

"No, that would just lead to his applying more pressure on you. Do you have a phone where he can be reached? Not at work?" Marc passed over the piece of paper with Danzig's private number on it. "Good. I'll have the appropriate book call him and arrange to take his bet in a way in which no one could be damaged. If he asks you, you gave his number to an anonymous voice on the phone." Silver looked at his silver watch. "It's almost two. Shall we go? My chauffeur will be out front at exactly two." He raised his hand for the waiter.

"No, let me." Marc protested. "You helped me tremendously."

"Can you put this on expense?"

"Not this. Mr. Witter doesn't even know I've spoken to you."

"Then I'll take it," Mr. Silver said. "I hope I've helped you sufficiently?"

"Well, someday, if I ever write an article on betting, I'd like to talk with you again, go over some of the fine points. As far as Madjeski's murder is concerned, you helped in a negative way. You destroyed a theory I had that Madjeski was killed because he was betting against his own team."

"He wasn't, Marc; that I am absolutely positive about. The head coach betting against his own team? That is something I would have known, no matter who the proxy was, or where."

"I don't mean he did, Mr. Silver. I meant he was thinking about doing it, but was killed before he was able to."

"Then how could I have known, Marc? Or anyone else, either?"

24

Marc didn't like the way Boom-Boom was looking at him. It didn't make any difference why Boom-Boom was annoyed with him, the Wizards or the situation in Albania, Marc was going to stay in the Orcas' area as long as possible. The Orcas were doing warm-up exercises, so Marc was able to buttonhole Scar Scorzetto. "My boss sent me to do a think piece, Scar," Marc said. "Like a survey. And I need a story too. What have you got for me?"

"If you had come with me on Tuesday, you could've written about a real Italian homecoming party and gone home stuffed for a week. You also wouldn't have to bother asking any stupid questions like did I go there direct."

"I really didn't— If the police are satisfied, so am I."

"Well, okay, I understand how it is with reporters. Look, if you want to see a real Napolitano victory celebration Sunday night, right after they run out of champagne in our locker room, a real feast, come with me to my mother's house. Food like you never ate before, real homemade, not like in a restaurant. And my father's homemade wine—it'll knock you on your ass, but good. Bring your girl too, anybody you want, there'll be plenty. I'll drive."

There was no way Marc was going to get into a car alone with any of the prime suspects, even if it was only Scar,

Suspect 5½. "It must be tough on your folks, Scar, that you're all the way out there in Oregon."

"Yeah, sure, it's real tough, especially with the grand-children. But it can't be helped. In this game, you go where you got to. When I was playing, it was only for six months, but as a coach, it's practically all year round."

"Wouldn't it be nice if you were hired away to become head coach of the Wizards?"

"Oh, sure, perfect, right here in Brooklyn. But it'll never happen. Gruber's too stupid to pick me."

"Why do you say that? Everybody I know is sure you'll be a head coach someday."

"Yeah, I think so too, but where? It could be Minnesota, Wisconsin, anyplace. But it won't be Brooklyn. See, Gruber doesn't know anything, and he's stupid on top of that. His barber tells him that defense is ninety-nine percent of the game—Gruber's going to believe him. If he's going to pick somebody who's not a head coach now, he gotta pick Tank or Boom-Boom. But he won't. He'll find a guy who's a head coach right now, even if he's a yo-yo, and wave a fortune in his face. Even if he's got more years on his contract, Gruber'll buy it out. That way, nobody will be able to crit-icize him. Some owners, the team is like a toy; they don't even like football."

"There still will be an opening for a head coach, then."

"Sure, but not in Brooklyn. And like I said, I'm offense. Right now, defense is in. What they, you media guys, espe-cially TV, did, is make the defense the king. But the head coach ain't defense, it ain't offense, it's everything. Your atti-tude changes when you're head coach. Look at Jimbo. He's good, right? The best, believe me. Well, he was a quarter-back; that's strictly offense. Then he was a quarterback-re-ceiver coach, which is still strictly offense. Then he was offensive coordinator. Doesn't that prove something?"

"Yeah, that's good, Scar. There's a story for the Sunday sports section. How to become a head coach. Great. Now I have to ask you my question: How will the death of Magic Madjeski affect the Super Bowl game?"

"Hey, Marc, maybe that's another way to become head coach. Nah, forget I said that. Only kidding." He thought for a while. "There's no doubt Madjeski's death will affect the game; no doubt at all. The question is, will it be better or worse? Hard to say, Marc. It's not a sure thing." Marc looked at him wryly. "Yeah, Marc, no kidding. Madjeski was a bastard but he was smart too. My first feeling is, and it's just a feeling, the Wizards got to do a little better without him."

"Why is that?"

"Well, because they all hated him, see? You hate somebody, you put out what you have to, no more. You love somebody, you put out everything, all the way. Carny and Boom-Boom, they're not soft on the players, but everybody likes them. Yeah, I think there'll be a different spirit, a better spirit, on the Wizards, and it makes a difference. It really does."

"But the Orcas will win, won't they?"

"You can count on it. Just don't quote me."

"Okay. Now, since I spoke to you last, did you notice anything, hear anything, that might be a clue to the murder?"

"Jeez, I heard you were on that kick. Let it lie, Marc. The world is better off without Madjeski, believe me."

"Everyone agrees to that, but still. . . . Do you remember anything, Scar? Anything that might be useful?"

"Come on, Marc, the game is tomorrow. You think I'm worried about Madjeski? In fact, you shouldn't be going around asking. You might be getting yourself in trouble personally."

Jimbo Tallifer was in a very good mood. "There's a book in Brooklyn giving the Wizards thirteen and a half points, would you believe it? Tomorrow it might even go to thirteen even. Those Brooklyn fans are nuts. Real nuts."

"Does that mean you're going to bet?" Marc asked.

"If I ever was going to, tomorrow morning's the time to do it and Brooklyn's the place. Trouble is, I don't know anybody in Brooklyn. You got any contacts, Marc?"

"Not a one, Jimbo. On my salary, I can't afford the tuition. Do you really think it's a sure thing at thirteen?"

"Like I said before—when was it?—last time you got me for a private interview, this game's going to be a lot tighter than most people think. But thirteen points? At thirteen, it's a lock."

"Not for quoting, right?"

Tallifer nodded.

"Okay. But I need something from you for quoting, okay? My editor has me doing a survey: Will the death of Magic Madjeski affect the big game, and how?"

"When a head coach is suddenly and unexpectedly removed from a team just before a major game, his team is likely to suffer. However, in the case of Madjeski, who due to his age and other failings that were hidden by the kindness of the press, the suffering will probably be minimal."

Marc had stopped writing at the start of the second sentence. "All right, Jimbo, enough bullshit. Will you just, for once, give me your honest opinion?"

"To quote? Never. The truth is, Marc, that the Wizards are a little better off, in my opinion, without Madjeski. How much? It's hard to say, but look around. You see anybody crying his little heart out? Players or coaches? Anybody? With Carny and Boom-Boom free to do what they think is right, adjust to conditions as they see fit, the coaching will be a little better too. And something nobody else thought of, I bet. Tilley. He's smart. Right up there with the all-time greats. And flexible. You never know what he's going to do. If he breaks loose, he could lose the game big, or he could come damn close to winning. Who knows, with a wild card like him?"

"But I can't quote that, huh, Jimbo?"

"Damn right, you can't. You even hint I said anything like that, nobody I know, not just the Orcas, nobody will tell you a damn thing ever again."

"Thanks, Jimbo. I always knew that behind that phony facade was a real facade. But it'll make a good story by the time I finish padding it out. Now, I'm trying to ask this casually, Jimbo, but it's become important to me and I need your help. Do you know anything about Madjeski's murder? The last time I talked to you, you told me practically nothing."

"You got a personal interest in this now, Marc? You really want to find the killer? What for? To turn him over to the police, is that it?"

"Yes, Jimbo. Yes to everything. I'm in real trouble, and if I find the killer I'll be out of trouble. Naturally, I'll turn him over to the police."

"Marc, whether you believe it or not, I don't know any more than what I told Lieutenant Danzig. You want to know what I told Danzig, you better ask him. And you're right, Marc, I didn't tell you anything much about the murder, and I'm not going to tell you anything much. Two reasons. One, I don't know a hell of a lot. And two, I hope whoever did it gets away with it. And if you want to quote me to Danzig on that, go right ahead; I already told him the same damn thing."

The two lines of men exploded at each other with such force that Marc, on the sidelines, was sure he felt a shockwave hit him. "Look at that fat tub," Tank Chrysczyk said, indicating his all-pro tackle. "Can hardly get his ass in gear. Move that beer belly, you big bum," he shouted.

"He looks in pretty good shape to me," Marc said.

"Good shape? That lard-ass put on three pounds in the past two weeks."

"Three pounds on a man that size is only one percent."

"Only one percent? *Only?* You know what one percent means, Burr? You ever take physics?"

"No, sorry. I was a journalism major."

"F equals MA, Burr. That's the whole story. Force equals mass times acceleration. The force stays the same; you don't get any stronger by putting on three pounds of blubber. So if mass goes up one percent, acceleration goes down to balance. See?"

"That's what I mean, Tank. It's only one percent."

"You win or lose games on that one percent, Burr. When two linemen impact, the momentum is what decides. Mass times velocity, that's what momentum is. You ever play pool, Burr? Ever see what happens when the cue ball hits the eight ball? They're both the same weight, but the eight ball, which is standing still, gets all the cue ball's velocity and shoots to hell and gone. And while my fatsos are still trying to get off dead center, the offensive tackles are already at max velocity and, one second later, my defense is lying on their backs while the ballcarrier is walking through the hole."

"Come on, Tank, you're exaggerating. He's an all-pro and still pretty quick. Nobody gets past three hundred pounds that easily."

"It ain't just the fat, Burr; it's the attitude. The worst thing on a team is overconfidence. Makes you sloppy; you lose the edge. In the locker room yesterday they were bragging about how many touchdowns they were going to score; how many times they were going to sack Tilley. I put a stop to that quick."

"You picked two of them up by the neck, one in each hand, and knocked their heads together?"

"Nah, that's crude. I let them all talk and I took notes. When they finished the bullshit, I went to each one and asked him to sign what he said. I explained that if they didn't perform the way they guaranteed, it might affect their contract negotiations next year. That was the end of that, I can tell you. Then I gave them all an extra half hour of jogging."

"Okay, Tank, you have my permission to worry. But in proportion, okay? There isn't one of your tubs of lard who can't sprint forty yards in under five seconds. Some of them can do it in four point eight. And your linebackers are good for four point seven or less. So you're okay in the velocity department."

"How long you been covering football, Burr? You don't know the difference between sprinting forty yards fresh, in a straight line and then collapsing for a half hour, and fighting your way through a seven-man line where everybody's holding you and the referee is blind."

"Tank, you've convinced me. I'm going to empty my bank account and put it all on the Wizards. What odds should I give? Orcas plus twenty?"

"The last time you talked to me, you also mentioned betting. What've you got on your mind, Burr?"

"Just trying to be funny, Tank. Actually, I'm looking for a story. Can I use what you told me about how your team is overconfident and how much they slacked off in the last two weeks?"

"Only if you keep it general. All athletes tend to relax after a game. It's not just physical, it's psychological too."

"Okay, I'll write it that way. One more thing. I have to do a survey. What do you think the impact of Madjeski's death will have on the Super Bowl?"

Tank considered this for a while, then said, "I don't think it's going to have any effect, Burr. I'll tell you why. If it had happened today, yes, the Wizards would have been completely messed up, confused. From shock alone, being unprepared for it. But on Sunday, five days later? They already have themselves organized. Even if it's with Gruber's stupid plan, still Boom-Boom and Carny are smart enough to work it out right. The players, hell, they couldn't care less. They all hated Madjeski anyway."

"Can I quote you?"

"Sure. All but that last part."

"Any more ideas on who killed Madjeski?"

"I already told you, Burr, it had to be that little guy I saw."

"Are you sure you didn't recognize him, Tank? Nothing familiar about him at all? His walk? Anything?"

"Come on, Burr. It was pretty dark, I didn't have my glasses on, and he was pretty far away. I saw him for only a second, then he walked into a tunnel. You've got to understand, I wasn't paying attention to him. Why should I?"

Well, Marc thought, that's a relief. For a while. He put his notebook in his pocket and picked up his computer terminal. "What happened yesterday? With your wife, I mean?"

Tank's big face broke into a smile. "Oh, I forgot to thank you, Marc. I should have mentioned it before. Sorry. My mind is on the game. I owe you one, Marc; I really owe you one. She's gonna have dinner with me right after the Super Bowl."

"Fantastic, Tank." Marc breathed a sigh of satisfaction. "Bring her flowers, Tank," he suggested. "And a bottle of wine. Two bottles. Champagne."

"Good idea, Marc. Thanks."

25

Crazy Al Tilley was getting a massage from Pusher Rybek himself, a hard, pounding normal massage, this time. Rybek was working on the quarterback's calves. "You got some real tight knots here, Tilley. You haven't been doing your gastrocnemius stretching every morning, like I told you. You think you can fool me?"

"Yeah, I know, Pusher," Tilley said. "But the last few days, everybody's been on me. The tension isn't just from lack of stretching."

"You're teaching me now, Tilley?" Rybek was amused. "I knew that from before you were born. But it works the other way too. You relax the muscles, the mind tensions relax too. You ever hear of the James-Lange theory? F. Mathias Alexander?"

"No, and I don't want to hear about them either. Isn't it enough that I drink your disgusting witches' brew?"

"That disgusting brew is what lets you keep scrambling when those three big guys are trying to break your stupid neck. Are you going to get a good night's sleep tonight, or do I have to slip you some knockout drops?"

"Don't worry, Pusher. I need the Super Bowl winner's bonus more than you do. I'll be in perfect shape."

"If you'd saved your money like I did . . ."

"Do you really think"—Marc broke into the banter—"the Wizards have a chance of winning, Al?"

"Anybody has a chance in one game," Tilley said.

"I'm not talking a statistical possibility, Al. I mean a real chance."

"Well, they never came up against anyone like me."

"You're right, Al. I forgot about your modesty."

"It's a fact, Marc. I scramble. I don't mean a rollout or a moving pocket, I mean real scrambling. Maybe I've slowed up a little, but those big baboons still can't keep up with me, especially if it's more than a few seconds. And sooner or later, a hole opens up, and I pick up a first down or else a receiver breaks loose. I can pass on the run and throw off either foot."

"Scrambling is dangerous, Al. You can get caught ten yards back completely unprotected. If two of them catch you between them, you could get killed, and I mean killed for real—those guys are *big*, especially on artificial turf."

"I don't do it for pleasure, Marc; only when I have to. And I don't intend to get caught. Worse comes to worst, I'll head for the sidelines or drop on the ball."

"You sound like you're really out to win."

"Damn right I am. You know, the Orcas usually win by such huge scores that nobody ever thinks about it, but their kicker, Alto Torrimaa, is not all that accurate."

"He's very powerful."

"Oh, sure, he can put one in the end zone from two thousand yards, but what's his record on conversions? I'll take our little Zoltan anytime."

"You really think conversions will make a difference, Al?"

"I think it'll be a lot closer than most people figure, and if it is, conversions will tell the story. Don't forget, without Madjeski's dead hand—I don't mean it that way; just a figure of speech—without Madjeski holding us back, we can play the kind of game we're best at: fast, tricky, flexible, and unpredictable."

"All right, Al. Now, I've asked everybody but you, and don't take it personally. Who do you think killed Madjeski?"

"Pete Sandor. Tell Danzig to arrest him right away."

"That's one way of getting rid of the enemy's star quarterback, but I don't think it'll work. I need a serious answer, Al. Who did it?"

"How the hell would I know? It wouldn't be one of the Orcas. Even those dinosaurs couldn't be so stupid as to think that eliminating Madjeski would hurt the Wizards. It couldn't be Boom-Boom or Carny. All they had to do was wait until Madjeski accidentally bit himself and died of poison. Nobody kills a guy because you don't want to wait one more year for him to retire. Or die."

"You know who that leaves as prime suspect, Al?"

"I don't need you to tell me, Marc. Danzig pointed that out very clearly when he called me in."

"Called you in? When? Where?"

"Tuesday, right after he got here. In Madjeski's office. All of us."

"Boom-Boom and Carny too?"

"Me first, then Boom-Boom. Carny last."

"Nobody said a word to me about that."

"Maybe they thought you knew it already, you being so close to Danzig."

"I'm not close to him at all, Al. Why should he tell me anything?"

"Well, we just assumed it, from the way you've been talking to everybody."

"You assumed wrong. What happened when you went into Madjeski's office?"

"Danzig gave me the third degree. The son of a bitch turned his back to the open toilet door and made me stand right where I had to look at Madjeski. I guess he thought it would upset me and I'd break down and confess."

"Were you? Did you?"

"I was upset, all right, but I'd be damned if I'd show that

to him. Not because Madjeski was dead—that was joy to the world—but because it's no fun to look at a corpse. That was when he told me not to leave town, the idiot—as though I'd walk out on a Super Bowl—because I was the prime suspect."

"Were you ever in Madjeski's office before?"

"Sure. I told you. Last week, right after the play-off against the Longhorns, when he threatened me."

"Just that once?"

"We weren't good enough to enter the throne room; he always had the assistants talk to the peasants."

"Except that Monday."

"Yeah, Monday had to be because he enjoyed threatening me or else because he wanted to tape me, just in case."

"Did you see anything, notice anything suspicious, different from before, when you were there with Danzig?"

"Come on, Marc. That Monday I was lucky to be able to see if it was day or night. Tell that to Danzig so he'll quit bothering me. Every day that man gets on my case."

"He was here today?"

"He left a message for me to call him. Before a game? Screw him."

Rybek slapped Tilley on the rump, hard. "Okay, glamour boy, that's enough for you. Any more and you'd have no more hide left. Besides, there's guys who need me worse. Triage, you know." As Tilley climbed off the table, Rybek reminded him, "And stretch that gastrocnemius, you hear? Especially the left one. You get a charley horse in the game, and I swear I'll pump you full of Novocain." Tilley walked off looking, to Marc, fully relaxed.

Rybek turned to Marc. "You shouldn't tease the animals like that."

"I have to stir them up a little, Pusher. How else am I going to get a story?"

"Do like the others: Copy the handouts from Verne Ketchel. You were lucky I had him flat and put my weight on

189

him, otherwise you would've had a busted nose. He's only small by football standards, and he's got a very fast release."

"He was that tense?"

"Everybody's that tense the day before a game, and this one's the biggest of the year. There's a lot of dough riding on the Super Bowl; a big difference between the winner's and the loser's share of the bonus. I'm trying to relax him, and you gotta stiffen him up again. Use your head, will you?"

"So feed him a tranquilizer potion, Pusher. You got to have one, if I know you."

"I've got a mixture for everything, but I don't want the players falling asleep in the middle of a play. I've got to keep them at just the right level of energy, no more and no less."

"So give them a little extra of your Super-Energy Potion just before the game. It worked for me. In fact, I'm going to take a couple of swigs myself before the game. I'm doing play-by-play tomorrow so I have to be really in top shape and alertness. How long does it last?"

"Eight hours. I told you it was good stuff; much better than drugs. But I'm not going to give them a double portion tomorrow. They're a suspicious bunch. What I'm going to do is to double the strength. Watch them; they'll be like tigers. I'm also going to try something new: liver."

"They're going to eat before a game?"

"Hell, no. I don't want any ruptured stomachs on my conscience. Dessicated liver pills. There's something in liver—nobody's isolated it yet—called the antifatigue factor. They think it's a new B vitamin or a combination of B vitamins, but nobody knows. It really works. Every player is going to eat a dozen of these tablets an hour before the game or I don't let him into the tunnel. You want some for yourself tomorrow?"

"Dahliah doesn't like me to eat meat, but I guess you could consider this therapy."

"Absolutely right, Marc, prescribed by Dr. Rybek. Take them with the Super-Energy Potion."

"Can I do a story on the Wizards' *braumeister*, Pusher? I need some copy, and this sounds good."

"Sure, Marc, but don't give away all the secrets. Just say some mysterious brown pills and a secret pink potion."

"Anytime you want to market the potion, Pusher, I'll hock my shirt for a piece of the action."

"Nah, I can't ever do that. The FDA wants ten years and ten million in testing before they approve something you rub on your ass."

"Yeah, well, my offer still stands."

When Carny saw who it was, he turned over the papers on his desk and motioned Marc to sit down opposite him. "Working on plays at this time?" Marc asked.

"Nah, I'm casting my horoscope to see if tomorrow is a good day for the Wizards or if I should postpone the game. What the hell do you think I'm doing, Burr?"

"When will you have time to practice them? The game is less than twenty-four hours away."

"They're not for practicing and they're not new. They're minor variations of our regular plays—with little changes to take advantage of some things I saw in the Orcas' defense."

"You were looking at game films last night. What about your family?"

"When else do I have time to really study the films? I look at game films every night; you never know which little detail you'll notice the tenth time you watch. Or the twentieth. Family comes *after* the Super Bowl; my wife understands that."

"You're lucky. Some wives don't."

"You mean Tank? Yeah, a real bum break. Tank's a straight guy, but his wife wasn't built for football. Chalk up another one for Magic Madjeski."

"Yeah, the more I check around, the more I find out about him. All bad."

"I told you he was no damn good the first time. Now do you believe me? Did you find out anything yet?"

"Not a thing. Everybody and his brother hated Madjeski and everybody, practically, could have killed him. But who actually did it is still a big mystery."

"Why don't you drop it, then? We're all concentrating on the game, and you come in . . . It's like biting down on a pebble in your sandwich. Don't forget, the guy who did it might resent what you're doing. It ain't safe, Marc. Leave it for the cops."

"I can't drop it, Carny. There are pressures on me too."

"Danzig? Yeah, he comes around and looks at you like he knows you're a killer and you feel like you ought to confess to something, anything, just to get rid of him. Ah, the hell with him. You want a drink, Marc?" He opened the bottom drawer of his desk and took out a bottle. He put two shot glasses on the desk.

"Thanks, but Dahliah doesn't like me to drink poison, even reversible poison. I didn't know you were a drinker, Carny."

Carny poured a scant shot and swallowed it slowly. "I'm not a drinker, but sometimes it helps me to relax. Boom-Boom's worked up some pretty good defenses, but there's no way we can keep the Orcas completely down. I've got to get some points on the board, and it ain't easy, let me tell you. Not with the size of their front line, it ain't."

"Well, I won't interrupt you much longer, but I really do have something I have to ask you. It's a survey. How, in your opinion, will the death of Magic Madjeski affect tomorrow's game?"

"I'm going to surprise you, Marc, I bet, and you can quote me: 'It'll have a slightly bad effect.' That's the quote. I always felt, and I still feel this way, that there's got to be just one boss, one captain on the ship. With all Madjeski's faults, he was the coach. So even though Boom-Boom and I are each going to do a good job and each work together, still, on the whole, we're going to be a little worse off than before."

"It's a reasonable view, Carny. By the way, did you talk to Danzig today?"

"Yeah, he called me. Same old questions; same old answers. What does he expect? I'm going to change what I said?"

"He hopes. He's trying to put pressure on everybody. He called Tilley today too."

"Yeah? What did Tilley tell him?"

"Tilley didn't take the call."

"I can't do that; a coach has got to act responsible."

"I heard he also called you into Madjeski's office on Tuesday."

"Yeah, and he tried to make me look at the body all the time. Screw him. I just turned the chair away and sat down."

"Another pressure tactic, Carny. Danzig is full of those little tricks. Did you notice anything different in the office?"

"You mean other than Madjeski? No, just about the same as that morning."

"You're in there every day?"

"At least once, sometimes more. You still playing detective?"

"I have to; Danzig is pressuring me too. I was the first reporter on the scene."

"That's bad?"

"Danzig picks on everything."

"Any luck so far? In your detecting, I mean."

"Not a bit. You got any ideas?"

"Damn little. Nothing I haven't already told you."

"That's what everybody says. Well, I have to talk to Boom-Boom. Good luck tomorrow, Carny."

"Yeah, thanks. I'll need it. And don't forget to mention that I'm getting offers from other teams. Firm offers."

*   *   *

Marc found Boom-Boom in the gym, hanging from the horizontal bar. "Pusher recommended it," Boom-Boom explained. "Supposed to relax you, but it isn't working."

"That's because you're holding yourself together," Marc pointed out. "The idea is to let yourself go all limp, completely loose. Then everything stretches, straightens out, gets in line—your muscles, ligaments, the spine. . . . Get off the bar, and I'll show you how."

Boom-Boom dropped to the floor, amazingly lightly for someone his weight, but for someone his height, it was not a long drop. Marc jumped up and caught the bar. "See? If I hold myself together, almost every muscle in my body is tensed. But if I relax—watch the bottom of my feet—you'll see I stretch out, get longer, everything relaxes."

"Yeah, I get it. No wonder it was so hard. I thought I was strong, but hanging was damn hard, and I was coming off the bar more tense than before. I guess it takes a lot of practice to do it right."

"Some find it easier than others. Believe it or not, football players, athletes in general, are so used to keeping their bodies together, under control, that letting loose, letting gravity take over, is psychologically difficult." Marc kipped up to rest position, hips at the bar, slightly bent. He swung around the bar once, did a giant swing, then performed a simple backflip dismount to a perfect landing.

Boom-Boom was impressed. "Hey, that was pretty neat. I didn't know you were an athlete."

"Once I was, a lot of years ago. I don't tell anybody; it's just for myself." He led Boom-Boom over to the rings. Marc gripped them, swung up to a rest position, and then lowered himself into an impressive iron cross. "Can I talk to you for a couple of minutes, Boom-Boom?" Marc said after he dismounted.

Boom-Boom seemed more open, now that he saw Marc

194

as a fellow athlete. "Yeah, go ahead. Better than sweating over the game."

"Carny's still working, did you know that?"

"Yeah, he's very conscientious. Also, he's a big worrier. I can't do it that way. I've got to have something active once in a while, something more physical, otherwise I'd go stir crazy. I used to come here at night, sometimes, lift some weights. It tired me out, all right, but I was still very tight. Tense."

"Hanging will help, Boom-Boom, but tranquillity ultimately comes from the mind. You have to practice relaxation techniques, mental as well as physical."

"When you're a coach? Forget it, Burr. This is a job that's all tension, twenty-four hours a day, all year round. When I was an active player, I could relax for six months, mentally and physically. Now that I'm a coach, I never get a moment's peace."

"You have tomorrow's game all set?"

"Sure. Stunts and games, same as we've been doing all season. What else can we do with what we've got?"

"You did pretty well this season; nothing to be ashamed of."

"I could have done even better with a little more muscle and size, but my guys are pretty quick, and that makes up for some of it. Also, they're pretty smart. They've got the right attitude. That I see to."

"No new stuff?"

"Oh, I always find a new wrinkle, that's my job, but it's more a case of how you do it than what it is you do."

"Can I quote you?"

"You think they don't know? I can give you the whole scene right now. Scar is going to try to go through me, and I'll try to go around him. So what else is new?"

"How will Madjeski's death affect tomorrow's game? We're conducting a survey. Give me a quote."

195

"We were all terribly shocked at Mr. Madjeski's death. This will put the Wizards at a great psychological disadvantage."

"Okay, good enough, Boom-Boom. Now what do you really think?"

"I don't think it'll make a hell of a lot of difference, if you want to know the truth. We've been together, me and Carny, and Magic too, for two years, two solid years. Everything is going to be just about the same. The only difference is that we'll make the decisions directly instead of advising somebody else."

"Who do you think is going to be head coach next year?"

"It should be me or Carny, but it won't."

"Even if you win tomorrow?"

"There's a very slight chance we'll win tomorrow—you never know, in spite of what everybody thinks. But that won't make any difference. If Gruber was going to pick me or Carny, he should've done it right away. Once he delayed it—I don't care what he says, he's going to get an outsider."

"You and Carny could still end up as head coaches."

"Yeah, but not with the Wizards."

"I hate to say it, Boom-Boom, but you're probably right. I heard you and Carny were called into Madjeski's office right after the murder."

"Yeah, Tilley too. Danzig was trying to read my face while I looked at Madjeski."

"Did he see anything?"

"I hope to hell he saw how mad I was at that cheap trick. He has no class, that guy; no class at all."

"Did you notice anything unusual, different, in Madjeski's office?"

"In the office? No, nothing. Well, the statue, naturally. Why?"

"Just curiosity. One last thing: Have you heard anything, learned anything, that might give you an idea as to who killed Madjeski?"

"You still on that kick, Burr?" Boom-Boom started to get red and roughly grabbed Marc by the arm. "Like I told you the last time, leave us alone. We've got enough headaches without worrying about shit like that. And if you know what's good for you, don't go looking for trouble around here. Somebody might decide he'd be better off without you. I'm telling you this for your own good, Burr. Get smart." He walked away fast, weaving around the closely packed conditioning machines.

Marc followed Boom-Boom closely. He decided to leave the stadium quickly, remembering what had happened the last time he had hung around after an interview with Boom-Boom.

26

"You've been under so much strain lately," Dahliah said. "I thought a special meal and a quiet evening at home would be relaxing. Hot borscht with sour cream and minced dill, potato *gnocchi* with Parmesan, dry-sautéed string beans Chinese style, and chopped raw cranberry-orange relish with honey. I even got some slightly fermented cider."

"Sounds great," Marc said. "Just what I needed."

"And I found a cassette of *Pygmalion,* with Leslie Howard and Wendy Hiller."

Marc's face fell. "I'd love to, Dahliah, but I have to bone up on bios and statistics for tomorrow. *The Sentry* is not *The Times*. We have to do everything ourselves."

"Can't you take even Saturday night off, Marc? You've been working without a stop for two weeks in a row. What difference does it make if you don't remember one minor fact? You can always look it up later."

"It makes the story better if you tie it in with some interesting fact about some player or some statistic about the team. Julius wants to get a special edition on the street right after the game, so I have to write it as it happens."

"You can't memorize everything, Marc."

"I don't even try, but if I know that it exists and about where it is, I can pull it out when I need it. Besides . . ."

"Besides, you're worried about the Madjeski murder."

"Well, of course. If I don't find the murderer for Danzig, he's going to frame me."

"He can't do that. The worst he can get you for is not reporting the crime."

"That's bad enough."

"Do you have any new ideas on who the murderer is, Marc? Who did you talk to today, for example?"

"All of them."

"All five?"

"Six. Scar too, just in case. It was my last chance. Nobody's going to talk to me tomorrow until after the game, and then it'll be too late. Besides, even then, all they'll want to talk about is the game: Who did what, what they should have done, that kind of stuff."

"Well, did you find out anything? How about the bookie I found for you?"

"He was very helpful, in a negative way. Madjeski was not killed because he bet against the Wizards. In fact, if Mr. Silver is to be believed, and I do believe him, no one on either the Wizards or the Orcas is betting against his own team."

"Then why was Madjeski killed, Marc?"

"We're still stuck at the same motive: revenge for something that happened in the past triggered by something that happened on the day of the murder."

"Or by something that Madjeski said or did immediately prior to the murder, Marc. Did you learn anything at all from the second set of interviews?"

"I'm not sure. Danzig made the three Wizards look at Madjeski's body during their initial questioning."

"How did they react? This could be important."

"Tilley hid his anger; he didn't want to give Danzig the satisfaction of seeing how upset he was. Carny refused to look at the body while Danzig was questioning him. Boom-

Boom let Danzig see how mad he was. Does that mean anything?"

"Of course it does, but exactly what, I'm not sure. I don't have enough information. It's very hard to do any analysis secondhand, especially when you've never even seen the people involved. It isn't a matter of a single characteristic; it's the accumulation of information and the weighing of the evidence. Tell me about all of today's interviews while we're eating."

"That's the second time Boom-Boom refused to discuss the murder with you, Marc. And this time he threatened you?"

"Not really threatened, Dahliah, more like a warning."

"It sounded like a threat to me, Marc."

"You have to know Boom-Boom. If he intended to threaten me, he would have done it directly, with his hand around my throat instead of my arm."

"Maybe he restrained himself because he didn't want you to suspect him of the murder."

"Maybe they all restrained themselves, relatively. They're all walking around like they're ready to explode. You have no idea what the atmosphere is like just before a Super Bowl."

"If you're any example, Marc, I have a very good idea."

"Every player, every coach, has his future riding on this game, this one hour of football. Justified or not, this game will have a great, maybe a decisive, effect on the advancement or destruction of a career, on the gain or loss of large amounts of money, on prestige, fame, everything that's important in football."

"All right, Marc, I really do understand. It's the same for everyone else in the world too, except that here it's concentrated into one hour."

"Exactly, Dahliah, a lifetime concentrated into one hour, the battle visible, right there in front of you, completely visi-

le, with instant replay, in front of over a hundred million
people. No way to claim it didn't happen, that you didn't do
, that it was an accident. How would you like to operate
nat way, Dahliah, in your profession? And the decisions, the
ctions, have to be made in real time, in a split second. Now
o you understand why everyone is so touchy, so nervous, so
ensitive?"

"I understand why you're so upset, Marc. Danzig."

"Not just Danzig—it's the whole situation. And the mur-
erer—on top of everything, he's got to worry about being
aught. He's ready to kill if you look at him crooked. I wish I
ould tell the murderer that I don't know a thing, that he's
erfectly safe from me."

"You already have, Marc. You said you told each one that
ou had no clues, no idea as to the identity of the killer."

"Sure, but did he believe me? Would you believe me if
ou were in his shoes? Wouldn't you rather play safe and kill
ne?"

"That isn't exactly playing it safe, Marc. Just trying to kill
ou may expose him to more danger."

"Or it might not. It's a gamble. And these guys are all
ootball players. They're used to making fast decisions and
cting on them immediately, violently. And he's already de-
ided to kill me, remember?"

"Look, Marc." Dahliah's beautiful face was serious. "We
an't go on like this. You have to get some protection. Let's
o to the police."

"Are you kidding? Danzig *is* the police. He's the one I
eed protection *from*. If it wasn't for Danzig, I wouldn't
ave gotten involved in investigating the murder in the first
lace."

"Exactly. You need someone to protect you from Danzig.
Someone he can't arrest for any reason, especially not for
mpersonating an officer."

"There's no such— You mean *another* policeman?"

"Do you remember the lieutenant I mentioned last

week? The one in my hostage situation class? I was talking to him yesterday. He's very nice."

Marc panicked. "You didn't tell him anything about me finding Madjeski's body, did you?"

"Of course not, Marc. Do you think I'm stupid? I just asked, generally, about police protection. He said if there's clear danger to someone's life, it's possible to get police protection for a limited period of time."

"How can the police protect me from Danzig?"

"They don't have to; they just have to protect you from the murderer."

"Did you tell him about Danzig? Does he know who I am?"

"Nothing. I only talked generally. He said I could come to him any time I needed help."

"No. Positively not, Dahliah. This could make even more trouble for me. He could be a friend of Danzig's."

"I doubt that Danzig has any friends. Besides, Lieutenant Brady works in Queens, not in Brooklyn. And he's in Narcotics, not Homicide."

"I don't care, Dahliah. I don't want to go near him. Besides, it's Saturday night; he won't be home."

"He's a grandfather and he says that his greatest pleasure is staying home with his wife listening to his record collection—operas."

"He's probably on duty. Saturday night is a big night for Narcotics. If Danzig ever hears about it . . ."

"Danzig won't hear of it. Why should he? Let's call and see if Brady is home."

"Because cops stick together, that's why. I don't care he *is* home, I can't take the chance. I am positively, absolutely *not* going to see him. That's final."

"All right, Marc," Dahliah said soothingly, putting her arms tightly around him, "it was just a thought. Don't be angry with me, darling. I was just trying to help. Try to relax. We'll think of something."

Sure, Marc thought. Something. I'll have eight hours to think of something. Eight consecutive hours in which my wonderfully concentrated mind will try to think of something. Eight full hours. While I'm lying there, trying to sleep.

The bullet crashed through the center pane of the front middle window and ricocheted off the ceiling bolt that supported the still rings. It hit the floor not twenty feet from where Marc was sitting and lay there, an ugly, distorted, dark silver slug.

27

"There's no way," Joseph Brady said thoughtfully, looking like Marc's recollection of his grandfather, "that you can get any police protection, Burr." They were seated around the Bradys' big old-fashioned oak dining-room table sipping tea, Marc and Dahliah at one side, with Brady at the head and Mrs. Brady at the foot. Irish tea, Mrs. Brady called it, and it was the strongest tea Marc had ever tasted. Brady pushed his glasses back on his stiff gray hair and continued. "You have no witnesses to the attack with the weight. No one has publicly threatened you. You are not a witness in a criminal case. On what basis did you think you could apply for police protection?"

Marc looked meaningfully at Brady, who blinked under standing. "I'm *sure* someone is trying to kill me."

"But only you saw or heard the attempts, Burr." Brady's big, round, red face was patient. "No corroboration of any kind."

"What about the bullet?" Dahliah asked. "Wasn't that a threat?"

"It was not a threat, Ms. Norman. It was a warning. Not by the murderer either. No connection."

"*I* see a connection, Lieutenant. It came through our window right after Marc interrogated the prime suspects."

204

"Look at it this way, Ms. Norman. The previous attack came when Marc was at the stadium. The attacker was near Marc and attacked him directly, personally." Brady held up his empty cup. Mrs. Brady, plump and gray haired, filled it with the almost-black brew. "This was at your home, Ms. Norman. There was very little chance of hitting Marc, much less killing him. A warning. Isn't it unusual for a warning to come *after* the attack instead of before? I'm sure the second party didn't even know of the attack on Marc, otherwise he might not have bothered with the bullet."

"You talk as though you know who it was, Brady," Marc said.

"Well, I don't *know*"—Brady took a long, noisy drink of the hot tea—"but it might be the Mafia."

"The Mafia?" Dahliah looked frightened. "What does the Mafia have to do with the Madjeski murder?"

"Not a thing, as far as I know, Ms. Norman. What I imagine happened is this: Marc said he spoke to Scorzetto today and that Scorzetto didn't want Marc to associate him with the murder of Mr. Madjeski. No doubt Scorzetto had mentioned to some of his friends that Marc was investigating the murder and had questioned him. In talking to others, the information got mixed up and it may have appeared to somebody that Marc was accusing Scorzetto of committing the murder. Somehow this got to a low-ranking hood, possibly one who had bet heavily on the Orcas and didn't want Scorzetto upset, and he took it upon himself to warn Marc to stop harassing Scorzetto."

"You mean Scorzetto is connected to the Mafia?" Mrs. Brady asked.

"Perhaps. You know the saying that there are only three people between any two people in this world. It's exaggerated of course, but I'll bet that if I had a list of all the president's acquaintances and made a list of all of mine, and then I made a list of all *their* acquaintances, there would be at least one person in this world who would know one of my acquaintances and one of the president's. So if I knew which these three were, I could get through to the White House in a very short time."

"Yes," Mrs. Brady said, smiling, "then you could ask him to do a bit more for Ireland or, if that's not in the cards, to see about your promotion to captain."

"All right," Dahliah said. "If that's the case, then we don't have to worry about the Mafia; Scorzetto's got a perfect alibi. But what about the murderer, the one who threw the weight at Marc?"

"Even if we had a man full time on Burr, we couldn't protect him against something like that." Brady looked knowingly at Marc. "You're lucky he's an amateur; just wants to kill you from up close. If he had a gun . . ."

"Sure, thanks, Brady. I feel real lucky. But what do I do?"

"At the earliest opportunity . . . I take it, you'll be safe in the press box during the game?"

"From everything but backstabbing. Only press will be allowed. The coaches and the players will be too busy to think of anything but the game."

"Good. What I suggest is this: Right after the game, go to the Orcas' locker room—they're sure to win, aren't they?" Marc nodded. "Fine. Go there and tell everybody, especially the prime suspects, that you are not interested in the Madjeski murder, that you don't know who did it, that you don't care, and that whatever Madjeski got, he deserved. Then go to the Wizards' locker room and do the same thing. But there you do it low key. Losers are not usually in a good mood."

"Sure, but what about Danzig? If it weren't for Danzig, I could have done that long ago."

"Well, you *have* broken the law, and it's going to cost you something, but you can keep it small. By the way, you were never here and you never spoke to me. I don't feel like tangling with Danzig myself. I wouldn't be doing this at all, if it wasn't for Ms. Norman."

"You always did have an eye for the pretty ones," Mrs. Brady said.

"I married you, didn't I?" Brady said. Mrs. Brady smiled contentedly. "All right, Burr, here's what you do. First thing Monday morning go to a good criminal lawyer—the bar association will give you a list of names—preferably one with an office near Borough Hall. Tell him that you'll plead guilty to the least the D.A. will accept. Oh, yes, he goes direct to the D.A., who he probably knows well, not the police, while you hide out in his office. The D.A. gets a conviction without lifting a finger, and you get a suspended sentence. You have a clean record, don't you?"

"Perfectly. Up till now."

"It'll all be settled in one day. If you can't get away on your own recognizance, have your lawyer arrange low bail. It'll never get into Danzig's hands again."

"How much will this cost?"

"Everything all together? Figure two or three thousand."

"Don't worry, Marc," Dahliah said. "I can get it from the credit union at school."

"And I'll have a criminal record."

"That's what a plea bargain means, Burr. You plead guilty, but to a lesser charge. It'll go down as a misdemeanor."

"And I'll lose my job."

"Not necessarily, if your boss likes you."

Julius Witter would be arrested as an accessory, and I would have to testify against him, Marc thought. After a moment he said, "Isn't there a cheaper way to do this? One where I don't end up with a record?"

"Oh, sure." Brady agreed. "All you have to do is figure out who the murderer is and give Danzig enough solid evidence to make the arrest."

"Very funny, Brady."

"So it's back to what I said in the first place, Burr."

"Yeah? Suppose Danzig arrests me on Sunday night? Right after the game, when I make my speeches. *During* my speeches."

"You said he wouldn't get there until six. If you write your story fast and make your speeches fast, you can be gone before Danzig gets there. Then hide out in some friend's apartment, or a hotel, someplace where Danzig can't find you. Then, on Monday morning, go to the lawyer's office."

"That sounds like good advice, Marc," Dahliah said.

"You listen to Joseph," Mrs. Brady said. "He's got a good head on his shoulders and he's got the experience too."

"All right," Marc said, "I'll do exactly that. I'll be broke, jobless, and have a criminal record, but at least I'll be alive."

Marc and Dahliah rose to leave.

"You can't leave now," Brady said. "You haven't told me everything *I* wanted. In this business, we trade information. You owe me."

Marc sat down again. "I don't think I can do you any good, but you're welcome to whatever I know."

"Burr, rumor has it that Danzig came across some evidence of drug dealing during his investigation of Madjeski's murder. Who's involved, and how much has Danzig told you about the drugs?"

"I have no idea, Brady. The impression I got was that Danzig was going to use the relatively small amounts of drugs he found to force the men to give him information about the murder. Or to frame somebody for the murder. Me."

"Did you ever hear or see anything that would lead you to believe that anyone on either team was selling drugs?"

"No."

"Do you think the Madjeski murder might have been drug related?"

Marc's eyes snapped open wide. "I—I never thought—

208

not the slightest idea. I always felt it was an act, a sudden act of anger, hatred of Madjeski. I think your approach—maybe because the idea is so new to me—isn't possible, Brady. It's just not possible."

"Anything is possible, Burr."

"Not this. That Madjeski was a drug dealer? No. Who would he be selling to? His coaches? The players? One sale and he'd lose control of that player. How could he fire a player, or a coach, if he had sold drugs to that man? Madjeski? No, I don't believe it."

"What about the trainer, Pusher Rybek?"

Marc smiled. "That's a joke, Brady. If you knew him . . . He's called Pusher because he's always trying to get people, everyone he meets, to take large doses of vitamins and things like that."

"You too?"

"Of course. It's good stuff too. For the last few days, I've been taking his special potion. Seems to work well too. I've been putting out an extraordinary amount of work lately, and I don't feel as tired as I used to."

"The Peruvian Indians, Burr, chew coca leaves. It gives them amazing energy and endurance."

"You don't really think Pusher would . . . ?"

"It's a common practice for a dealer to give free samples. Then, when the dependence is established, he gets his money back a hundred times over."

"But this is not— There are no symptoms."

"None that you'd notice. In the early days, Coca-Cola was made with an extract of coca leaves. Many people believed it gave them a lift, more energy." Brady looked at Marc calmly. "Give me the bottle."

"No," Marc said. "It was given to me in good faith," he said lamely. "He's a . . . I like him." Brady kept looking at Marc, no emotion on his face. "I guess I owe you, don't I?" Brady nodded. Marc took the bottle out of his pocket. "Leave me enough for tomorrow; I have a real hard day coming." Mrs. Brady took the bottle and went into the kitchen. She returned a minute later and gave it back to Marc.

"Can you—will you let me know if there's—if you find anything?"

"In confidence?" Brady asked. "Absolute confidence?" Marc nodded. "Tomorrow. I'll phone Ms. Norman."

"Is that all, Brady?" Marc felt very uncomfortable, confused, upset at this turn of events, at the way the grandfatherly Joseph Brady had controlled him.

"Yeah, I guess so, Burr. Stop sweating. I helped you, you helped me. Maybe. That's the way the world works. If Rybek is clean, you'll know it in one day. Also, I'm not asking you to spy on your friends either. All I want is, if you come across anything that might interest me, you let me know. I'll get somebody to take a peek at Danzig's files; see if there are any real leads there. Probably not, but you never know. One last thing. Did Madjeski ever stiff any people?"

"Why, yes, Brady. He seems to have done it at least once before. Gambling. Why? Do you think he was killed because he didn't pay a gambling debt?"

"No, it doesn't usually work that way with people in his position. What I was thinking of . . . did it ever occur to you that Madjeski was not a dealer, he was a user? Didn't he have big swings of mood? Cocaine—maybe he thought it gave him energy or something else stupid like that. And that he bought a big amount and then didn't pay?"

"No, Brady, it never occurred to me. It still doesn't. If he was a user, wouldn't that have showed up in the autopsy? Danzig never mentioned that to me."

"Danzig tells you only what he wants you to know."

"Everything I know, Brady, points to Madjeski's being killed by someone he knew well, in a fit of anger."

"Maybe his supplier was someone he knew well? Alvin Tilley, for one? Crazy Al?"

"Do you really believe that, Brady?" Marc asked heatedly. "Because I don't."

"I don't believe anything. I'm just keeping my mind open. You should do the same." He sat back heavily. "One more little reminder. Nothing we talked about tonight goes outside this room, right?" He sounded just like Danzig. "If anything goes, *everything* goes." He no longer looked like Marc's wise old grandfather; he looked more like a man who had a hook into Marc, a big hook. Another master of Marc's fate. "And you've got a lot more to lose than I have," Brady added. Unnecessarily.

28

Marc carefully arranged the papers—the records, bios, and statistics—around the computer terminal keyboard within easy reach and waited for the formal introduction of the players on the field. He had decided to enter each set of plays, and each outstanding play, as they occurred and to tie the story together at each break in the action, using the terminal as a word processor. That way he would have his story sent in a short time after the game ended.

Marc had no solution to the murder and, with the game ready to start, had no time to think of one.

The kickoff teams took the field. The Orcas looked powerful and dangerous in their blue-black and white uniforms, with the leaping killer whale emblems on their helmets. The Wizards were noticeably smaller, but looked very sleek and fast in their deep red uniforms sprinkled with blue-white lightning flashes. Their helmets had the Merlin insignia, complete with pointed hat and wand.

The Wizards seemed to Marc to be even more energetic, more electric than usual. Pusher's pills and potions, double strength, were clearly working well. And why not? They had worked well for Mark the past three nights. Marc swallowed a dozen of the liver pills—forgive me, Dahliah; they're therapeutic—and hoped she would not smell them on his breath when he got home. If he got home. He took two swigs of the pink potion. Then, on second thought, he took two more.

Alto Torrimaa, the Orcas' powerful but erratic kicker, pumped one into the Wizards' end zone. Not neat, but the Orcas had not had a kickoff returned for a gain in the past two seasons, and were well content to let their opponents start from their own twenty-yard line.

The Wizards' offensive team and the Orcas' defensive team trotted out to the line of scrimmage. Marc settled back, relaxed. The opening moves of any football game were as stylized as those of a game of chess. The offense would probe the defense, testing, checking for style, feeling for weaknesses. An end sweep, a slant off tackle, a plunge left and right, to see how the defense flowed. If it brought a first down, there'd be a little more probing and a little more opening up after the play crossed the thirty-yard line. If not, a punt would give their opponents an opportunity to go through the same ritual. Of course, with Crazy Al at quarterback, there might be a short pass, a dissection of the zone defenses to uncover the holes, the hesitations, the relative quickness of action and reaction that might permit a long gain in the next round of offense or, if the Wizards got lucky, when the line of scrimmage was past the forty-yard line.

Marc grabbed his binoculars and checked the unfamiliar numbers again. It was true; the Orcas had put in their whole second team of defense. He remembered another reporter once suggesting it as a joke to Tank Chrysczyk. Could Tank have taken him seriously? And Jimbo? Impossible. There had to be something more to it than a wish to appear chivalrous, but what? Marc decided to watch carefully, but he did not know for what. You did not do anything to give an advantage, even an *apparent* advantage, to your opponent in a Super Bowl game. Jimbo Tallifer must have something up his sleeve. Not that the advantage was all that obvious. Some of the Orcas' substitutes were even bigger and stronger than the first-team players. Marc also remembered that Tank had told him: The difference between the first and the second teams was a matter of very small percentages. Still . . .

Tilley had clearly noticed it too. Coming out of the huddle, Tilley hesitated for a fraction of a second as he saw the new faces. Marc was sure that Tilley, acknowledged as the fastest thinker, the most experienced quarterback in football, would change the play, would call an audible at the line of scrimmage.

Tilley looked left, then right, then put his hands into the center's crotch. He barked out the signals left, then right. At the snap Hector "Speedy" Gonzalez dashed straight ahead. He was bumped once by the Orcas' cornerback, then went on.

Tilley backpedaled into the protective pocket, took a quick look left and right, and saw Waldo Freen, the Orcas' big end tearing at him, barely held in check by fullback Brick Brancusi. Tilley left the pocket and scrambled left. Freen got past Brancusi and began closing in on Tilley. At almost the same time, the Orcas' tackle, Mel Lyon, broke through and ran toward Tilley. Tilley ducked under Freen's clothesline arm and ran right, fast. There was a hole at the right sideline and Tilley went for it, pursued by Lyon and Freen. Speedy Gonzalez slowed down as he neared the Orcas' safety, Brian Caeser, as though he was going to come back in a hook to catch a fast low pass. As soon as Caesar jumped forward—the Orcas were using man-to-man coverage Speedy noted, surprised—Speedy turned on the jets and flew. When Tilley reached the right side of the field, Gonzalez was two full steps ahead of Caeser and gaining. Tilley threw with all his might, going almost fifty yards from the line of scrimmage. The ball settled like a feather in Gonzalez's outstretched hands. He tucked it in and sped across the goal line. Touchdown! First play! The Wizards! The Wizards leading 6–0!

The crowd, 70 percent Brooklyn fans, went crazy. It was unbelievable. Marc could hear even some of the reporters talking, the out-of-town reporters. The locals were reassuring them, yes, Tilley *could* throw a long one, once in a while. Not really *long*, but long enough. Got to give the guy credit. The Wizards had done it again. A big surprise, a *really* big surprise, but that's what the Wizards were all about.

Zoltan Szomodji, the plump little Hungarian soccer player with the big black mustache, strolled into kicking position. He moved calmly, like the Magyar king he was. He didn't have the power of a Torrimaa, or of half the other place kickers in the league, but he rarely missed inside thirty yards. So unless there was a sudden gust of wind, or the line let a blocker run through them, it was a sure conversion. Unlike the three-step kickers, Szomodji took only one step with his left foot, swung his right in a sweeping arc, and the ball went through the goalposts. Tilley held, the snap was good, and the ball went through the goalposts. Only a few seconds into the game, and the score was Wizards 7–Orcas 0.

Szomodji walked calmly to the Wizards' forty-yard line to prepare for the kickoff. At the signal, the Wizards' line moved forward, a step behind Szomodji, who put a beautiful high kick near the left sideline. Unfortunately, the kick was caught at the fifteen-yard line and returned to the twenty-five.

The Orcas' offensive team trotted out, the eligible receivers waving to the referee. Marc was shocked to see that this too was the second team. Big bruisers all, but not the usual starters. Not even Pete Sandor, the regular quarterback. Ken Dunbar was competent, but Pete had four more years under his belt than Ken. On the other hand, Ken was over six four, had arms like an ape, and could throw over most defenders. Still, Marc wondered, had Sandor been injured? And if he had, why hadn't the Orcas reported it, as they were required to do? No, Pete hadn't been hurt. He

215

was sitting on the bench, numbers clearly visible, not even warming up.

Dunbar played a conservative opening. The Wizards' defense was shifting in and out, crossing and recrossing, more than Marc ever had seen them do before. Dunbar picked at the defense, but with power. A ride left, a flow right, and a slant left picked up a first down. The Orcas were moving in their usual overpowering ground game. Like a well-oiled machine, Marc thought tritely, but what better way to say it?

A counter right, a plunge left, and a dive left would have picked up another first down, but an offside was called on the Orcas and the ball was moved back five yards. Dunbar tried a short pass that was knocked down by linebacker Delbert Prior, and the Orcas had to punt. The special teams came out, and Ralph Grimaldi, the Orcas' all-pro punter, put a beautiful high ball on the Wizards' thirteen, which Earlon Cambridge could bring back only to the nineteen-yard line.

In deference to the bomb Tilley had thrown, the Orcas' defense had spread out deeper. There would not be another successful bomb caught by the Wizards that day, that much was clear. Tilley took advantage of the dispersion of the Orcas' backfield and began testing for holes in the defense. Two short passes, left and right, picked up a first down. An end sweep was stopped after only two yards, but two more short passes, the last one a slant left over center in combination with a cross right, got another first down. The flanker, "Slippery" Sam Eustis, was tackled hard, and Spencer Rippler came in. Tilley's line was being hit violently on every play; they were beginning to move with a little less bounce.

Tilley tried another end sweep, just to keep the Orcas honest—no sense trying to go through that stone wall— which picked up only three yards, then he went back to his short passing game to get another first down. The Wizards were now in Orcas territory. On the next play, the Orcas blitzed two linebackers. Tilley, anticipating this, called a draw play, and Twister Jericho picked up eighteen yards right down the middle, putting the Wizards on the Orcas' twenty-four. Slippery Sam Eustis came back into the game. Tilley hit him with a flare pass for ten, and now the Wizards were on the Orcas' fourteen.

The Orcas' backfield was getting too tight for the easy short pass, so Tilley tried a power sweep. It was stopped with a gain of three; power did not work too well against the Killer Whales. A screen pass to Eustis picked up another four, so the teams were packed on the seven-yard line. Tilley sent Speedy Gonzalez and Hawk Munro for a combination slant out and slant in across the center and Twister Jericho and Slippery Sam Eustis on flares right and left, leaving himself completely undefended but tying up the entire Orcas pass defense. At the snap, Tilley ran back fast. With three Orcas chasing him, he scrambled right, then threaded the needle between the mass of struggling men directly to fullback Brick Brancusi, who had quietly slipped into the far left corner of the end zone. Touchdown! The second amazing touchdown of the first quarter, and both by the incredible Wizards.

Zoltan Szomodji unemotionally put the ball through the goalposts and, as before, Szomodji calmly, as though leading the Orcas by fourteen was the normal state of affairs, walked back to the Wizards' forty for the kickoff.

Aaron Tuesday, another of the Orcas' old reliables, caught the low kickoff at the nineteen and had time to run it back to the thirty. The Orcas' fresh first team ran out on the field. Clearly, Jimbo Tallifer had decided that enough was enough—time to teach the upstarts a lesson. Pete Sandor called a series of plunges, end sweeps, and slants off tackle to get two first downs in five plays and penetrate Wizards territory. Having discovered a weak spot in Burdin Vole, the Wizards' left tackle, Pete began a methodical attack at the hole in front of the right side of the defense. A plunge off tackle, a ride, and a slant, all through the battered Vole, brought another first down. Sandor ran an end sweep right, which picked up five yards and gave the offense a good reason to slam it into Vole again. Another dive through Vole left him stretched out on the ground. Oscar Colwell came in in Vole's place.

Pete Sandor continued the ground attack. An end sweep and a flow left and the Orcas were at the Wizards' eighteen. The Wizards' defense tightened into a six-man line and the backfield closed in, leaving only the safety in the end zone. With the momentum the Orcas had, Pete Sandor was obviously going to continue his power game and not take a chance on an interception.

Now Sandor unleashed all his power, picking the tired Hank Kuwalik as his next breach in the wall. Sandor ran three consecutive plays through the big tackle, double-teaming him each time and making sure the offensive tackle, guard, and end slammed Kuwalik hard on each play. It was now first down on the Wizards' six, goal to go. The Wizards' defense, now in a seven-man line, had no room for stunts: This was power against power. They put two linebackers behind Kuwalik and prayed. Taking up the challenge, as though contemptuous of the Wizards' concentration of men, Sandor sent his big fullback Lester "Steamboat" Willis crashing against Kuwalik, picking up four yards. Lined up in the same formation, Sandor sent Willis through Kuwalik again and was within inches of the goal. A third time in the same formation, Sandor faked to Willis, and Jordan "Snake" Bloodworth ran, untouched by human hands, around the left side of the scrimmage for a touchdown.

Torrimaa ran out and took his position for the point after touchdown, Sandor holding. The snap was bad, Sandor could not get the ball turned and erect in time, and Torrimaa's kick was far to the left. Score: Wizards 14–Orcas 6.

Torrimaa kicked off into the Wizards' end zone, and the ball was brought out to the Wizards' twenty. The Orcas' first-line defense was on the field and had shifted from a 4-3 defense to a 3-4, three men in front with four linebackers behind, in reaction to Tilley's short passing game. The two cornerbacks were a little closer than usual, the two safeties out a little deeper than they normally would have played Tilley.

Tilley hit Hawk Munro with a short pass up the middle for five yards, and the quarter ended.

Marc began typing on his keyboard, taking advantage of the time between quarters for the change in field position. How to explain was the problem; how to justify the weak Wizards being eight points ahead at the end of the first quarter. "The weak bamboo bends with the wind, the mighty oak breaks" kind of approach? But that wasn't quite true. The Judo analogy? To use an opponent's strength to defeat him? Not quite applicable. The hedgehog and the fox? "The fox knows many tricks the hedgehog but one, but that one he knows exceedingly well?" Not really. The truth was that the two teams were playing two different games. When the Orcas used their power, they were invincible. Boom-Boom would have to change his defense or else the Orcas would simply, every time they got the ball, run their steamroller over the weakest spot in the Wizards' defense and score at will. The Wizards, when they played their magical tricks, were unstoppable. And Tank had better figure out how to stop them, or else. But how do you stop what you can't see? Block what isn't there? How do you come to grips with empty air? Marc decided to write it that way. Let Julius cut it if he wanted to.

The whistle blew, and the Wizards had the ball on their twenty-four, second down, five yards to go. Tilley sent both his receivers downfield and threw a long pass to Hawk Munro. The Orcas' safety, prepared, knocked it down. On the third down, Tilley set up for a short pass, but all his receivers were covered. He scrambled right, fast. The cornerbacks were covering the receivers, and Tilley picked up fifteen yards for a first down before being forced out of bounds.

On first down, Tilley called for another pass, back-pedaled, and was tackled hard by Nick Solomon, the Orcas' big left end—sacked for a nine-yard loss. Getting up slowly, Tilley ran another short pass and, though blitzed, got the ball off to Twister Jericho for six yards. He was blitzed on the third down too, completing a pass to Hawk Munro in a hook pattern for a twelve-yard gain, but it wasn't enough for a first down, and Hosmer Keeley, the punter, came on.

Keeley put a good high punt, forty-five yards, near the left sideline, which was run back by Aaron Tuesday to the seventeen. Pete Sandor began his calculatorlike ground game again: counter, slant, plunge, dive, slant, sweep, ride, plunge, flow, slant—dividing the work between Steamboat Willis and his halfbacks, Snake Bloodworth and Roscoe Blades. Happily and steadily, they picked up three, four, five yards a play and, not incidentally, beat the Wizards' defense into the ground, always advancing toward the goal, yard by yard, play by play. Not once did he put the ball into the air, not once did his robots fumble. In the middle of the march, the two-minute warning sounded, but that did not change anything for Pete Sandor. He did not need any time-outs and he did not call for any. The Wizards' hope was to delay the juggernaut until the end of the half, so they did not call any time-outs either. They used every delaying tactic they legally could, but that didn't help. The Wizards, in fact, pulled 2 five-yard penalties, an offside, and a defensive holding. The Orcas boringly and predictably scored on an off-tackle plunge by Steamboat Willis. This time, Torrimaa's kick was good and the score was now 14–13. Brooklyn was still ahead, but barely, and the tide had turned.

Torrimaa's kick was short, for him, a low, fast kick caught at the two-yard line by Earlon Cambridge, who, running around the complacent Orcas tacklers, made it all the way to the forty before running out of bounds to stop the clock, but it was too late. As expected, the Orcas blitzed. As expected, Tilley got off a forty-yard pass to Speedy Gonzalez, and not as expected, Wayland Alexander, the Orcas' strong safety, intercepted the pass and took off, only to be tackled at the Wizards' forty-five by Twister Jericho.

The half ended, Brooklyn still leading, 14–13.

Marc watched the Wizards walk slowly, heads down, off the field. They did not move like players who were ahead; add a few chains and they might have posed for the march to the scaffold. The Orcas had given them a tremendous beating, physically and psychologically, and the second half promised to be worse than the first.

Marc started typing, writing the story directly as he saw it, cold and factual. If he finished this part before the second half started, he'd have that much less work to do after the game ended, and might even have time to catch the tail end of the Orcas' victory celebration in their locker room.

At least no one would try to kill him in that crowd. The greatest danger would be from flying champagne corks.

29

Szomodji got lucky at the beginning of the second half, and his kickoff bounced into the end zone. The Wizards' defense ran out on the field, bounding like teenagers. Burdin Vole, looking hale, hearty, and angry, was back at left tackle. Pusher must have pumped them full of super-concentrated magic potions or else Boom-Boom had had a long, serious talk with them. Probably both. The Wizards had shifted to a nine-man front, five men on the line of scrimmage and four linebackers, to contain the Orcas' ground game. The new formation was more vulnerable to passing attacks than the 4-4 the Wizards had used in the first half, but it was clear that the Wizards would not continue being flattened under the Orcas' steamroller anymore. If this defense forced the Orcas to go into the air, maybe it would be a change for the better. It certainly couldn't be worse.

Pete Sandor was not swayed. His first play, a power sweep around his left end, picked up six yards. Then, in rapid succession, Sandor began calling plunges and dives, picking up three, four, and five yards with regularity. The Wizards' defense began stunting in earnest, blitzing at least one linebacker on every play. Occasionally this broke up a play, sometimes for a small loss, but the Orcas' march down the field was steady. Two five-yard offsides by the Wizards were more than balanced by a fifteen-yard penalty for illegal use of hands by the Orcas, but the march went on. Near the goal line, the blitzing Delbert Prior hit Steamboat Willis hard enough to cause a fumble, but it was recovered by Snake Bloodworth and, on the next play, Roscoe Blades flowed right and went over the goal line upright. Torrimaa's kick almost hit the left goalpost, but it was good, and the score was Wizards 14–Orcas 20.

Torrimaa, as usual, kicked off into the end zone, and the Wizards started on their twenty. Melvin Bainbridge was at the left side in place of Speedy Gonzalez. Just as he had done at the beginning of the first half, Tilley sent Hawk Munro out for a long one, streaking down the right sideline. Wayland Alexander was ready and, not fooled by Munro's fake at a hook, was half a step ahead of the Orcas' receiver. When Tilley rolled out right, Herman Terress, the Orcas' weak safety, ran hard to the other side of the field to double-team Hawk Munro. Tilley's pass was underthrown. From far down the field, Munro and the two safeties started walking back to the twenty-yard line.

Suddenly, without calling a huddle, the Wizards lined up. Speedy Gonzalez had run out from the sidelines to the left side of the line and waved to the referee. As soon as he reached position, Munro stepped across the sideline. The Wizards took the stance, Tilley barked a single "Hut," and Gonzalez started flying along the left sideline. The Orcas, straggling back to position, were caught flat-footed. Terress and Bainbridge started running back, but it was too late. Tilley threw a forty-yard pass along the left sideline that Gonzalez caught without breaking stride. Run as they might, the two safeties didn't get near Gonzalez as he crossed the goal line for a touchdown.

The Orcas surrounded the referee, who calmly repeated what they already knew: There were only eleven Wizards on the field in their proper positions; Munro had stepped out of bounds on the Wizards' side before the play started;

Gonzalez wore the proper number for ends, had signaled the referee, and was at the end of the line; it was the responsibility of the defense to be in position when the play started; the Wizards had scored a touchdown. And, if he heard any more nonsense, he would call a penalty on the Orcas for illegal delay of game.

Szomodji methodically kicked the point after touchdown and the score was Wizards 21–Orcas 20. The Wizards were in the lead again.

Szomodji's short kick took two bad bounces. By that time, the Wizards were surrounding the ball, and it was grounded on the Orcas' nine-yard line. This was the end of the quarter, and the two teams changed sides.

Marc started typing his story. The theme was the amazing Wizards, the Davids who were leading the Goliaths—by only one point, true, but still leading—at the end of three quarters of play. Marc played up the natural sympathy everyone had for the underdog who fought his way to victory, for the little guy who took on the big bully and won. He emphasized the cleverness of Carny Quigley, whose brilliant innovations at exactly the right moment brought two of the Wizards' goals, of Boom-Boom's defense, which had held the Orcas to three touchdowns in three quarters, of Tilley's effectiveness in working the unusual plays, of Szomodji's steadiness and dependability in providing the points after touchdown that gave the Wizards their lead.

The fourth quarter began. Pete Sandor started his standard ground power game, but now the Wizards were blitzing two linebackers on every play. With at least one enemy in his way most of the time, Sandor had to mix up his plays by throwing short passes, usually over the middle. This led to his receivers and halfbacks being hit hard from the side after the catch, sometimes by two defenders at once, and they began flinching each time they reached for the ball. This did not stop the Orcas' progression to the goal line, but it did slow it down, and it took sixteen plays and two near interceptions before the Orcas scored a touchdown on a fourth-down center dive by Steamboat Willis. Torrimaa missed the conversion again, and the score was Wizards 21–Orcas 26.

Torrimaa kicked off, and the Wizards took possession on their twenty. Short passes and two scrambles brought the Wizards to midfield when Tilley was caught on an Orcas blitz and sacked with a loss of nine. On the next play, third down and fourteen to go, Tilley tried a long pass. It was intercepted by Bainbridge, who ran it back to the Wizards' sixteen before being brought down.

Pete Sandor called for three power sweeps in a row around his right end to make an easy touchdown. This time, Torrimaa did not miss. The score was now Wizards 21–Orcas 33.

The Wizards started their run at their own twenty. Tilley used a series of short passes and reverse to pick up two hard first downs, then scrambled for a third first down, putting the Wizards on the Orcas' thirty-seven yard line. The Orcas blitzed the next plays so successfully that Tilley had to throw the ball away both times. On the third down, Tilley called a draw play, but the Orcas were waiting for it and held Twister Jericho to a two-yard gain. Zoltan Szomodji walked out, stood farther back than usual, took three steps, kicked, and missed the goalposts by two yards. The score was still Wizards 21–Orcas 33.

The Orcas took over on their own thirty-five. The Wizards continued to blitz one or two men on every play and, as a result, Pete Sandor was throwing short passes half the time. Two sets of third-down first downs brought the Orcas to the Wizards' thirty-eight yard line. The Wizards' safeties were moving a little closer to cut down on the short passes, and their cornerbacks were working a little closer to the middle to reduce the yardage gained on the runs made possible by the blitzing middle linebackers.

Sandor sent Hotdog Jahnke on a cross left over the middle, and simultaneously Chimp Carter ran a flag pattern right, flying. Sandor laid the pass perfectly on Carter, who outjumped the Wizards' safety and put the Orcas on the five-yard line, from which they scored easily. Torrimaa kicked the extra point perfectly, the ball going high into the stands, and the score was Wizards 21–Orcas 40. The badly outnumbered Oregon fans in the stands made almost as much noise as the entire Brooklyn majority had made before.

Torrimaa kicked off, and the Wizards were on their twenty again. Tilley had successfully completed two short passes and an end sweep to pick up a first down when the two-minute warning sounded.

After the teams got back on the field, the Orcas went into a short prevent defense, permitting the Wizards to pick up another first down at midfield. There the Orcas went into a 3-4 defense and pulled in the safeties a bit. Tilley completed a short pass to Slippery Sam Eustis, who promptly stepped out of bounds to stop the clock. Tilley then had another pass knocked down and, tired as he was, had to scramble on third down with only a four-yard gain. There was no choice. Hosmer Keeley was brought in to punt. Keeley sent a good high kick to the left side of the ten-yard line. Taking no chances, Aaron Tuesday made a fair catch easily.

Pete Sandor called for a center plunge and Steamboat Willis, with a tremendous second effort, fought his way to a five-yard gain. Sandor then pulled back six yards into a shallow shotgun formation. Thurston Washburn and Fulvis Sterling, the Wizards' safeties, went back another five yards in preparation for the bomb.

At the signal, Chimp Carter sped fifteen yards into the hole and hooked, as two Wizard linebackers blitzed Pete Sandor. Pete's rushed throw was wide, and Chimp Carter dived for it. His fingers just touched the ball and deflected it upward toward the hands of the racing Thurston Washburn.

Washburn jumped, caught the ball, and ran for the goal. He was tackled hard at the four-yard line.

There were forty seconds left, first down, goal to go, when the Wizards took their positions. Tilley sent Brick Brancusi off tackle to pick up one yard, and immediately called a time-out. Tilley ran to the sideline for a quick conference with Carny Quigley. He came back, called a quick huddle, and ran a reverse around his left end. This picked up another yard and a second time-out. Another conference, and Tilley came out with Hank Kuwalik and Burdin Vole. They lined up behind Tilley in I-formation, with Brick Brancusi dotting the I, the same formation the Wizards had used two weeks before to fool the Texas Longhorns. Tilley faked the handoff to Kuwalik, who crashed into the line left of center, then to Vole, then handed off to Brancusi, who dived into the hole. Tilley backpedaled slowly to the right, but it was wasted. The Orcas' defense was prepared for both eventualities. One linebacker followed Tilley as Brancusi, who this time really had the ball, was stopped dead one yard short of the goal line. Fourth down, goal to go. The last time-out was called, and Tilley ran to the sidelines.

Marc watched Carny talking rapidly to Tilley and using lots of body English. Tilley ran back to call a huddle with his regular offense as Kuwalik and Vole ran off the field. Tilley went into a shallow shotgun formation. Slippery Sam Eustis was in motion to the right. The ball was snapped. Tilley faked a handoff to Eustis as he was passing. The Wizards linemen hit the defense once and pulled out right to form a power sweep in front of Eustis as Twister Jericho passed in front of Tilley going left and faked taking a handoff. Tilley jumped left, then flipped a screen pass over the heads of the charging defensemen, back to Eustis in a perfect screen pass. The defensemen wheeled around Tilley, careful not to touch him, as Eustis began running around end behind his blocking wedge. Just before he reached the line of scrim-

227

mage, he jumped up and threw a hard, straight pass t[o] Tilley, who had, unnoticed, quietly slipped over the go[al] line at center. Tilley jumped, caught the ball, and lande[d] with both feet in the end zone a half second before a line[-] backer hit him from the side and knocked the ball out of hi[s] hands. The field judge had his arms up. Touchdown!

An angry crowd of Orcas formed around the referee, wh[o] explained that Tilley's pass to Eustis was a lateral, that Eu[-] stis had made the forward pass from behind the line [of] scrimmage, that Tilley was an eligible receiver because h[e] had started the play five yards behind the line of scrimmage[,] that the moment both of Tilley's feet touched the ground i[n] the end zone while he was in control of the ball it was [a] touchdown and therefore the fumble was not a fumble, an[d] that he was sick and tired of having his judgment questione[d] by amateurs who had never read the rule book.

Zoltan Szomodji kicked the point after touchdown an[d] the score was Wizards 28–Orcas 40.

Aaron Tuesday took Szomodji's short kick at his seven[-] teen and ran it back to the thirty-two. There were twelv[e] seconds left to play, time for two quick plays and, if the[y] produced a touchdown, a try for conversion would be a[l]lowed even if the clock ran out. A football game is not ove[r] until it is complete. There was time, if Jimbo wanted to gam[-] ble, to put seven more points on the board.

The Orcas took their positions, Pete Sandor put hi[s] hands in the center's crotch, barked "Hut," received th[e] ball, and immediately sank to one knee, grounding the ball[.]

The game was over. Oregon had won, 40–28. The Orcas[s] fans in the stands booed Tallifer's cowardice; the Wizards[s] fans booed their losing team. Marc was filled with admira[-] tion for both teams. He was sure, from his investigations[,] that Jimbo, probably Scar and Tank, and many of the Orca[s] players, had bet, possibly heavily, on themselves, giving th[e] Wizards fifteen, fourteen, but certainly no fewer than thir[-] teen points. Every one of them had lost his bet whe[n]

Oregon beat Brooklyn by only twelve points. In terms of betting, Oregon had lost the game. In terms of betting, Tallifer had nothing to lose by running the last two plays. If he scored, the Orcas would have won by eighteen points, nineteen if Torrimaa had been able to find the goalposts. If he hadn't scored, Jimbo would have lost no more than before. Even if Sandor had had a bomb intercepted that the Wizards ran back for a touchdown and conversion, the Orcas would have won, 40–35. But Jimbo's pride and sportsmanship won out over the money. If the Wizards had intercepted and scored, Tallifer would have beaten a markedly inferior team by only five points, in his eyes a humiliation. He had the game won by twelve points. Why risk injury to any of the players, his or the Wizards', who had proven themselves gallant foes, in order to rub their noses in an extra seven points of defeat. Marc couldn't help thinking of how Magic Madeski had acted in similar situations.

Marc felt proud of the Wizards too, proud to know Carny and Boom-Boom and Tilley, especially Tilley. Happy for Pusher Rybek and his miraculous pills and potions. Working with what they had, what little they had, the Wizards had fought the most powerful team in football, one of the greatest teams in history, to a relatively close loss, and had done it with their courage, their spirit, and their desire, and by using the assets they had well and intelligently.

Marc turned to his keyboard and began composing the story of that great last quarter, then stopped. Suddenly he knew—it was perfectly clear—who had murdered Magic Madjeski.

30

- - - - -

Marc dawdled over the game story as long as he could, but as hard as he tried, he couldn't make it take very long. The story was three-quarters written before he started, and the last quarter just flowed. He didn't want to leave the press box, now deserted by all the reporters who wanted to be in on the victory party in the Orcas' locker room. There the champagne would flow, but the smiles would be tight, shame at the closeness of the score, regret at the bets lost. Jimbo would say, "I told you so," the score was much closer than anyone would have dared predict, but he and everyone would know that this was not the Orcas' finest hour. Scar and Tank would have their hopes for new jobs as head coaches severely damaged, if not totally destroyed, and their contracts for next year would not be for as much money as they really deserved.

There would be no joy in the Wizards' locker room either. Any toasting would be with Gruber's Lite Beer and, given Gus Gruber's ignorance and insensitivity, there might not be any of that either. In fact, the team would be lucky if Gruber's tongue-lashing was short, mentioning, in passing only, the failure of Zoltan Szomodji to connect on every kick, Tilley's negligence in not making every bomb a touchdown, Brancusi's inability to smash his way through three layers of rcas, Vole's incompetence at crushing two three-hundred-pounders at a time, Boom-Boom's delinquency in devising evices to stop the Orcas dead, Carny's dereliction in the roduction of surefire scoring plays, and Rybek's lack of success in turning every player into a rhinoceros. After Gruber nished with them, they would all feel lucky to be allowed buy tickets to next season's games, provided the minimum-wage laws, a holdover from the socialism of past radical dministrations, was still in effect at that time.

Yes, a few reporters would come in for postmortem interviews—in no other field of medicine is the opinion of the orpse solicited—and for quiet but sincere congratulations n the magnificent showing the Wizards made but, unfortunately, in football as in other, less important, aspects of fe, losers are not awarded laurel wreaths or showers of old. On the other hand, there was still the considerable, ough not as large as the winner's, bonus for playing in the uper Bowl. And, for those who had had the foresight and e connections to bet on their own team: bets. These were ell and honestly won, bets paid for in blood, sweat, and ears, and in risk from a hypocritical, outwardly upright orld, but bets, thank God—won. The players and the oaches, everyone, would dress and leave as soon as possi-le, quietly, as befitted losers.

The reporters would certainly be gone from the Wizards' cker room by now; the stories and the histories are written y the winners. Maybe, with a bit of luck, everyone would e gone. Maybe, if Marc waited at the main gate for Lieu-enant Danzig to arrive, maybe he could explain it all to Danzig.

The trouble was, Marc had no evidence, no real evi-ence, to present to Danzig—nothing, that is, that a D.A. ould use and therefore nothing that Danzig would accept. Maybe if Marc spoke to the murderer—after all, we're all easonable, intelligent people, aren't we?—pointing out hat, at worst, eight years in jail isn't all that bad and, at best, a plea of temporary insanity . . . ? With Marc telling the murderer he would give the defense attorney all his notes—the stories gathered from the others about what a monster Zachary Madjeski was, what a vicious monster— augmented, no doubt, by statements from the dozens of others Madjeski had destroyed? With Marc convincing the murderer he would be helped by extremely favorable news- paper stories—written by Marc of course; Marc was *not* his enemy—that would turn public sentiment his way?

Marc found himself leaving the elevator at the ground floor and wandering into the Wizards' locker room: empty and messy, pieces of uniform scattered all over, but no empty bottles, not even beer. The laughing cavalier, Au- gustus Gruber, shining knight *sans peur et sans reproche*, strikes again.

"I've been waiting for you," Carny Quigley said. "After we scored, I knew you'd come."

"Yes, well"—Marc hesitated—"I wanted to talk to you too, Carny, but I thought it would be too crowded before."

"We're alone now, Marc. Sit down. We can talk pri- vately."

Marc put the computer terminal case on the bench be- tween them. "I don't know where to begin, Carny. I do ad- mire you very much. You're the best offensive coordinator in the business. Gruber should have named you head coach."

"Yeah, I think so too, and if he had, I think Boom-Boom would have stayed. We make a good team."

"Those long passes? Really brilliant. All yours?"

"Completely. Madjeski hardly ever designed a play any- more."

"That last play?"

"Also mine. I gave it to Madjeski three months ago, as a desperation move, to be used only in the last ten seconds. It was much too complicated for normal use; everything had to fall into place perfectly for it to have a chance, including some luck."

"And a quarterback like Alvin Tilley."

"That too. That bastard's got guts and balls; played a terrific game. If I had made head coach, and he had straightened out his head, I would have made him quarterback-receiver coach next year and, from there . . . well, look at Jimbo Tallifer."

"Madjeski took that play as his own?"

"Partly because he was getting old, memory going, and partly because he could never admit, to himself even, that he didn't do it all by himself." Carny paused for a moment, then said, "You're the guy who erased the play from the blackboard."

"I didn't know at the time, Carny, what it was. I thought I'd get an exclusive. Every reporter wants an exclusive." Marc paused too. "Why did you try to kill me, Carny?"

"You got a tape recorder in there, Marc?"

"No. Really." Marc opened the computer terminal case and put it on Carny's lap. "Here, see for yourself."

Carny ignored the case. "That's all right, Marc. I know you're straight. The trouble is, you were trying to find the murderer; everybody knew that. I was scared, Marc, that's all. Nothing personal."

"You scared? When you were an all-pro receiver, you used to go right down the middle on a short slant, knowing that if you caught the ball, two linebackers would slam you between them."

"That was different, Marc. I went into that with my eyes open. But to go to jail for losing your mind for a second? That son of a bitch, you have no idea what he did to me, what he wanted."

"I have a good idea, Carny. I've found out a lot. You could have talked to me; I would have helped all I could."

"I'm talking to you now, Marc. How are you going to help me?" He looked straight into Marc's eyes. "Are you going to tell Danzig what you know? Can I bet my life you'll never tell him, Marc?" He saw the answer in Marc's eyes.

"See, Marc, you're too straight. You can't even lie to yourself to save your own life."

"Wait, Carny, don't make it worse. There's something you don't know. Even if you kill me now, it won't help. I took a picture of the blackboard. It will still hang you."

"But the picture is in a safe place, isn't it, Marc? Where nobody will find it? Even if somebody does, your girlfriend or even Danzig, will he or she know when it was taken? Danzig wouldn't even know what he was looking at." He took a deep breath. "Relax, Marc, I'll make it quick, put you out first. No pain, I swear, Marc. No pain." He started to put the computer case on the bench next to him.

Marc jumped up and ran away from Carny. Blocking Marc was a bank of hydrotherapy tanks. Trapped. He turned around to see Carny coming toward him, confidently, slowly. Marc turned again, took three running steps, and dived over the tanks, arms first. He hit the floor, tucked under into a roll, continued to upright, and ran left, into the gymnasium. Mistake. There was only one exit from the gym, but Marc had no choice, Carny was blocking the other direction.

Carny ran back around the tanks and followed Marc into the gym. Marc ran forward, jumped up, and caught the high horizontal bar. Looking back, as soon as Carny entered the gym Marc reversed his grip, kipped up into a handstand, and went into a backward giant swing, his heels catching Carny in the chest, knocking the big man backward. Marc dropped to the floor and began running again. Carny got up slowly and started to come after him.

In front of Marc, transverse to his path, was the parallel bars. If he ran under them, Carny, who was still moving relatively quickly though appearing a bit dazed, would duck under too and catch him in a corner of the gym. Marc jumped up to rest position on the near bar, brought his torso and legs forward to a pike position, then at the right instant snapped his legs backward to catch Carny's shoulders hard. Carny staggered back several steps before sitting down; this time he took two seconds to get up again. Marc continued to swing his legs upward, holding on to the near bar until, overbalanced, he flipped over the far bar and began running again.

Ahead of Marc, between two lines of equipment, was a dead wall. On his left were end-to-end racks of vertical barbells; on his right was a line of Nautilus machines and Universal gyms. But going right, between the machines, led to another dead end. The only exit from the deadly gym was to the left. Twenty feet before the end wall hung the still rings, pulled all the way back to the right in a loop, held by a hook at the end of a thin cord. Without breaking stride, Marc jumped on the seat of the first Nautilus and kept running and leaping upward until he stood on top of the Universal gym opposite the hanging rings. He unhooked the rings and let the near one go. Grasping the far ring with both hands, he threw himself forward and down. Carny's sudden dive missed Marc's swinging feet by inches, and the swing continued until Marc was at the weight racks. He let go as he swung into a backflip over the racks, landing clumsily on the other side. He took two steps to regain his balance—that dismount wouldn't even score a five, Marc thought crazily—and ran to the gym exit. Carny, having to retrace his way around the racks, was a good ten yards behind, but now running fast.

In a few seconds, Marc saw the entrance to a tunnel on his right. Once in the open, on the field, Marc could make for the Orcas' locker room and be safe—there had to be lots of people still there. Even on the field, there might be a cleaner, a security guard, somebody. He made a quick right turn and dashed into the tunnel.

Halfway through the tunnel, Marc stopped dead. The grille was in place; the tunnel was closed. He ran to the grille and tried to lift it. Impossible. Locked. Even unlocked, too heavy, thirty feet wide and twenty feet high, to roll up by hand. He was caught, really caught, this time. He was dead.

Marc turned around. Carny was walking toward him slowly, slowly. No need to hurry; no need at all. Marc backed into the far corner, his back against that damn grille, his arm against the rough concrete wall. No way to get past Carny now.

Like a bolt of lightning Marc started running, with all his might, diagonally toward the wall opposite from where Carny stood. Marc jumped up, his body horizontal, as high as he could, his feet running on the concrete wall as though it were a floor, running as fast as they could. Higher he climbed, forward he moved, trying to maintain momentum, but it was useless. As he reached the point where Carny stood, waiting, he began to fall, his feet pulling away from the wall, unable to keep driving forward. He tried to tuck into a roll to prevent his head from hitting the floor, but Carny caught him, his right forearm across Marc's throat. Carny put his left arm over Marc's shoulder and, with his right hand, clasped his left elbow. Bringing his left hand to the back of Marc's head, Carny applied the tremendous leverage the choke hold gave, forcing Marc's head down. At the same time he pushed his right forearm against the side of Marc's neck. Marc began jerking his body back and forth, but the big man was holding him off the ground, helpless. Marc's ears were roaring with a tremendous banging, his lungs fighting for breath; he was being hit all over, hard, and he couldn't breathe, he couldn't move, and it was all dark.

31

- - - - -

Marc opened his eyes; the light was blinding and forced them closed. He opened one eye a bit, then gradually opened it a little more. Green. Light green and very bright. He closed that eye and opened the other a bit. Same light green, too bright. He closed both eyes and reached for the light. Couldn't move his arm. Both eyes wide open. Dahliah leaned over him and held his head. "Oh, Marc, you're all right," She was crying. He wanted to hold her, but couldn't move his arms. He felt nauseous and very tired.

Slowly he looked around. It was a hospital, and he had a tube up his nose. "It's all right, darling, it's all right." Dahliah said.

"Water," he croaked. He was very thirsty.

Dahliah put a piece of ice in his mouth, a very small piece. He sucked it gratefully.

"Why can I talk?" His voice was settling down. "I thought when you're choked, it breaks your larynx."

"You weren't choked," Julius Witter said from the foot of the bed. "The doctor explained it to me. Carny was compressing the carotid artery. It cuts off the supply of blood to the brain and, in a very short time, you lose consciousness. Then, I suppose, Carny would have bashed your head in."

"Then why am I here?" Marc asked. "More ice,

Dahliah? . . . Did he break anything? My neck? Is that why I can't move my arms? Tell me now. I can take it."

"You're all taped up," Dahliah said, "and stitched up. It's only temporary."

"Stitched up? Why am I stitched up?"

"Well, actually," Lieutenant Danzig said from near the door, "I saved your life."

"You? Really? Thank you, Lieutenant. Thank you from the bottom of my heart."

"Yeah. Traffic wasn't too bad so I got there on time. Just in time. But you've got to give me a few answers, Burr, right? In return, know what I mean?"

"Gladly, Lieutenant. Anything you want. But if you saved my life—another piece of ice, Dahliah—why am I here? What happened?"

"Well, see, I hear the noise when I come down the hall to the tunnel and I see Carny is choking you. So I says to him, 'Stop.' Twice. Loud. Good and loud."

"You *yelled* at him? While he was *killing* me?"

"Hey, I'm a servant of the people, you understand? I've got to follow regulations. You can't just go around shooting people in this town. You could lose your pension that way, know what I mean?"

"And if he's killing me?"

"Hey, I did it, right? Didn't I do it? I shot him and I saved your life."

"He's dead?"

"Yeah, that's how it happened. I didn't mean to, but it was pretty dark in that tunnel, right?"

"Well, okay, I can understand that. But why am I here? The hospital?"

"Like I said, Burr, it was pretty dark in that tunnel. I didn't hit Carny with the first three shots, know what I mean?"

"No I don't—" Suddenly it dawned on Marc. "You mean *you* shot me?"

238

"Only with the first three shots, Burr, while I was saving your life. Like I said, it was pretty dark, and I was pretty far away."

"Far away? Why didn't you come closer, Danzig?"

"Well, you know, he's a pretty big guy, and he's fast for his size. If I came close, he could've grabbed me, and then who'd be there to save your life, huh? You was in no condition to save *my* life, right?"

"You were only thirty feet away, Danzig. You mean to say you couldn't hit a guy his size from thirty feet?"

"Oh, sure, I could. I did, didn't I, when I had to? The thing is, I was trying to wing him. You know, they give you a very hard time in this town if you knock off a civilian. Besides, if I killed him, how could I close out the Madjeski case? I'd never be able to get a confession if he was dead, right? All I could get him for was attempted assault, maybe, of you, which don't close out the Madjeski case, see? And some wiseass lawyer would get ten guys to swear Carny was a nice guy who was only trying to teach you football tackles. My word against theirs, you know what it's like in this town, and bang, there goes my pension."

"You son of a bitch. You didn't care what happened to me as long as you closed out your case."

"Hey, don't get mad. If it wasn't for me, you'd be in the tunnel right now with a flat head. And I didn't even mention—maybe you don't know it, but in this town, if you're on the force, you've got to pay for your own extra bullets, right?"

Marc turned away in disbelief. "Give me some more ice, Dahliah. When will I be able to move?"

"Another day or two, that's all."

"Uh, Burr," Danzig called out, "the case, you know, it's still open. Did Carny say anything to you I could use? As long as you're up, I could get a stenographer in to take a deposition right now. Okay? Just in case, know what I mean?"

239

"Why should I tell you a thing, Danzig?"

"Well, you know, I had a talk with Chrysczyk after you went in the ambulance, right? I was pointing out how the guy he saw coming out of Madjeski's office had on exactly the same clothes you did, and he looked exactly like you, and he was refreshing his memory, know what I mean?"

Julius Witter coughed gently from the foot of the bed. "You'll have to tell me, Marc, sooner or later. I need the story. If Lieutenant Danzig's superiors read it in the papers rather than hearing it from his own lips first, he might be embarrassed. Do we really want that, my boy?"

Marc glared at Danzig. "I want it in writing. That in return for my cooperation, there will be no charges filed against me for withholding evidence, or anything else. Right?"

"Oh, sure, Burr." Danzig soothed. "Just don't raise your voice now. Strains the stitches, know what I mean?"

"Can't you leave him alone?" Dahliah pleaded. "He's still not in good shape."

"I'm feeling much better now, Dahliah; just give me a little more ice. So start writing, Danzig."

"I would take Lieutenant Danzig's word for it now, Marc," Witter said. "I'll make sure it will be in writing, though I doubt, if he gets the information you have against Carny, that he would bother annoying you."

"And you, Julius?" Marc asked. "What do I get for breaking the case? And almost getting killed?"

"For almost getting killed, Marc, my heartfelt sympathy. For putting yourself in that stupid position unnecessarily, particularly after I ordered you to stay away from the murder, I should fire you. As for breaking the case, I haven't heard a word. All *The Sentry* has is what every other paper has: that you were attacked by Edward 'Carny' Quigley and almost killed. By the way, Lieutenant Danzig, neither *The Sentry* nor any other paper has a word on *how* Marc was almost killed, and by *whom*. There won't be any difficulty, I take it, with who phoned the police, and when, to notify you of Mr. Madjeski's murder?"

"Oh, no, Mr. Witter, definitely not. *You're* in the clear. I gave my word, right?"

"So you did, Lieutenant. And now, Marc, may we have your lucky guesses?"

"A raise, Mr. Witter?"

"Certainly not, Burr. If you get another raise, you'll be making more than any other reporter in your position."

"You mean up till now I've been making less?"

"You never asked, Marc. *The Sentry* doesn't volunteer raises, you know."

"Fifty."

"Twenty-five is my limit, as you well know."

"Twenty-five today and twenty-five if you put my story on the front page."

"Materialism does not become you, Burr."

"Do you want the story or do I go to Rupert Murdoch?"

"I should let you go, but okay—twenty-five and twenty-five."

"And I'm now an investigative reporter?"

"It seems I cannot stop you, Marc, no matter what I say. You realize, the next time the killer may not miss?"

"Which killer, Danzig or an *unlicensed* murderer?"

"Hey, wait a minute—"

"Be quiet, Lieutenant. Trust Burr to dig his own grave."

"And I want a column, Julius. Three times a week."

"You will have that much to say, Burr?"

"There's plenty to investigate in sports, Julius. I'll fill a column three times a week; don't worry."

"Let me guess the title you've chosen in your childish little fantasies, Burr. It wouldn't be 'Meditations,' would it?"

"It's a natural, Julius."

"Ninety-nine percent of our readers won't understand the allusion, Marc."

"Mr. Heisenberg won't get it either, but I don't care. It's for my father. He loved Marcus Aurelius."

"What are you two gabbing about?" Danzig asked. "What's so funny about this Marcus guy?"

"Marcus Aurelius Antoninus," Julius Witter said, "was a Roman emperor who lived about eighteen hundred years ago. He wrote a book, his diary, called *Meditations,* which is read by foolish people who think that knowing the innermost thoughts of a wise man will help them understand themselves a little better. 'Meditations,' I assure you, is a very poor name for a sports column."

"Yeah, I think so too," Danzig agreed. "So why don't you pick a different name?"

Julius turned back to Marc. "You realize you'll have to handle your regular assignments as well? With the raises you've extorted from me recently, I can't afford another warm body."

"Sure, Julius, I'll handle everything. Now for the story. Take notes. First, why he did it. Aside from the usual tortures, Madjeski called Carny in to give him a new play. This was a desperation play—to be used when the team is near the goal line and a touchdown, not a field goal, is needed, but the defense is impregnable, unbreakable."

"Isn't that the normal function of a head coach, Marc?"

"Not necessarily. In this case, it was a play that Carny had given to Madjeski three months before, which Madjeski had appropriated as his own and would take credit for if it worked. Carny would of course take the blame if it didn't."

"I presume something like this had happened before too, Marc? Possibly more than once? Is this reason enough to kill a man?"

"No, I'm mentioning it because this is what led me to know that Carny was the murderer."

"Ah." Witter's face lighted up. "That was the last play the Wizards made, wasn't it? The one they scored with?"

"Yes, exactly. Well, not exactly. The play I knew about

was a little different. The diagram showed the quarterback—a heavy line going diagonally down to the left—indicated that the quarterback ran away from the line of scrimmage and did not go across it to catch the pass from the halfback he had just lateraled to. It didn't even show a pass from the halfback to the quarterback, just a screen pass combined with an end sweep. But I remembered that the line showing the quarterback's movement started forward and broke down hard, and there was also a piece of chalk on the floor. This proved that Madjeski was hit just as he began to draw the quarterback's run into the end zone. The heavy diagonal line was made as he fell, and the chalk on the floor dropped from his hand. After Carny dragged Madjeski into the bathroom, he was concerned only with wiping off his fingerprints and getting the hell out fast."

"I still don't believe Carny would have killed Madjeski for a little thing like stealing his play."

"He didn't. There was a much better reason. It was only during the drawing of the diagram on the blackboard that Carny snapped, could no longer control himself."

"Marc, you're talking as though you actually saw this diagram on the blackboard. I don't recall any mention of this anywhere in your story or your talks with me," Witter said.

"Yeah, Burr"—Danzig chimed in—"and I didn't find no chalk on the floor."

"I erased the blackboard," Marc said calmly, "and I put the chalk back on its ledge."

"You what?" Danzig grew red. "The deal's off, Burr. I'm gonna read you your rights and—"

"Do you want the evidence, Danzig, or do you want me?"

Danzig took a deep breath, looked around the room, and, said quietly, "You got proof? Hard evidence, or is this just talk?"

"I have a photograph of the blackboard with the statuette from the desk missing, to establish the time, with other shots of the office and the photo session on the rest of the roll. I have a close-up of the blackboard itself, everything sharp and clear. And you can fit the cut parts of the negatives—the three shots you have of Madjeski—into that roll. They match."

"Now you're withholding evidence from the legal authorities, right?"

"Calm down, Danzig," Witter said. "You'll get the pictures. Where are they, Marc?"

"Safe. Fifty?"

"Is this the last raise, you avaricious little mercenary?"

"For this case, my word, Julius."

"Very well. Twenty-five on presentation and twenty-five if it is used on the front page."

"Stop kidding, Julius. You know you'll have to use them on the front page. I'll tell Dahliah where the negatives are hidden when she leaves. But I want you to write the story personally, to show Carny in a good light. He didn't have to use that play, you know. He had already won his bet, and I'm sure he had a lot of money riding on the game."

"What do you mean, won his bet? The spread was down to plus thirteen for the Wizards. If they hadn't scored that last seven points, the score would have been forty–twenty-one. Carny would have lost. He took a chance and exposed himself as a murderer out of greed."

"The spread in Oregon was the Wizards plus twenty-one. When Carny was in Boise, he must have established a relationship in Oregon. It's just across the border, and I don't think Idaho has a big enough population of gamblers to support a lot of bookies. Besides, it's not a good idea for a coach to do any betting, even by proxy, in his own backyard. It's certain that Carny had a bookie in Oregon to handle his betting."

"You mean the spread in Oregon was twenty-one points?" Danzig was incensed. "And you let me bet in Brooklyn?"

244

"No one *made* you bet, Danzig." Marc shot back. "And if you did bet with a bookie, why didn't you arrest him or report him?" Danzig closed his mouth. "Besides, you won, didn't you?" At the look on Danzig's face, Marc smiled. "Don't tell me you bet on the Orcas, Harvey?"

"Where did you learn so much about gambling, Marc," Witter asked.

"Oh, we investigative reporters have our sources."

"You haven't told me," Witter continued, "why, after he tried to kill one of my reporters, I must canonize Ed 'Carny' Quigley."

"Not for that, Julius, no. But if he hadn't used that play, I never would have known who killed Madjeski."

"If he knew that someone had seen that play, and he must have known—when Danzig called him into Madjeski's office, the play was gone, and he wouldn't have erased it—if he knew this, why did he use that play?"

"Love of the game, desire to win, the wish to help his team, the need to do the best one can, pride, responsibility, self-respect, because that's the way the game is played—any one of these, and probably all of them. With all its faults, football does build character, cooperation, team spirit, lots of good things. In most players."

"I hate football," Dahliah said. "It's brutal, vicious."

"Not brutal," Marc said, "violent. There's a difference." Marc turned back to Witter. "Other than what he did to Madjeski, Carny was a good man. Even when he felt he had to kill me, he went out of his way to do it without pain."

"You still haven't explained why he killed Madjeski in the first place," Witter said. "Was it the accumulation of a lot of straws that broke the camel's back?"

"Yes, mostly, but there was a triggering incident; Carny wasn't that unstable. This is conjecture, but I have good reason to believe that it happened this way. There was a similar incident that . . . Anyway, Madjeski didn't call Carny into his office to discuss the new play; that was secondary. He called Carny in to ask him to place a bet for him in Oregon, where he could get a much bigger spread."

"That's pure guesswork, Marc. There's no way you could have known that."

"Deduction, Julius, not guesswork. Madjeski had used that technique before. I have a source who told me all about it. Boom-Boom had come from Georgia, where he had been for years. Carny had been playing with Boise for quite a few years. Carny was the only one who would have had access to a bookie in Oregon."

"And for this Carny killed Madjeski? Because Madjeski asked Carny to place a bet in Oregon for him?"

"Oh, no, not just for that. First of all, there's the danger of placing a bet—I'm sure it was a big one—on credit, in your own name, for another person you don't trust. Carny was smart enough to have figured that out himself. Second, Madjeski had to have told Carny, when he refused, that he would not recommend Carny for head coach when he retired, and probably also said that he would fire Carny after the Super Bowl. Then Madjeski had the effrontery to show Carny, as though it were his own, the play that Carny had given to him months before. Carny must have steamed for a minute or so while Madjeski was diagraming the play, and then blown his top."

"It sounds reasonable," Witter said, "and it fits the facts. Do you buy it, Lieutenant?"

"Yeah, I guess so. Yeah, it'll work; I'll close the case with it. That way, no one can call me for killing a murderer who I caught in the act of perpetrating another murder. Okay, that's it. But tell me something, Burr, why didn't you tell me about that play on the blackboard right away? I could've closed the case in twenty-four hours."

"Twenty-four hours? Impossible. How? Madjeski drew it himself; I'm sure you found chalk on his fingers. Until Carny used that play at the end of the Super Bowl, I didn't have the slightest idea who the murderer was. Even when I saw it layed—and it was a substantially different play from the one on the blackboard—it was about ten minutes later that I realized . . ."

"The trouble with you, Burr—and I said it before, remember?—is that you like to make things complicated. Life ain't complicated; it's simple. Especially murder."

"Yeah, sure. When you know who the murderer is."

"Always making it complicated." Danzig sighed. "The play on the blackboard, that was a play to make a touchdown?"

"Of course. I just said so."

"Right. I heard you. So who was Madjeski gonna show it to, huh? An Orca? Hell, no. A player? You told me the head coach, he don't talk to players direct. So who? Drogovitch, the defense guy? Nah, it had to be the offense guy, Carny, right? So all you had to do was tell me it was Quigley and I'd have pressured him till he cracked. Then I would've take him downtown and sweated him till he confessed. Case closed, right? That's it. One day, two days, case closed. You know how many cases I got, huh? Why'd you waste my time?"

"You sound like a brute, Lieutenant Danzig." Dahliah was really angry. "I'm ashamed that people like you are on my police force."

Danzig looked pityingly at Dahlia. "You're a professor, right? At Holmes Criminology, right? Well, let me tell you, professor, if it wasn't for guys like me, you'd have a lot more killers knocking off a lot more civilians than you even got now. You got a better way to get them animals off the streets, you've got my permission to do it yourself. What do you think you're dealing with here, schoolbooks? You're so sure you know what you want is better, I'll take you out there and leave you alone for ten minutes. See who you start screaming for when they go after you. That bullshit—"

"Wait a minute, Danzig," Marc said. "You can discuss crime later. Let's get back to what you said before, about your being able to close the case in twenty-four hours because I knew who the killer was. When I saw that play on the blackboard, I had no way of knowing it was done just before the murder; it could have been drawn two weeks ago, for all I knew."

"Did you ask anybody, Burr? Did you ask what was on the board the day before? Or that morning? Whenever they was in there?"

"No. Did you?"

"I didn't know there was anything on the board to ask about, Burr. You should've told me."

"It wouldn't have made any difference if I had. In fact, it would have guaranteed that we'd never find the murderer. If I'd asked Carny about the play, he would have told me it was from earlier that day, an hour or two earlier, or more, depending on when anyone else had been in there that day, *if* anyone else had been in there that day. I would have believed him—I had no reason not to—and then he never would have used that play and I never would have cracked the case. For which you're getting all the credit. It's lucky for you I didn't tell you about the play, so be grateful and stop hounding me."

Danzig, for once, was speechless. Dahliah gently smoothed the hair back from Marc's eyes. "Don't yell, darling. It's bad for you to get excited. You have to rest." She kept her hand on Marc's hair for a moment, then said, "Oh, I forgot. Would you like some of your pink medicine? It'll make you feel better."

Marc looked at her, questioning. "Is it okay with the doctor?"

She smiled reassuringly. "No artificial ingredients." She took the bottle from her bag and held it to Marc's lips. He swallowed, then took another swallow.

Julius Witter cleared his throat. "I think we better go now. I'll be back tomorrow, Marc, to bring you a copy of the story; show you how it should be written." He picked up his

248

hat and coat, took Danzig by the arm, and opened the door. "One more thing," Witter said, holding the door open. "What with your regular assignments and your investigative reporting and your column, which, may I remind you, was your choice, Marc, you will still remember one very important thing."

Marc smiled, for the first time in a week. "Yes, Mr. Witter, I'll remember. On time."

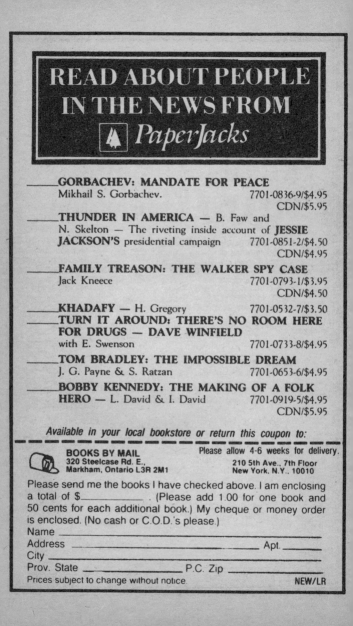

FREE!!
BOOKS BY MAIL
CATALOGUE

BOOKS BY MAIL will share with you our current bestselling books as well as hard to find specialty titles in areas that will match your interests. You will be updated on what's new in books at no cost to you. Just fill in the coupon below and discover the convenience of having books delivered to your home.

PLEASE ADD $1.00 TO COVER THE COST OF POSTAGE & HANDLING.

BOOKS BY MAIL

320 Steelcase Road E.,
Markham, Ontario L3R 2M1

IN THE U.S. -
210 5th Ave., 7th Floor
New York, N.Y., 10010

Please send Books By Mail catalogue to:

Name _____
(please print)

Address _____

City _____

Prov./State _____ P.C./Zip _____

(BBM1)